Trouble In Monarto Revenance

~

Unfinished Business

by

Thomas James Taylor

Published by DIVERSE BRANDING
www.diversebranding.net

ISBN: 978-1-0881-7954-3

ALSO AVAILABLE BY THE SAME AUTHOR

⏮ — ⏸ — ⏺ — ▶ — ⏹ — ⏭

For Your Pleasure & Questionable Behaviour

A Montage of A Mauve Reality

Trouble In Monarto

Star-Crossed

Pursuit: Life the Big Game
(a heads-up for the uninitiated)

Rambling Ways

Variations On a Theme

An End to Certainty

Of Echoes & Shadows

McKinney's Growth

Contents

*DEVILS are created within the hearts of men
by the manifestation of the Id.*
                        . . . unknown author

FOREWORD

My name is Alex Jaeger. This account is being initiated for two reasons. One is for personal reasons. I find myself troubled of late. I suspect it's no more than a sense of loss connected to the natural process of growing older, a circumstance every human being must confront with the passage of time. It may not make immediate sense to anyone who may stumble across this account and reads it without having known me as a younger man. My life was, then, lived with constant certainty that this world was balanced on a fulcrum, teetering between good and evil. I chose sides early in life and devoted all my energies to fighting negative forces in all its forms. The easiest course to serve the purpose when I was a young man was to enlist in the armed forces, to do the difficult and dangerous work required wherever the physical clashes occurred. Looking back on it now I see how naive and cocksure I was of myself, the way I viewed most things in black and white. That was to change as the world itself changed, the real battle not occurring out there on the ground, but revealed to me to be within the minds of men and women. The heart of the problem could, back then, still be seen simplistically. There are times when it is best to do so, but only after attempting to untangle the deeper complexities of the human mind, what surrounding environmental factors come into play in fashioning any human mind capable of the kind of cruel injustices such as I have witnessed.

While touching on the subject I must not overlook the theological aspect. It occurs to me that the kind of evil I have both witnessed firsthand and heard tell of is a thing not seen anywhere else in nature but in the human realm only. I have, at times, when given opportunity to reflect, perhaps while sheltering throughout a long night in some godforsaken land in a forward defensive line, come to contemplate the existence of, and the visible actions of these fundamental forces as are described in religious texts. Though I cannot be accused of being a religious man, I find it not so difficult an exercise to attribute actions so heinous, egregious, complex and vengeful in their planning and execution, to something beyond the nature of humankind, a creature born of an Earth which onetime must have been analog to the fabled Garden of Eden.

Attempting to fathom all that is involved in the process of creating true evil, which, in a person often traces back through many generations of conditioning. . . Well, as I have discovered, for the sake of sanity and of clarity it is sometimes best to view the whole subject simplistically, in black and white, as a contest between good and evil. Prior to being impelled by forces outside of my control, and adapting to my new, more sedate manner of existence, my mind was never given reign to digress or further explore such things in any depth. Given that such time is now available to me, and that recent events have provided reason for further, vexatious contemplation on the phenomenon, I am embarking on this written description of recent past events in hope that it will allow me to better understand myself, and maybe to resolve why I took the actions I did.

The second reason for committing this account to the written word? The quest for knowledge and understanding is one of the better human traits. I hope that somewhere in the pages to come resolution will be gained. Whatever it is that is bugging me, it feels important that it is examined and that understanding be reached, at last to provide some lasting peace. There is then the possibility of it furnishing similar for any others struggling with a similar plight within themselves.

*

I begin the account by stating that this city, Monarto, a satellite city of Adelaide, South Australia, holds many memories for me. Some good. Some not. The city grew large and prosperous with the influx of migrant workers coming to this country looking for somewhere peaceful to settle down, working hard while raising their families. For them it was, and still is in many cases, a place far away from the war-torn homeland many had fled. Monarto grew rapidly, with heavy industry, allied industrial engineering, foundries, businesses, and housing sprang up all around for the accelerated rise in population. With the burgeoning wealth there soon followed the kind of people looking to take advantage. The usual array of parasitic infestations tapping into the general prosperity and rapid accumulation of wealth. Night clubs and gambling houses followed, built by entrepreneurial types wanting to expand their interest.

Later came the bordellos, doss houses where drug traffickers began plying their trade, getting a foothold before spreading deeper into the general population. The rapid growth, seen as a prime opportunity for already powerful, wealthy interlopers is what led to people like Spinoza and Zendell coming here, bent on sucking the life out of the place with their incessant lust for ever greater wealth and power, and gained by whatever means they saw fit.

It was in this city that I met my wife, Janie; and Took, the loner biker with a penchant for solitude and an appetite for beer, Asian cuisine and a chance to stick it to *the man*; always one to be counted on in a tight spot. James and Patricia Harris (Jim and Pat) live here too. *Jimmy* is the son of a long-time soldier friend of mine. We served together in many shitty theatres of war around the globe, places where armed conflict became the only means of communication between countries on opposing sides of an argument. We served with the Australian Special Air Service, occasionally under the direction of US Military Intelligence within the long standing ANZUS treaty, which, I must admit, is a most sensible and effective alliance.

When my friend was KIA in Bolivia, South America, it was behooving of me to deliver his parting words, softly spoken to me and intended for his son, Jim, whom I continued quietly to watch over, supporting the boy from the wings, as it were. Such things as financial help to assist him through his education, a word here and there in the right ear, in order to keep negative influences impinging upon his developmental years.

Whatever he needed until he grew man size, I did what I could to assist.

Jim and his wife Pat worked hard to succeeded in cutting out a good living for themselves, here in Monarto. An electronics retail and maintenance shop, managed by Pat while he provided the expertise gained from his night school training and after hours studies, working through the days, often on day and night home repair call-out jobs, business installations and the like. Last I heard, and despite the trouble I had managed to bring to their doorstep, they were continuing to thrive peacefully, and with two little additions they are, these days, a successful and happy family of four.

Our exploits here are documented; sealed files kept in some dark basement within the corridors of the Australian Armed Services archives building, Canberra. The whole deal kept under wraps as much as possible after we three, Janie, Took and myself, perceived malcontents and misfits, managed to thwart, almost entirely on our own, the machinations of that warped runt, Guido Spinoza, with his inflated ego and giant sized case of megalomania to match. Him and his mentally deficient nephew, a nasty piece of work, one Vincent Zendell.

When the shindig was over and the dust began to settle it was impossible for me to continue with my usual mode of survival, that of being a free agent and opportunist, targeting those in positions of power gained through corruption, the inordinate use of hired muscle, threats against the innocent and physical bullying of honest folk in pursuit of whatever kind of happiness they sought. It was always a joy for me to annoy and relieve such people of their ill-gotten gains, and it did pay quite well, while allowing me to exercise my natural talents and dislike for piss-ant gangsters surrounding themselves with sycophantic hatchet men.

Like I said, that line of work has since been taken from me, following what happened here some years ago. The powers that be would never take their beady eyes off of me after that, though they did allow me to walk free when it was all over. I should be grateful for that, I suppose. I had to find something else to do—something which would fill the void left after my usual, adrenalin fuelled line of work was taken from me.

Janie and I found a perfect house to live in out in the country, and for some years I was happy enough just taking life slow while easing into a less exciting existence. We married, something I thought I would never do, but married life has its good side if one is lucky enough to find the right person, which, I'm glad to say, I did. Before we met, Janie had stumbled into drug dependency after her life had been turned upside down by a run of bad luck, much of it the fault of that poisonous pipsqueak, Spinoza. Before that she had been attending university, studying veterinary science and doing very well. She went back to finish her studies after cleaning up, and is now a licenced vet, with a practise which keeps her happy and feeling fulfilled. The same could not be said for myself, however. No matter what I tried to occupy myself with, it never quite filled the need for excitement after having my wings clipped by the Government. It about drove me nuts, until I happened upon an advertisement one afternoon in a local paper. Someone had their very expensive car stolen, which the cops could care less about. The owner advertised for anyone capable of tracking down the culprits and returning their beloved Austin Healy sports car. It took me less than a week to find it, parked and covered in a nearby barn on a property a couple of miles out of town. I received the thousand dollars reward, and, being on the hunt again, it went a long way towards filling that hole I mentioned a while ago.

It was then the idea sprang on me. I would take up private investigating. The licence was tricky, full of paperwork, of checking my police records and having to go, cap in had, to Pritchard, the guy in Canberra who could sanction or quash my quest to work a job which might put some of the old pepper back in my life. Damned if he didn't approve. Said he'd even use his influence to wipe my criminal history clean so I could get my investigator and firearms licences.

I began working as a private snoop. I had a badge and everything, but I got into hot water pretty quick; an unfortunate affair involving the death of a particularly unsavoury character by the name Mihail Draganov. Yeah, I know: Draganov, a villain's name if ever there was one. A real piece of work, too; master at arms of a motorcycle club called the Devil's Deciples. Again, a name not exactly inspiring a warm, fuzzy feeling, and one not likely to be overlooked by any law enforcement outfit on the lookout for odious characters with a bent for criminal mischief.

The Devil's Deciples. One might wonder at the mentality of those choosing the appellation. I'm always put in mind of naughty twelve year-old boys with a predisposition for going against the grain, if only to attract attention, egging one another on toward evermore antisocial and, later on down the line, violent behaviour; boys who never really grew up, only to the extent they were prepared to go in venting their deeper hostilities. It's a comic book evaluation, I know. I'm no shrink. The truth might be way more complex, but I don't see it, and I don't much give a damn. Fact is I have good friends within the ranks of motorcycle clubs; free spirited and fun-loving, well balanced and not in the least out to rattle anybody's cage. But the Deciples? They're just plain bad news. And Mr Draganov?

After an inquiry, and, after that, the dreary criminal proceedings, I was *officially* deemed to be no more than loosely connected to his demise. When the coppers pulled his remains out from under the garbage at the municipal tip, they had found my name and contact number scrawled on a slip of paper in his breast pocket. That plus the fact that his mobile phone record indicated I had been the last person he had talked to before going missing, the cops found it irresistible. They poked, probed, prodded and outright threatened, until they figured they had enough to link me to Draganov's well deserved and sticky end. Lucky for me, and with the help of a surprisingly good defence lawyer, they were never able to make anything worth a damn stick, and they were plenty pissed off about it the day I walked out of that courtroom with a free pass.

The lead detective on the case was a certain Detective Sergeant Carruthers. He was so disappointed at seeing me walk away from the unsolved shemozzle, he managed to pull strings enough to have my licence suspended for a full two years. The prick.

The office space I found here is sufficient for my needs. I purchased a desk, a few comfortable chairs, a couple of filing cabinets, a table to sit a coffee pot on and a fridge, placed here in the corner by the window, where perishable food items might necessarily be stored. A new communications line was installed to connect me to the outside world: a telephone and internet package; and, importantly, a secondhand airconditioner installed to combat the fierce summer heat of this place. There's outer office space here, too. Perfect for a secretary, a position I have yet to find a suitable, full-time candidate for. Janie likes to come in and help out when she can find the time, and she does a great job. I try as much as I can to keep her away from goings on here, in case things get dodgy. Besides, her veterinary work is demanding of her time and I don't like to take her from it, not if I can manage without her.

After putting an add in the local business directory and having myself re-listed, I had cards professionally made which I had a kid stuff into letterboxes all over town:

Jaeger, discreet investigations.
No job too small/No job too large.
Hourly or weekly rates.

A week after setting up, my first client walked up the stairs and into my office.

ONE

Jaeger Investigations sits at the top of the stairs on the third floor of an old, stone built building at 144 Argyle Street, above a street level dry cleaners, and, above that, a second floor importing business called Southeast Mercantile, where they sell handicraft: painted crockery, wood carvings, statues intricately carved in wood, brass and china ware, colourfully printed clothing and assorted knickknacks. There's a lift between floors. It works, at times, but rarely when one needs it to. The stairs provide a little exercise when I'm stuck, waiting for the phone to ring, when I need to go down to street level to buy lunch, or just to take a walk in order to break the tedium. I sometimes go down one level to browse the goods in Southeast Mercantile, talk with Eddie who works there, shooting the breeze about whatever comes to mind. His old man was a soldier. For some reason the fact was enough to provide sufficient common ground and strike up a friendship, despite the fact of Eddie being a devout pacifist.

On this particular morning Janie had driven me in to the office. She came up the stairs with me to spend half an hour helping, sorting paperwork and such before taking off to her veterinary clinic in time to open at eight thirty. She had been gone five minutes when I heard a woman's footsteps come back up the stairs, pause, pass through the outer office, pause again, and continue to the doorway of my inner sanctum.

'What'd you forget?' I asked, not bothering to look up from studying the chess game on my pc monitor. I had begun a game with someone calling themselves Chaz, a casualty of war over there in the Ukraine. He had paid his own passage in order to help defend against Vlad's bastard invaders, and collected a half ounce of Russian steel for his trouble. It lodged, hot and painful near his spine, taking away the use of his legs. Temporarily, I very much hoped.

When no response was forthcoming, I glanced up, discovering a woman standing at the threshold, the open doorway framing her like a portrait. Here I must explain that I came to trust my instincts a long time ago. They had, after all, managed to keep me on the happy side of mortality through many military engagements, and several more pinches since leaving the service.

Standing there as she did, in relaxed pose, wearing an elegant black dress, heals, with bronze coloured hair tied up, perfectly coiffured, and clutching a pocketbook against her thigh while the other hand rested under the elbow at her waist. I was initially very much taken by her poise. Calm, cool, confident; and with clear, deepest blue eyes contributing to a thoughtful expression on her pale, attractive face. The package added up to all the things usually *not* associated with a girl her age. She might have climbed off the cover of one of those women's fashion magazines one sees displayed at newsagents; that, or she had dodged her college classes and dressed in her mother's expensive raiments before finding her way here, to be framed in the doorway of a freshly re-licenced PI at the top of a dusty staircase inside a dilapidated building on Argyle street. That is to say, this picture somehow didn't jibe. A fact which immediately had me guessing.

'Am I addressing Mr Jaeger?' she asked, a trace of apprehension betraying her practiced demeanour.

'I am he,' I responded, already wary. It was now clear to me this girl applied every ounce of determination she could summon, attempting to maintain the steely grip employed in playing a role she had tasked herself with. Before she broke and ran, I stood, slowly, lest I spook her, waved a beckoning hand toward the armchair I had scrounged from the secondhand store not fifty metres up road, and had placed, not directly in front of my desk but in a less interrogative position, a pace away and to one side, a position I had given some consideration to, given the nature of the business I was now in and my natural bent for self-preservation. With the furniture arranged thus, I could easily maintain attention on whomever occupied the chair while maintaining good observation of the outer office, and, potentially, anyone coming stealthily up the stairs with anything other than friendly conversation in mind.

'Please. Make yourself comfortable,' I coaxed, wondering if she would make the four short paces to the armchair. She covered the distance with surprising aplomb, managing to disguise her difficulty, lowered herself into it, crossed her legs and demurely pulled down at the hemline of her dress.

Applying further bonhomie, I asked, 'I was about to pour myself a guzzle. What can I get you, miss. . . ?'

'Zendell,' she replied, and at that my blood near froze, causing a chill to course along my spine. 'Matilda Zendell,' she elaborated. 'You wouldn't have a brandy at hand, would you?'

'I think I do. A splash of ginger ale, perhaps?'

'Please.'

'My wife recently stocked the cabinet. I'm quite sure she did include brandy.'

I moved to the inbuilt cabinet recessed within the wall opposite the street-front window, pulled open the twin doors. Delaying recovery of the nominated spirit, I feigned difficulty in identifying the relevant label as my mind whirred crazily, speculating as to the likelihood of this girl being related to that cur, Vincent Zendell, Guido Spinoza's twisted, sycophantic nephew and co-conspirator in the insane game of Monopoly, which, years ago, near cost me my life. That plus their part in a ghastly conspiracy concocted by the enigmatic monster, code name Cassandra. Had it not been for the dogged perseverance given by Took and Janie, they might well have succeeded in unleashing their diabolical nightmare of a scheme, killing millions of those they and their kind considered dead-weight and superfluous human beings, people in need of a hand up who they saw as nothing more than a financial drain on the pockets of powerful plutocrats; the filthy rich, the so-called elite populating the world, caring nothing for anyone but themselves. How close they had come to unleashing their horror but for we three pulling on the single exposed loose thread?

I turned, the poured drinks and in hand. 'Matilda?'—handing over the brandy, adding, 'Zendell, you say? From where do you hail, Matilda?'

'Nowhere in particular,' she answered, taking possession of her brandy and ginger. After taking a healthy swallow, she breathed heavily; a sigh indicating some decision had at last been reached. 'I flew in from Lisbon, Portugal, after receiving news of my mothers passing. A long, ongoing battle against time,' she preempted, with a smile. 'She lived a long and pampered life, and simply grew old. Her heart stopped beating a week ago, as she slept.'

'*Mm,*' I responded, attempting to impart the right amount of sympathy. Since she didn't appear much upset by the event, why should I? I reasoned. We should all be as lucky to die so easily. 'Sorry to hear it.'

'She lived in Melbourne. I flew over for the funeral.'

And the reading of the will, no doubt, I thought to myself.

She looked at me then, thoughtfully, in a manner suggesting an appraisal, attempting to get my measure and maybe deciding how much more she might add to the subject.

'Melbourne?,' I prompted. 'We're quite a ways from Melbourne.' 'Since I was in your country I decided to take a look around, and at my father's remaining properties.'

'Makes sense,' I responded, waiting. But why had she said it that way? I wondered. "*Your country.*" Was it a slip? Why hadn't she said, *"Since I was in Australia,"* or, *"Since I was here?"* The implication being she either knew or knew *of* me, and in that moment I switched automatically to **anything-could-happen-here** mode.

I assessed the size of the pocketbook resting on her knee. Big enough to accommodate a handgun. A commonly carried woman's pistol like a point two five would easily fit within, and easily turn my brains to *foie gras*. I made a mental note: *Consider carrying a concealed weapon.*

'. . . the club,' she was saying. 'I was thinking about purchasing it for myself. Clubs are always such a good investment, but I heard they're discussing tearing it down. The council, I mean, because it's an old building and it has structural problems. The *Blue Parrot* was a favourite of my father's.

This had gone on long enough. Her father *was* Vincent Zendell. No doubt now. The Blue Parrot *was* one of his earners, before his scrawny arse was dragged off to prison. So what the hell was his daughter doing here, right now, in my office?

'Miss Zendell,' I interrupted, 'why exactly are you here? You do know who I am, don't you?. . . how your father and I are connected? I'm responsible for your father being brought down. He and his uncle, Guido Spinoza. You must know it. Why then would you come here? Revenge? Do you intend revenge? Is that it?'

There was a moment's pause as she appeared to consider this. Then, replying in a quiet, steady voice: 'Yes, I know who you are Mr Jaeger. I know that, if not for you and your companions, a terrible crime might have been perpetrated on a great many unsuspecting, innocent people. One cannot choose their relatives, Mr Jaeger. I cannot help being connected to my family, the terrible thing he was a part of.'

She paused again, once more thoughtful, and I watched as her face revealed fresh commitment. 'I know how this must appear, how strange it is for me to be here, talking to you, after all that happened between you and my father, and my uncle Guido. So many times I almost turned back while on my way here, but. . . Look at this,' she said, and snapped open her pocketbook to retrieve something from it.

I was waiting for the merest glint of gunmetal, readying myself to launch forward and disarm the girl as she delved within. When she withdrew the hand, it grasped a folded envelope which she extended toward me.

'Read this,' she instructed. 'I received it just two days ago, pushed under my hotel room door.'

'Which hotel?' I asked, leaning forward and taking possession.' 'The *Oceanic,* Saint Kilda, in Melbourne.'

I slid the note paper from the envelope, unfolded it, noticing first the letterhead: *"Oceanic Hotel. Be our guest."* A short, pencil written note had been scribbled below, reading:

Tell Vincent, "The sins of the father. . ."
He will know EXACTLY what I mean.

Cassandra.

My blood was already running cold, but at reading the name at the bottom of the note, a name I had not contemplated in so a long time? Were chickens coming home to roost?

'Do you know the author?' I asked, flipping the paper over, looking for anything else capable of yielding a clue.

'Not really,' she replied, studying my response.

'*Not really?*' I repeated, not at all believing her. 'You've not ever heard mention of a Cassandra?'

'I know the name, in connection with Greek mythology, of course. The disbelieved prophet of doom. Is that what you mean?' she returned, breaking eye contact with my inquiring gaze rather too quickly.

I was annoyed—annoyed at her obvious attempt of deceit, and, although I wasn't fully aware it then, far more annoyed that she had brought this to *me*, with all the unwanted baggage it contained.

'You can lie all you want, miss,' I told her. 'You brought this to me, remember?' Without intending to be, I was up, out of my chair and at the window, looking out on the street below, with images of the past looming up from where I had buried them years ago.

Without turning to my visitor, I told her, 'If you want me to believe you don't have any knowledge of the name on that piece of paper, it's your prerogative. You come to me with a scrap of notepaper containing a weirdly cryptic message scrawled on it, and you're asking me to accept that you don't understand what it's about. Is that what you're telling me?'

She did not respond, but I watched her reflected image in the glass of the window I stood at. Her head lowered, with her chin almost resting on her chest. She looked to me as a girl caught in a lie, attempting to summon a suitable response as to why she had come to me with this. If she did not understand the message, why was she here?

'Why would you come with this, to *me*, of all people, if, as you say, you don't understand what it's about, miss

Zendell? I mean, please. Really? What the hell were you thinking? What game *is* this?'

She began to cry; at first the kind of cry women perform when they don't mean to, attempting restraint as they hasten to find a tissue or something to keep the tears from spoiling their eye makeup. Unable to locate a tissue, she broke into sobbing, her hands raised to her face as she gave up trying to hold back, her shoulders heaving with the quiet sobbing behind her perfectly manicured fingers.

So what can I say? There's not a man alive who is not affected by a weeping woman. Some will feel alienated, finding themselves baffled, not knowing know how to respond. Some will be disarmed, given to sympathy, feeling a need to comfort the distressed damsel. Me? I was completely and utterly confounded. It was the last thing I expected and I wasn't at all prepared. I could only stand, flatfooted, wondering what the hell should be done to make it stop. When it continued I finally succumbed to convention, approached hesitantly, moved to grip her shoulder, baulked once and completed the manoeuver.

'Alright, miss,' I relented, still annoyed but managing a soothing tone. 'I see you're under some strain here. Let me get you a top-up—' retrieving her glass with my free hand, the other still clutching her shoulder. 'Liquid courage, eh? What do you say?'

She accepted the recharge, steadied herself after gulping it down in two swallows. I remember the determined expression as she applied what she had left of her courage, and at that moment. . . *Yes,* it was right then. I felt the world shift, albeit ever so slightly under my feet. A mere tremble though it was, when the world shifts beneath one's feet, even a little bit, it's a moment remembered. It marked the time, precisely, when I ceased viewing everything around me in so objective and dispassionate a manner. The girl was not playacting, I decided.

~

I must remind myself at this point, and anyone stumbling across this account, that these pages are undertaken as much to document the event as it is to allow me to view and better understand the event, as well as my thinking and actions, in a manner which might explain why it all unfolded as it did. *Greater clarity!* I say clarity, when, in fact, there is no clarity at the moment of invoking these words.

I mentioned how I saw the world in black and white as a younger man. I chose to see things that way, only because I recognised the pitfalls awaiting me should I choose attempting much deeper comprehension of all that surrounded me. When things are black and white it's easier to understand and to choose sides. There are so many things, often confusing, perplexing things where human beings are concerned, needing to be understood and to choose sides over. I was happy in the simplistic black and white view. For me the world consisted of those seeking power, control, wealth, and on the other side were those dedicated to supporting humanity—their fellow human beings—looking to somehow level the playing field where the rules had long ago been decided by those with all the power, all the money and influence.

Looking back at the way I was now only amuses me, the same way it amuses me to observe any young person, so full of fire and enthusiasm, looking for that one challenge, a means of making a mark on the world by exercising whatever inherent talents are gifted from birth. The words *'Life is wasted on the young'* come swiftly to mind. I wouldn't wonder the adage was coined many millennia ago, and so sharp and apt is the observation, it rings true to this very day.

Black and white was the only way I could navigate so grey and complex a world. I guess it's true for many, especially those needing order and reason; justice even; watching despairingly as things like greed and despotism always seem to overpower and win out while only sporadically and unimaginatively challenged without any real force of conviction, crushing life's spark out of those fated to accept the responsibility of carrying the real load when it comes to our continued survival.

That today I find myself scribbling these things is a total mystery to me. It's a mark of the gradual change occurring in me, especially during this last year or so: I guess since putting down the tools of my trade, marrying a girl who had suffered and survived a climate created by the likes of Spinoza, Zendell, and that supreme bastard, Cassandra. To me it's the lame leadership offered by our elected representatives, and not just in this country but everywhere I look. It's exactly this allowing these parasites to exist and all need to be brought to account.

~

Matilda placed her emptied glass on the small table beside her, appearing to have regained composure. I returned to my position behind my desk, hoping to appear less confrontational.

She look up. 'I'm sorry,' she began, her voice sounding smaller now, lacking the previous pretense. 'The truth is, I'm completely out of my depth. I don't know who I can turn to. You are the only person who might understand the meaning of it. With my father in prison and my mother now gone, I came here to Monarto to ascertain the viability of the club, nothing more. Nothing more until I discovered that you were still here in town. Your flier,' she explained.

'You might imagine that my father left me well able to cope, financially. It's not the case. I was hoping to salvage what I could from the *Blue Parrot*, invest something to survive on. The courts took almost everything, leaving me little.' She nodded to the piece of notepaper on my desk. 'When that came, with *that* name on it. . .' she paused, searching for words that would not come.

'. . . I used to spend a lot of time with my father and uncle Guido. More time than maybe I should have. I had no idea what they did, at first. It was fun for me to be around the action, you know? I was only little. As I grew up, the picture began to take shape. I was a bright girl for my age, I guess, and, yes, I pieced together that something awful was about to occur. I had no concept of *conspiracy*. I was nine years old then. Not the whole story, just pieces, enough to recognise something horrible was about to be unleashed. And the name,

Cassandra. It was mentioned just the one time, but it stuck in my memory.'

At this point she reached for her glass, realised it was empty and returned her hand to her lap.

'Perhaps just one more,' I suggested. 'It's not a great habit for a young lady to engage in, but we can make an exception today,' I told her, and afforded the girl a genuine smile.

'Thank-you,' she said, blushing slightly, and I came around to retrieve the glass, mixing a last, weak brandy and dry as she continued the story.

'The name was uttered only one time in my presence, eliciting a terribly threatening look on the face of my uncle. My father had uttered a name that should never have been mentioned. Of that I was certain, and I was never to forget it. It was Cassandra behind everything, wasn't it?'

It wasn't so much a question as an assertion. At nine years-of-age she had picked up on something dark in design, the name Cassandra at its heart.

'Yes it was,' I responded, handing her the refreshment. 'And you've had all these intervening years to dwell on what happened to your family, I guess. I can see how that might. . . *niggle?*'

The reply elicited a short laugh, lighting up an attractive face. 'Niggle,' she repeated, again laughing, but then her face clouded over once more. 'Yes. When my father and uncle were arrested, there were all sorts of strange goings on around me. People died. They were killed, mister Jaeger, just to keep secrets. My mother and I moved to a Sydney suburb, before Melbourne, into a much smaller house. Suddenly money was very tight.

Mother started drinking. More than ever, I mean. She always had a problem. It's what killed her in the end.'

'And the thing with Cassandra?' I interceded. 'Did you pick up on anything else, anything of importance regarding it?'

'No. Nothing. There was nothing in the newspapers or on the television concerning any of it. I wondered why that was. Later I worked it out. Obviously the public weren't to know. I was very grateful for that, but. . .'

'But?' I quizzed after a moment.

'It haunted me, mister Jaeger. It did, does, and it probably always will. I never really learned what happened. What was going on, I mean. Something dark and horrid, I'm sure, but I never learned the full breadth of this terrible hidden something that my family had become a part of, and what tore my life— *all our lives apart.*'

She halted there, looking me directly in the eye, the unasked question poised in the air like some very large but invisible, levitated elephant hanging there in the room. She was asking me to reveal the story— the *full story* involving a diabolical global conspiracy I had been sworn to secrecy over, and with the risk of instant internment in a Federal prison attached, should I be so foolish.

TWO

I wound up my preliminary meeting with miss Zendell on rather an unsatisfactory note, for both of us, I'm afraid. If I were to believe everything she told me, the girl had a dilemma. The mysterious note might have been written as no more than a scare tactic, aimed more at Vincent Zendell than his daughter. It was possible nothing untoward would occur after its delivery, the purpose having been achieved. That is, to put the wind up her father, Vinnie the viper, as I used to call him.

What worried me was the message, quoting, *'the sins of the father'.* I remembered something similar to it being from a Shakespear play. I looked it up before leaving for home that afternoon, and what I discovered did little to instil cheer.

Excerpt: Shakespear's *Merchant of Venice.*

Yes, truly; for, look you, the sins of the father are to be laid upon the children; therefore, I promise you, I fear you. I was always plain with you, and so now I speak my agitation of the matter: therefore be of good cheer; for, truly, I think you are damned.

I asked Matilda to return to my office at eleven in the morning, at which time I would give her my decision regarding whether or not I could provide her the assistance she was looking for. Had I no idea what was attached, I would have accepted the commission without further thought, but that was very far from being the story. If the threat was more than an empty threat and turned out to be real, this was a can of worms. Nasty worms at that! It was something I wished no part of, but. . .

Yes, there was a *but*. A small and near innocuous word, usually. This time, however, it was packed full of concern for a young lady barely out of her teens who had been dealt a life blow, not by anything she had done but by her thickheaded father's penchant for nastiness. In addition, it was connected to certainly the biggest, ugliest conspiracy it had ever been my misfortune to be caught up in, and chock full of foreboding. The latter was something new to me, and I did not like it one bit.

Foreboding is a word way too close in relation to another word. Fear— a condition I was familiar with—as in mortal fear; fear for one's safety; both being a healthy enough condition and able to be put to good use whenever finding one's self caught in dodgy situations. What I experienced, and for the very first time, I might add, was a fear of loss. To lose the manner of existence I had become so used to these past years suddenly became an issue: a comfortable life, a wife I loved and cared very much for; all the trappings and responsibilities attached to this new way of existing. It was no longer about only myself and I didn't much like risking any of it. The loss would be much more than if I were the lone ex serviceman gone rouge I had been, living a chancer's life with little thought to the future.

It hit me hard then, how much I had changed, but hell, I was already poised at the pool's edge, ready to jump into this PI thing, and, at the risk of destroying further an already lame metaphor, with a toe in at the deep end of the pool. I had the afternoon, the night and the following morning to decide what I would do.

I arrived home before Janie, having ridden in a taxi, and pushed open the front door at three in the afternoon. Our dwelling on these ten acres of unspoilt countryside lay a twenty minute drive from my office. Every time I rolled and bumped along our four hundred metre driveway, passing beneath the overhanging gum trees to finally see come into view that secluded, colonial style home, it did absolute wonders, reminding me of how fortunate I had been to arrive at this restful, comfortable, if, perhaps, undeserved chapter in my life.

I dropped my briefcase on the table by the door and strolled on down the central corridor, emerging in the kitchen with a view out into our enormous back yard, full of fruit trees, overhanging grape vines growing over trellises, and, in the distance, under clear, blue sky, were those rolling green hills that stretched right across the distant horizon.

I took a home baked oat cookie and a large mug of coffee out to the table under our verandah, and sat. Having not realised quite how wound up I had become, the moment I took the weight off, a huge sigh escaped me, and for a long moment I continued silently soaking up the ambience; a transcendent tranquillity only the countryside can offer.

I was halfway through the giant sized cookie when I heard Janie enter the kitchen behind me.

'You're home early.' she called.

I checked my wristwatch, discovering that it was not yet four o'clock. 'As are you. Everything honky dory at work?'

'Peachy,' she called, amid the clatter of crockery and the roar of the *express-boil* kettle in preparing her own brew.

She came out, five feet five inches of gorgeous. Brown hair tied back in a ponytail, smiling sweetly while, with a cookie on a plate and mug of coffee in the other hand, she rounded the table to sit down alongside me.

'How was your day? Do you have a client yet, or—' she began to giggle '—are we still paying rent to fulfill your private dick fantasy?'

I didn't want to do this, but it was now or never, and screwing up my courage–.

'*Hey! Get down from there, you little so-and-so!*' she called out, reproving our tabby cat who had made a comfortable nest for itself in the window box, plumb centre of the flowering chrysanthemums.

'We've got to stop feeding that animal,' I said, seizing on the distraction in cowardly avoidance. 'I've never seen a cat as big. What does he eat, anyway? Rabbits? Wild dogs? He's a beast.'

She had risen to fetch the cat down, set it down on the ground. It ran off, and as she sat back down, she insisted, 'Well?'

'Well what?'

'A client. Any luck yet?'

'Oh. I was about to tell you-'

I didn't believe my good luck. From the front yard there issued the sound of probably the loudest car horn on Earth. The recognisable window rattler had come from off a diesel locomotive, but it was now attached to the roof of a early model Ford truck owned by my old compadre, Took, whom neither of us had seen in quite a stretch.

'My god, that thing nearly causes me a heart attack every time,' she responded, clutching her chest and laughing.

We called to him from where we sat, to come on in when he banged at the front door. We hadn't seen him since he departed for his annual jaunt to Indonesian shores, where he enjoyed the good life, the women, the customs and the generous exchange rate of the Australian dollar which went a long way toward affording him a kind of luxury he would never find for the same money here in Oz.

Emerging on the verandah, he halted, the great, six foot seven inch galoot dressed in denim jeans, black t-shirt and denim jacket, his enormous beard, shaggy brown hair and those crazy eyes, one blue one brown in colour, both full of some barely contained mischief. In his arms before him he supported a stack of gift wrapped parcels which threatened to tumble at any moment.

'Yo, guys. Glad to see you taken' 'er easy. Here, grab this lot before I drop 'em.'

'Hello, Took,' Janie greeted. 'Janie. Lookin' good, girl.'

'What's all this?' I wanted to know. It's not my birthday.'

'Just a couple of items I picked up. Them duty free places are full of good stuff, and cheap.'

He unloaded the packages onto the table, grabbed Janie in a big hug, lifting her feet from the ground. 'It's good to see you, girl. You behaving yourself? He then turned to me and we exchanged blokey thumps about the body and shoulders.'

'Everything sweet with you, brother?' he asked.

'Yeah, you know. Same old same old. Can't complain. Who'd listen anyway?'

'Yeah, right. But why would you, man? What would you possibly have to complain about? Look at this place. You really landed on your feet.'

'I guess so,' I had to admit.

Janie made sandwiches, which we washed down with light ale as we listened to Took relate to us, and as he would have us believe, his adventures in paradise: the people he met, new friends he had made, the markets, the forays into the mountainous countryside, black marketeers toting M16's and Kalashnikovs. He had even befriended, or been befriended by, some crazy warlord with a million dollar price on his head, a man who had evaded capture for many years by moving from one hideout to the next, via a network of secret trails throughout the densely covered Banjan ranges.

'Yeah, that dude was crazy alright,' he was saying. 'But they loved him, the hill-tribes people. That guy ain't never gonna be captured. He's like the Robin Hood of the Banjis. Of course, the opium fields he controls, the money they pull in, he can well afford to splash it around.'

'Here, check this out,' he said, pulling from his pocket a small amulet on a short string of beads, the figure carved from what looked to be ivory, into the shape of a grinning, somewhat menacing looking skull. 'It's *bookoo*,' he explained, gingerly. *Powerful medicine.*

It enables the owner to strike down his enemies with the aid of the spirits of dead warriors which he himself killed in battle. How cool is that?'

I didn't buy it. Why would this warrior or maybe bandit king guy give away something supposed to hold power like that? Of course, I wasn't going to tell Took I didn't believe it.

Janie wasn't as tactful, laughing outright. 'You can't believe that mumbo jumbo, Took.' She looked at him, disapproving. Do you?'

He shrugged. 'Maybe. Why not? *There are more things in heaven and Earth, dear Janie, than are dreamt of in your philosophy,*' he returned, borrowing from Shakespear, and that made twice, today, I had come across Shakespearian quotes.

Janie pretended amazement. 'You've read Shakespear?'

'Don't look so shocked,' Took replied. 'I have a pretty reasonable education, truth told. And I've been around, enough to have greater respect for the powers of belief, I can tell you, Janie. There's some strange shit happens in our world.'

'Hell, I've witnessed, first hand, what belief can manifest in someone believing in this sort of thing,' I chimed in. 'I knew a Caribbean guy, years ago, who carried a woven lock of hair. It was, supposedly, a gift from a powerful witch, and he believed it would render bullets unable to find him in a firefight. That guy was fearless, and one hell of a good soldier.'

'Do I want to hear how this story ends?' Took asked nervously. 'I suppose you're going to tell me he was hit by a bus the day he was demobbed from his outfit.'

'Not at all. No.' I told him, dropping it, but he remained watching me, waiting for the punch line. When the strange look continued, I relented. 'Well, actually.'

'I knew it. You can't help yourself, can you? I was quite prepared to let myself believe this thing had good mojo for me, protecting me from my enemies and misfortune. Go one then, if you must. What happened?' he insisted.

'Truthfully? He never got so much as a scratch in all the years I knew him.'

'Ah-haa! *See!* There you go then,' he returned, gleefully. 'These things work. All you gotta do is have a little faith.'

'More than *a little*, I would imagine,' Janie rejoined. 'Given the choice of a kevlar vest and that thing, what would you choose to wear if someone had a gun aimed at you and was squeezing the trigger?'

'Oh, no,' Took replied, laughing. 'I refuse to play that game.' He held the amulet up by the threaded bead loop, allowing it to swing before our eyes. 'This thing has mojo to spare, I'm tellin' you guys. It was a present from Barry, and I choose to believe it has power.'

'Barry.' I repeated.

'Yeah. *Barry*, warlord king of the mountains.'

Took still had his Vincent Black Shadow motorcycle, the one Guido's goons had banged up pretty good, the time they knocked him off it the day he went off to search for their secret base of operations. It was worth a fortune in today's money. He didn't ride it often these days, for fear of having it be damaged. The old Ford truck was his standard mode of transport. He had a small property of his own, only eight miles up the road from us, where he kept himself busy and in pretty good shape selling or trading firewood. He felled trees become dangerous for their age, cut, stacked and transported many tons of the stuff. On his property he had built a large shed cum workshop, filled it with wrecked and restored motorcycles which pulled in a handsome reward when it came time to sell a completed project. He still had the yellow school bus; the one we hired from him when we made a move on Guido's place of residence, *Villa Vulgar*; the beginning of the end for Mr Spinoza.

It was a pleasant evening. We caught up over the passing hours. At around nine, having consumed the carton of beer, we concocted a giant pizza in order to christen a brick pizza oven I had finished building only days before. I had apparently used the wrong mortar mix in its construction and the thing began to crack, threatening to collapse on our pizza, but it held well enough and we had our late night snack.

At around midnight I realised we hadn't opened the presents Took had bought us from the duty free. Most of it was alcoholic in nature. In attempt to help me give up the my nicotine habit, so he says, he bought a bunch of vapes. I'd never heard of them before, but he insisted it was what people were using these days to wean off of tobacco. Janie received a jumbo sized bottle of perfume, which, surprisingly, didn't smell half bad and which she delighted in. After the pizza oven incident and consumption of the crusty creation, Janie excused herself, explaining that she needed sufficient sleep in case of early morning emergency cases coming to her at the clinic, when she would need to be at the top of her game. She hugged Took goodnight, told him, 'Don't be a stranger. We would love to se more of you.'

To me she said, 'Don't make a night of it, okay?'

When she had been gone a few minutes, Took turned to me, asking, 'What is it, buddy? Something on your mind? I caught you brooding from time to time, all through the evening, and don't be tellin' me it's nothing. I know you, man, and I know that look. What's eatin' at you?'

I didn't deny the fact there was something on my mind. I needed someone's input in order to get better prospective, but still, dragging up the past was difficult. I could only lean forward in my chair, elbows resting on knees, give an affirming nod. But where to start?

'I got my first client, this morning. Well, *prospective client*,' I amended.

'Good for you,' he replied. 'Or not good for you?' he decided. 'Not that great,' I clarified, and he waited as I dithered some more. The situation had really scrambled my ability to apply my usual brand of logic to it.

'Damn it,' I at last voiced. 'A girl came to me with a note she had discovered pushed under her hotel room door. A girl around maybe nineteen, twenty years-old.'

At this point I pulled my tobacco from my pocket and began rolling a cigarette. Took waited patiently, watching in silence as I finished construction, lit up and took a long draw.

'The note was some kind of threat, saying to pass on a message.' I reached into my pocket and retrieved a copy. 'Here. I photocopied it.'

Took looked it over:

Tell Vincent, "The sins of the father..."

He will know EXACTLY what I mean.

Cassandra.

He looked at it for a long time. Handed it back to me, and we looked at one another in shared, mute silence. He was doubtless going through all the mixed emotions and processes of confused thought I had, the moment of my own first viewing.

'The girl was. . . Vinnie the Viper's kid?' he asked.

I nodded. 'I ran a search immediately after she left my office. Her credentials check out. Photo and everything. She is Vinnie's daughter.'

He though for another short while before saying, 'Why the hell would you give a damn? Why do we care if someone's got it in for him and his family? It's no business of yours, buddy.'

'Isn't it?' I replied.

Again with the silence. I tried to look at it from the prospective Took had suggested. He had a valid point. Why make it my problem? I owed them nothing. So why was I having such difficulty?

Dumb question. I knew very well why. I just had trouble admitting it.

'What's the problem,' Took wanted to know.

'I can't walk away from this. That's the problem,' I answered, grinding out the words angrily. 'It's not her fault she has a rotten family, is it? The threat is directed at her, not her father. You didn't miss that, did you?'

'No, I didn't miss the fact. I remember my Shakespear. It's from the *Merchant of Venice*. But, hell–' and he stalled, apparently thinking better of the proposed retort.

'You were about to say?'

'I was going to say, we all came from rotten families, and look at how we turned out.'

We laughed together at that. All of us, Took, Janie and myself, we had come from dysfunctional families; ignorance, negligence, full of crime, violence and general abuse. As for the way we had turned out? It had taken a lot of years, effort and a lot of difficult times before arriving where we now found ourselves; and, even then, that wasn't so very special a place. Still we counted ourselves fortunate. We were the lucky ones, even to survive as long as we have.

'So now you're a social worker.' He said it flatly, not as a question, and it nettled considerably.

'You know what you can do with that remark,' I told him, feeling rising anger.

'Okay, sorry. I'm only trying to play devil's advocate here, let you view this thing from other than where you're seeing it from.'

'You think I haven't tried to do that? The kid has her whole life in front of her. Her mother died recently, her miscreant father is in prison and there's no one she feels safe in turning to.'

'You haven't changed.' Took observed.

I wasn't going to respond to the statement, but I couldn't resist. 'Meaning what, exactly?'

He had the beginnings of a wry grin emerging on his face. 'Ever since I first met you, I knew. Took, I said to myself, this guy is trouble.

. . . but a good kind of trouble. You gotta poke at things with a stick, looking for, I don't know what exactly. . . authenticity?'

'*Authenticity*?'

'Authenticity. Yeah, I think so. I think you're the *reallest* person I know, and when you don't see it in others, it gets your goat. You never can stand things like inequity, injustice and all the other bullshit things in this world. You just can't walk past it, can you? You gotta poke it with a stick, in hope it will lash out at you. That way you've got an excuse for getting involved, maybe stomp on it, put things to rights.'

'Yeah, sure,' I scoffed, but it was a shock, suddenly to hear something approaching the truth pointed at me. Maybe having a mirror placed before me is what ignited my self-examination in recent times.

'Seriously,' he continued. 'You're like some crazy middle order angel, all bottled up inside and permanently angry, demanding fairness and justice in a world that refuses to live up to your expectations.'

The smile had spread right across his face while witnessing my growing discomfort at his oddly penetrating caricature.

'And you,' I rejoined, 'pseudo aesthetic, fringe dwelling agent of karma that you are. Put a sock in it, and tell me honestly—' I had my head in my hands at this time— 'What do I do?'

He sighed, shook head head. 'Come on, man. You've already decided. You're looking for me to talk you out of it. To find some compelling argument why you can't go in to bat for this girl. I've given the only argument I have. Well, that is the only argument apart from the bleeding obvious.'

'You mean, that it quite possibly a trap, a means of Spinoza and Zendell getting even?

'That's the one,' he replied gravely. 'You can't tell me those guys haven't been stewing on it all these years.'

'It is a dilemma,' I responded quietly. 'And if I misjudge, think it's a trap and turn my back? Put yourself in her position.'

'But not forgetting: Why do you owe her anything? It's a good question, don't you think?'

'I guess,' I told him, but it's just another question, not an answer.' 'I know,' he replied, himself beginning to feel the gravity of the decision at hand.

We studied one another in sustained, tense silence, attempting to glean any hint of fresh, emerging insight from the little we had to go on. Nothing tangible came to mind, but there was in the air a gradual and growing understanding; that gathering sense of inevitability we both recognized and were only too familiar with in our lives; knowing better than to try and resist, or even to question it. In unison stupid smiles emerged on both our faces.

'God have mercy,' Took uttered. 'A bloke should have his head read. 'We're decided then?' he asked.

'It appears that way.' 'And the trap thing?'

'We'll be cautious,' I assured him; and, as if by the hand of providence, my pizza oven chose that precise moment to collapse in on itself.

THREE

I boarded a bus without knowing where it was going. On it with me were many familiar faces, people I had known throughout my life, several of them close friends. Where we were travelling to, I had no idea. The diesel engine droned in the background as I looked from face to face. No one spoke yet I felt I was being made welcome. They had been expecting me, although the fact seemed entirely irrelevant. There was a feeling of comfort and safety until it dawned on me that everyone of them had been dead for many years. The vehicle travelled onward, the motor droning as we all sat, silent and at ease. The destination didn't much matter, although one destination in particular seemed obvious to me.

I awoke earlier than the usual time of six-thirty, after a night of sporadic sleep broken by a number of unsettling dreams. The one I remembered involved a bus ride.

Janie was not yet awake. I climbed out of bed as carefully and quietly as possible, pulled on my robe and slippers before sneaking out to the kitchen.

I had not much of an appetite this morning, I recall, but toasted a slice of bred anyway, slathered it with butter and jam while brewing coffee as usual.

I knew I had to appraise Janie of what was going on, but it would doubtless put some strain on the domestic calm we had cultivated for so long. It bothered me that I was worried about upsetting her. Not in the usual way. It worried me that I was worried about invoking her displeasure; one of those ridiculous situations scriptwriters with no imagination love to play with in daytime soap operas. That I was that guy, worrying about displeasing the missus, it caused me concern. What the hell had I become? I had always ridiculed the behaviour whenever I witnessed it, and now, here *I* was, doing exactly that.

My usual remark whenever a saw something like that was: 'Grow a pair of balls, fellah.' I had always been a fierce advocate for the truth, allowing the chips to fall where they may, as the saying goes. If one has to appease their partner whenever decisions are made, the whole deal is destined for the scrapheap. So why the hell was I even thinking about this? I had made a decision, for better or worse, and that was that.

Maybe it was the better or worse bit? That was the problem. Events might go in any direction and this, what we had here, could all go tits up in a heartbeat. Hell. . . What was I thinking about? I needed to tighten my grip on myself, discard these wayward thoughts and focus.

I was on my second coffee when Janie entered the kitchen. 'You're up early,' she said, as she walked by and began preparing her breakfast.

'Didn't sleep so well,' I explained, 'and then woke earlier than usual. 'Equinox,' she replied, switching on the kettle while waiting for her bread to toast.

'Equinox?' I asked.

'It's the same every year, dear. Today is what, the twenty-second of March? You're right on queue. How can you not know?' 'Know what? Are you speaking in riddles or something?'

At this, she rolled her eyes in frustration. 'Alex, dear. You know what an equinox is, I hope.'

'Of course. The position of the sun crosses over the equator twice a year. . . Oh, yeah. I do remember. We had the same discussion this time ast year. Didn't we?'

'And the year before that, and the one before that' she added, catching the toast as it popped out. 'How could you forget? You're like some kind of defective equinox alarm. Your diurnal clock or internal calendar or whatever. Ever since we've been together, you've had strange dreams and restless nights every year at this time.'

'I have strange dreams anytime.'

'Maybe, but you only ever mention it around this time of the year.' 'Really? Hugh. Yeah, I guess that's right.'

Janie brought her breakfast over to the table and sat opposite. 'You sleep well?'

'I slept great,' she said. 'Why?'

'Why do you ask, *why?*' I answered. I wondered, is all.

She was watching me over her piece of toast and yeast extract spread as she bit into it. *Observing*, actually.

'What?'

'*Nothing—*' shaking her head and shrugging simultaneously, but she still held me in that steady, uncanny gaze I hadn't seen since the first night we met; the night I found her in a cabin at the Old Coach, zoned out on the blue stuff, when her colleague had his face blown off after two of Guido's men stormed their cabin to rip off the drug takings. How far she had come, I was thinking; how proud of her I was for beating a terrible addiction few others were able even to attempt to do. She was really something. *Is*, I corrected myself, and here she is, sitting with me after all this time.

She finished her toast, and reaching for her English Breakfast tea to wash it down with, asked: 'What are you thinking right now?'

'*Nothing,*' I told her, emulating, in an exaggerated manner, her own response of a moment ago.

It made her laugh; a bright-eyed, wide smiling laugh which never failed to cheer me up. It was time to fess up.

'Janie, about that client I was going to tell you about yesterday before Took dropped by.'

'I was wondering when you were going to get around to this.'

I told her how the young woman had arrived soon after Janie had left for work, after helping out in the office yesterday morning. That was the easy part, now it got difficult. The best way to proceed was to produce the note miss Zendell had shown me. This I did, pulling it from my shirt pocket, unfolding and pressing it flat on the tabletop, spinning it one-eighty for her to read.

She read it, remained quiet for a moment as she fully absorbed it's meaning. Then raising her gaze: 'The woman received the letter and brought it to you? Presumably Vincent Dell's daughter?'

I nodded. 'She found it a couple of mornings ago, pushed under her hotel room door, down in Melbourne. The Oceanic Hotel, in Saint Kilda.'

'And she brought it all the way here, to you. Why do you suppose that was?'

'She told me she didn't really know what to do, but she was coming here to settle some business concerning winding up her father's business holdings. The Blue Parrot club. . . or pub, I forget which. She was left with little means of support when the courts took all they could of Vinnie's amassed cash and assents. The council are considering tearing the place down, for structural safety reasons.'

'And you believe her? I mean, she brings it to *you?* You don't think it sounds even a little bit fishy?'

'I did. Maybe I still do. She told me she spotted one of my advertising leaflets here in town and. . . Well she told me her mother had recently died. There was no one besides her father, I guess, who she could turn to who might understand the significance or who might help her. She obviously didn't want to go running to dear old dad with it, causing needless concern if it might be nothing more than some kind of vindictive hoax. I guess that makes sense, and discovering I was still here in town and running a detective agency.' I shrugged insouciantly. Even to me this was all sounding a bit of a stretch. But life was like that. Not everything came neatly packaged. People certainly don't always follow logical guidelines.

'She almost chickened and didn't come,' I continued, 'but you do see how she might think I would understand better than most. Better than anyone else in her life, without worrying her father.'

'*You,*' Janie enunciated with emphasis, 'after your part in her father's arrest and conviction?'

'Yeah, I know. It's exactly what I thought, but as she explained, people don't get to choose their families. She seems a nice enough girl, and genuinely upset by the whole thing. She was only nine years old, I think, when all that stuff went down. Quite separated from all the mayhem when it was playing out, and knowing nexttonothing about it. I think she tries hard to divorce herself from it all. There's no real reason, necessarily, to hold a grudge against me. She acknowledges the narrowly averted horror. Her father's role in it all.'

'You think there's no resentment?' Janie replied.'You're responsible for putting daddy in prison, never to be released.'

'And her uncle Guido,' I was impelled to add. 'They were the two male role models in her life, I guess.'

Janie rolled her eyes in an amusing fashion. 'And you are believing her because, and I quote: *'She seems a nice girl.'*

I lifted one of those vape things Took had given me from the table-top, intending to try it. I looked at it briefly and discarded the thing, opting for the real thing. Nicotine may have it's drawbacks, but hampering clear thought processes was not one of them.

On the face of it, Matilda Zendell having come to me with a note and a story spelled *trap*. At the very least, *be wary*. No denying it. On the other hand, there was just enough imperfect logic to the story. That, to me, gave it a patina of authenticity. I never much liked perfect logic. It's too predictable, too precise for human reality. There had been several instances in my life when I had been fed false information. It had always been designed perfectly logically. It was that perfect logic, in the end, which had been the flaw and given it away. The game of war is stuffed full of disinformation and I had grown adept at sniffing it out. Right now I was locked in a mental stalemate, attempting to identify the clever deception or what might well be an imperfect truth. I lit up my cigarette.

Janie, meanwhile, had been patiently allowing me time to work through it. She glanced between the clock on the wall and her wristwatch, exclaiming, '*Wow!* I gotta dress for work,' and hurried off towards the bathroom. I was still sitting at the kitchen table when Janie emerged, dressed and ready to go.

She sat herself across from me again, placed her handbag and car keys on the table. Pushing them to one side, she said, 'I guess you're taking a cab in to work, later. Unless I'm dropping you off in your dressing gown?'

'I'm meeting her at the office. She'll be there in a little over three hours. I'll book one in a minute.'

'Look,' she said, reaching across and grabbing my arm. 'You know I'm nervous about this, but it's your decision. There are many possibilities. Of course most of them are coloured by the past and it would be crazy not to consider them.' She reached for and relieved me of the cigarette between my fingers, took one drag before crushing it out in the ashtray. 'You'll do what's right,' she reassured. 'You always do.'

With that she stood, came around the table and kissed me on the cheek before retrieving her keys and bag, leaving me siting, alone and undecided as she departed for the veterinary clinic.

In the time remaining before I left, I dressed to spend some time in the garden. A warm autumn morning, it was pleasant to be out in the air. It helped to clear my head as I roamed about the flowerbeds Janie loved to tend, while mulling over all I knew of events surrounding the girl, Matilda. With an hour left to go, I called the cab company, booking a ride for ten thirty, shaved, showered and dressed. Nothing flash: dark coloured sneakers, grey cotton trousers, woolen shirt and jacket. About to leave the bedroom, I suddenly recalled my mental note of the previous day. A working PI should carry protection, I figured, and to that end I opened the little safe in the walk-in closet. My needle gun lay on the top shelf within. A piece of nostalgia these days, nothing more. Perhaps I would have it framed as a memento to crazier, more exciting days. I selected my Glock 32, shoved a clip of .357 magnums into it. A beautiful but deadly package most would think was fiction, but surely was not. It fit snugly into a clip holster, suitably well hidden, clipped under my belt at my back. About to exit the closet, I paused, catching glimpse of my kevlon, teflon compound vest hanging on a hook. I hadn't had one of these moments for some time, but that same old oddness I once relied on was back again. Anyone who knows what I'm talking about will understand. A thought will enter one's head for no apparent reason, sometimes as a flashing vision, barely lingering long enough to be seen, let alone understood. It is nearly always accompanied by a brief feeling of s omething impending. The usual thing is to ignore something seemingly as silly, brush it off, to be forgotten as quickly as it comes, but a long time ago I started paying attention to these anomalous impulses.

The very first time I did so—as an experiment, really, though the feeling was potent—it involved an armoured vehicle, a Bushmaster. We had abandoned it outside of a village in Turkestan when a fractured fuel line leaked, draining the reserve tank, and we abandoned it overnight, returning at five next morning with replacement hose and a can of diesel. It started, fine, and we were about to move off when just such a fleeting feeling struck. The guys laughed, naturally, saying I'd had a common bout of the *eeby-jeebies.* I climbed out of the vehicle to closely inspect everything from engine compartment to drive shaft and tyres. I discovered a tiny movement device sitting atop a tyre, hidden from sight by a low, armour-plated guard panel. The movement detector would have energised a radio circuit attached to a rocket launcher mounted a hundred feet off in a thicket, the moment we inched forward.

No one was laughing then, and the instinct only developed as time went by. Every patrol team from then on tried having me assigned with them like some kind of good-luck mascot, and I have obeyed the uncanny, inbuilt warning device ever since.

Hence, despite the outwardly illogical and improbable need for it, I slipped the lightweight vest on under my jacket and shirt. It spoiled the appearance of my clothing, but I just could not bring myself to ignore the habit of obeying this strange, fleeting feeling which had served me so well in the past.

FOUR

I climbed into the back seat of the taxi at ten thirty and asked the driver to take it slowly. This morning I was in no hurry to get to work; besides, our deciding to move out here had not been without thought; a leisurely, daily commute through the rural landscape was a consideration since day one. Of course, candidly, today it was not as much to do with appreciating the landscape as the fact of my struggle with what I would tell Matilda when I saw her.

The driver was a big guy, around fifty year-of-ages: chubby, kind, smiling features, poorly groomed, with shoulder length, pale ginger hair thinning on top, and a three day growth on his face.

He offered a wide, friendly smile as he twisted about in his seat to address me. 'Sure thing.' His pale eyes appeared bloodshot under heavy lids. 'Slow and easy suits me too, mister.'

There was something up with this guy; as if he hadn't slept in a long while. There was the distinct odour of burnt marihuana in the cab, poorly concealed by a cheap, pine scented air-freshener. I watched frequently through the rear vision mirror to make sure he didn't doze off while I rode in back. He glanced up a couple of times, catching me watching him. His eyes seemed to be making special effort to focus in on me.

'I know you, don't I, mister,' he said at last. 'Couldn't say,' I replied. 'Do you?'

'You're that guy. The guy who came to the station that day. The radio station. You and that chick, and a big guy. A biker dude. You said there was a bad batch of *blue* on the streets and for folk to avoid it unless they had a death wish. It *was* you. . . Wasn't it? UM-FM Radio. University of Monarto.'

'Joe Grummen,' I uttered, gob-smacked. You're kidding me. It's you?'

He laughed, hard, his voice loud and gravelly. 'In the flesh. Man, I can't believe it after so long. That was a time, wasn't it?'

'It was, Joe. What happened to your disk jockeying career? Or should I say, *radio announcing*?'

'All the same to me, dude. I was fired. Can you believe it? They actually fired my arse over a public safety announcement.

'*No, hey!*' he protested, seeing I was about to apologise. 'We had to do it. No choice, dude. We must have saved thousands of lives that day. I'd do it again. Shit, eh? What a bummer that was.'

'What're the odds, Joe, me climbing in your cab this morning? I'm surprised you recognised me.'

'You look almost exactly the same,' Joe all but bellowed from the front seat. 'Hardly changed at all, dude. Unlike myself,' he continued, self-mockingly. 'I must have put on at least sixty pounds since them days.'

'That was a tough break, Joe. Unjust. I *am* sorry. *Really. . .* What did you do after the radio announcing?'

'*Ooh*, this and that. Not a great deal. Jobs were hard to come by after the riots,' he said, laughing. 'Shit, the uni was so badly busted up I had to transfer to another, if I wanted to finish my doctorate. In the end I just didn't bother going on with it. I picked up a part-time gig, sound engineering for a band called DOA. Remember them? They cracked it big, and they dragged me along for the ride. I got lucky. Right place at the right time, you know? Money rolling in. Fat city for a while, man, but fame is fleeting, right? And money, too. Now I own this cab. Life, man. Fickle as fuck sometimes, *ain't it?*'

'It is that, Joe Grummen,' I agreed, smiling and pleased as punch to see him again.

Joe pulled up to the curb in front of my building at around five minutes to eleven. I gave him a tip, for old times sake.

I was standing at the curb beside the driver's side door, telling Joe good-bye, wish him well and that sort of thing. I chanced to look up and caught sight of Matilda, walking along the pavement on the opposite side of the street. I let Joe go with a parting *'Good luck, '* and a final wave, watched as he accelerated away to merge with the traffic.

Matilda stood across the road, waiting for the traffic to thin before crossing, and I moved to wait, to greet her at the building's entrance so that we could ride the lift up to the third floor together. She recognised me only after crossing the road and looking up; a short smile emerging, but vanishing as quickly.

'I've only just arrived, myself,' I told her as she neared. 'We'll go up together.'

'I never did ask you where you were staying while you're in town,' I said to her as we rode in the lift.

'I'm renting,' she told me. 'I discovered a reasonably cheap, unoccupied rental. It's quite close by, on Rosetta, in Ravenswood.'

We emerged on the third level, walked the four or five paces to my office door, which I unlocked, bade her enter.

'I usually have a coffee, first thing. Can I get you one?' She nodded. 'White with two, please.'

She waited within my inner sanctum, occupying the same chair she had the previous day. Coffees prepared, I seated myself behind my desk.

'Well,' I began, not at all sure what was to follow, and pausing briefly. I noted her chosen attire and appearance this morning. The bronze coloured hair was tied in a ponytail. There was a minimum of makeup. Her clear, deep blue eyes needed no accentuation. She wore a colourfully printed dress; autumn leaves in browns, yellows and dull reds on a white fabric, suitably warm for the time of year. About her neck hung an elegant pendant on a fine, gold chain.

'Did you sleep well?'

'Not really,' she replied. 'Too much to think about, Mr Jaeger.' 'It's not easy to know how to respond to something like this,' I sympathised. 'I've been struggling with it also. Before I go on, has your thinking changed overnight? You're sure you want to engage my services and not go to your father with this?'

'I think this is a better solution than worrying my father with what might be, as you yourself proposed, no more than a hoax. You probably think I'm being overly dramatic, Mr Jaeger. I hope you're right, but. . .'

'Not at all, miss. Cautious is never a bad thing to be in a situation such as this. Although, it occurs to me that your father has a right to know the score. We cannot help worrying him. Circumstances are as they are, though no fault of your own. If my family were being threatened, I most certainly would want to know about it.'

She was shaking her head determinedly: 'No. It's not fair. He's suffering enough already in that horrid place. I won't do anything to make it worse for him. You must understand.'

'Alright. I had to put the option forward. After all, despite his location, I'm sure he still has connections on the outside. Connections capable of exploring the same options and avenues available to me. Perhaps better options and avenues?' I had posed this a question, hoping like hell she might reconsider, but again with the shaking of her head.

'If you'll excuse me for saying so, do you really think someone like your father is so easily shaken? The Vincent Zendell I know is someone not so easily rattled.'

This comment at last got a rise from her. 'And what exactly do you mean by that?' she demanded. 'He's not some kind of monster, you know. He was ambitious, and doing his best to get ahead in the world. What makes him any different than anyone else? That business was the doing of Cassandra. Guido got caught up in it somehow, and, of course my father was dragged into it. But he could not have known where it was leading. He couldn't have, Mr Jaeger. I know my father, and better than you. He's not that sort of man.'

'What sort is that?' I was impelled to ask. I wanted to know what sort of ground I was standing on. I still had not convinced myself that what I was seeing was the way things really were. If I were being suckered into a trap, I needed to know it. The whole exercise could so easily be the baiting of some elaborate trap, meant to entice me out into the open, perhaps in seeing me jumping through hoops for the entertainment of Vinnie the Viper and that pernicious pipsqueak, Guido Spinoza.

At my pointed remark her eyes shone with unbridled anger for the briefest of moments, an anger she extinguished so rapidly that, to me, revealed exceptional force of will. Just as quickly she looked flustered, as if caught out for her exposing so furious emotion. In that instant I was reminded of her father; his quick temper and desire to inflict harm. The resemblance was uncannily striking.

The result was brief silence, as we both seemed to be assessing the dynamic of what had just occurred; *re*-assessing our individual positions.

'Why do you toy with me?' she voiced softly, suddenly calm again. 'You meant to anger me. Why?'

'I meant to *bait* you, miss Zendell. There *is* a difference.' She did not respond to this second, less obvious probe, as might have been expected. In a calm, and, I hoped, conciliatory tone, I said to her, 'You need to consider my side of, shall I say, this unusual situation we find ourselves in? Give it a little though and you might understand where I'm coming from.'

'It is kind of unique,' she responded, managing to sound somewhat appeased, and even affected a smile. I see your point, I think. Do you actually suspect this is some kind of contrivance?"

'Contrivance?' I repeated, weighing the word carefully. A curious word for the young lady to use. Not one I would expect to emerge in conversation. 'What an excellent word,' I commented. Then rejoining our exchange, 'Honestly?'

'Yes, honestly. I'm sorry, it has only now occurred to me the way my situation and my coming to you for help might appear to another.'

'Then honestly is how I will answer. 'Of course I'm suspicious. And very much caught off my guard after all this time. After all these years.'

'It was stupid of me. Of course you are suspicious. All I could think of was my own situation. I was frightened, confused, and I really should have given more thought. . .' She lowered her head, watching her entwined fingers, fidgeting on her lap. 'I think, maybe, on some level it crossed my mind, but really, I suppose I was far too involved in my own mind, my own troubles, and couldn't see it clearly. I didn't consider all the ramifications, Mr Jaeger. I'm sorry. I should have.'

I might well have been watching the performance of an actress auditioning for a possible Oscar winning role in some tawdry drama. I was suddenly certain of it now. The warning alarm was going off in my head like crazy and all I wanted to do was get this antipersonnel mine out of my office and further think things through. I needed to remove her subtly while convincing her I had bought into the story. It would be to my decided advantage.

'You can be forgiven for that, miss Zendell. You should not be saddled with such burdens at your age. I hope you can forgive my manner. I needed to be sure, is all. If you still desire my assistance, I'm happy to offer it to you. For a fee,' I added. 'Three hundred dollars a day, plus expenses. Does that suit?'

She appeared relieved. 'Thank-you. It's a great comfort knowing a man of your calibre and resourcefulness will be at my back. Truly.'

'Do me a favour,' I asked in response. I pushed my note pad and pencil across the desk to her. 'Jot down your address and contact number for me. I'll come visit, at the earliest convenience.

'Meanwhile, I'll need to formulate our strategy. We'll discuss it further when next we meet. Oh, and if you could? A week's advance? My experience is that information costs money. You understand.'

She did as I asked, wrote a personal cash cheque for twenty one hundred dollars, although I would have preferred cash money, and I bundled her out as quickly as I could, hopefully without revealing anything of my intent.

She asked if I would accompany her down to the street, wanting to continue our discussion as we went.

'I'm feeling less vulnerable, already,' she confided, standing beside me as we descended in the lift. 'I'll sleep so much better tonight, I'm sure.'

'I'm glad,' I replied, distracted. By accepting the commission I had set my feet on a path leading I knew not where. I had no real choice though, I remember thinking. I was in someone's cross-hairs. Maybe hers, maybe her farther's, that vindictive viper Vincent Zendell, maybe Guido's. Very likely all three. I had Janie to consider, our life together. This was not a job I could very well turn my back and walk away from. I could only make the best decisions available, given whatever opportunities were available. Refusing the commission would leave me almost totally blind. With Matilda close, she might prove an asset, besides being the danger she most certainly was.

'Do you live here in town, Mr Jaeger?'

'I have a residence quite close by,' I lied.

'Oh, that's handy for you. Are you married?' She actually produced a *come-on* look, one she might have picked up watching too many old black and white movies. It lacked all sincerity and left me feeling nothing but cold. It gave me the creeps. Already the reptile in her was beginning to show.

I pulled open the heavy, manually operated door when we had reached ground level. 'I'm still looking for that special girl,' I answered, heading for the street.

I stepped out onto the pavement with her, and stopped. 'I'll be in touch the minute I have anything for you, Miss Zendell. Remember to keep your eyes and ears open. Oh, and I should have mentioned, I can have personal protection assigned to you, if you feel you need it?'

We were standing outside, the bright sunlight reflecting from the acres of plate glass making up the display windows, causing me to squint after coming from the shadows. I had stepped to the side, near the base of the archway providing access into the building.

She appeared to think of a last minute something and opened her handbag to rummage through it, searching.

The first hornet exploded against the stone wall near my face, with shards flying, cutting and stinging as they whizzed by. I instinctively threw myself against Matilda, attempting to get us out of the line of fire. The second round hit me as I stood, square in the middle of the chest, the impact like that of a body blow from a heavyweight boxer, throwing me backward beneath the sheltering archway and out of sight of the gunman. A final, parting shot ricocheted from the pavement, smashing a plate glass window and showering us with a glistening shards, but I was more concerned with trying to suck air into my lungs.

Flat on my back, somewhat dazed, I lifted my head, and with my eyes stinging from the exploded stone, I caught sight of Matilda. She was putting good distance between herself and the scene, quickly disappearing into the crowd. I couldn't criticise the girl's instincts, but, *goddamnit*, there were wounded lying here in need of attention.

FIVE

Janie was less than impressed about my work injury. She left the veterinary clinic to come down to the hospital after my nurse insisted she telephone her, let her know I would be held for observation til morning. I had already been x-rayed. The nurse assisted by another was about to commence bandaging as Janie entered the treatment room with a look containing desperate concern mixed with unrestrained anger on her face. I'm not often intimidated but I almost considered jumping from the table and backing up against the wall.

Hi, dear,' I greeted, attempting a smile, but which came off as being rather lame. 'You really don't need to be here, you know. I'm fine.'

'What the hell were you thinking?' she responded, disregarding the medical staff as she closed on me.

All I can say is thank God I decided to don the vest. My chest was already blooming with intense bruising over the greater portion of my chest and upper abdomen; purplish colour, perhaps more puce. It surrounded the centre which already was turning black where the slug had impacted. A high velocity round, no doubt, fired from a building across the street by an unknown bastard who could have done better. A novice? I considered.

Someone with an axe to grind and wanting to do the job themselves? Janie had not yet finished with me.

'Took told me all about it,' she almost hissed in derision, but then the tears started, and if I didn't already feel like a heel—

'Oh, Alex. Why? My God, you could have been killed. What then?

What's wrong with you?'

'Me? Killed? Hell, I'm the nemesis of bad guys; the name striking fear into evildoers everywhere. Come on baby, if I was going to be killed it would have happened years ago.'

It was meant to be funny; to lighten the mood; a means of defusing the emotional stress the poor kid felt. I was hoping for a laugh, but I guess I knew it was the wrong the moment it was uttered. Even the nurse who had begun bandaging my ribs gave me a disappointed, disapproving look.

'I'm sorry, hon,' I attempted, but, already she had about-faced, and I could only watch as she stormed back out of the room.

The nurse, a big aboriginal women, responded with, '*Mm-mmm*, you sure did miscalculate that, fellah. She your wife and she's scared.'

I told her, 'Yeah,' feeling surprisingly much worse. 'I blew it alright.'

Nodding agreement she instructed, 'Lift up your arms while I wrap the stupid person.'

'What do I do now?'

'I'm guessing you put yourself in harms way without consulting your other half?' She interpreted my silence as confirmation. 'Well, she loves you. You got that much going for you. If she didn't she'd be somewhere else, stead of comin' all the way from her work to be all the way over here. You got kids?

I shook my head, discovering that doing so caused substantial discomfort.

'No kids,' she noted, inauspiciously. 'Too bad. There goes one mitigating circumstance.'

'Are you a lawyer or something,' I asked, irritated.'

She chuckled at that, and answered, evidently concealing something amusing. 'Not any more—' and securing the bandage with a tiny grapple, 'You can put your arms down now. Try taking a normal breath.'

I did, stupidly over-expanding my rib cage, resulting in, '*Ah-ee-ooh-eow.*'

'Less ambitious,' she advised. 'Loosening it won't give the support you need. Again? Not so much air this time.'

I took a more sedate breath. At least it felt better than it did when I first arrived. It would do, so long as I didn't laugh, sneeze, cough, bend, lift, walk without the smoothest of gaits or allow anyone to jolt or brush against me, attempt anything requiring flexibility or do anything inordinately stupid.

'Comfortable?' she asked.

'*Ha!,*' I replied, and immediately paid the price.

'You poor thing,' she crooned sympathetically. 'You really have been in the wars, haven't you. You'll mend, dear, I promise. Just go easy, okay?'

I was about to reply with a nod, but didn't.

'See?' She smiled broadly. 'You're getting the hang of it already. Just a minute and I'll be back,' she told me.

Entering her tiny office, she closed the door and lifted the receiver of her phone. Meanwhile I experimented with how much air I could inhale before the pain prevented further expansion. I would have to think about my reception upon returning home. I would ride a taxi home, but this was the first time I had seen Janie behave this way. It was worrisome, and not the sort of thing I usually allowed to happen. I had never stuck around anyone long enough for things to deteriorate, not that I could count this as deterioration. This was something I had witnessed before, but never intended experiencing myself.

This was one of those symptoms of change in me I referred to earlier. Life for me had, until now, been a series of events, chapters, separate and isolated from one another but for their similarity in providing excitement and challenges. With my life experiences being compartmentalized episodes of anything involving risk and desired adventure, I seldom made attachments. Nor had I put down roots, as described by those living a normal existence. The women I had known were never more than fleeting intermissions, meaning I always moved on before any relationship came close to resembling anything like what Janie and I share.

Now that old instinct to remove myself from the equation raised it's gorgon head once more. The instinct to remove myself from the picture presented as a painful choice. Truth was, the mere idea of abandoning Janie evoked unpleasant emotions and I knew that even considering any such option had already vanished, and quite some time ago, though only now did I realise the fact. The life of serial adventuring I had always treasured was no more. I had already, and without noticing, changed, I realised with regret, and even a feeling of loss.

Grow up, a voice told me inside my head. If you've been here too long, move on, get back to who you really are. But it was false advice and I recognised it immediately. I knew because I had long ago learned how misleading one's thought can be. Gut feeling, on the other hand? Not once had it ever let me down. Today was a perfect example. I would not now be alive, sitting here, twisting my brain with these bothersome thoughts if I had not expressly decided to always trust gut instinct.

The nurse came out of her cubbyhole of an office, pulling the door closed behind her as she regarded me wearing a curious smile on her dial.

'You asked me question, earlier, and I didn't reply: *What do I do now?* There's not a woman alive who isn't moved by flowers from the man she loves. Even when that person has done something hurtful. If you like, you can give me cash enough to cover the cost of flowers and I'll have a florist deliver, on my card, to your home address, which I have in your file. They'll be there within the hour.'

'I can get some on the way home,' I told her. Wondering why she would ask for cash money.

'No you can't. It would spoil the surprise. Your wife is waiting for you, out there, in the waiting room. She never left. It will be just what she needs right now, dear. Trust me?'

'You think?' I responded, feeling completely out of my element. I had never in my life done anything which could even remotely be described as romantic.

Although, *appeasement* was the word coming to mind in the moment.

I found Janie in the waiting room, sitting, brooding, it looked like to me. I had been given a stick to walk with and I made my way over to stand in front of her, reached out for her to take my hand, helping her up from her seat; a gesture I hoped she might appreciate, and a gesture she accepted, a small, rueful smile appearing on her face.

On the ride back to the house we made small talk, avoiding broaching the obvious subject. We pulled up at a takeaway near home to purchase Chinese, eliminating the unneeded distraction of cooking a meal. I grabbled a couple of bottles of good wine; to my mind the perfect lubricant to help process and come to terms with the day's events.

The minute we entered through our front door, Janie surprised me by saying, 'I'm going to call Took and have him come over.' To my questioning look, she continued, 'You think you can handle this on your own? Who else would I ask?'

'Fair enough,' I replied, placing the items we had purchased on the kitchen bench. Janie had obviously done some thinking while in the waiting room, and if she had made some kind of decision involving no drama, I was for it. Anyway, Took had always been useful in coming up with ideas less ordinary and out of the box. We would be working pretty much blind. At least, more blind than the last time we had pooled our resources. Every angle needed to be covered before blundering into this thing.

SIX

The delivery arrived about an hour after we had arrived home. Janie answered the door, returning to the lounge room carrying a colourful bouquet and a box of chocolates, but with a very confused look on her face.

'A secret admirer?' I asked, feigning irritation. 'Who is the scoundrel? I'll tech him to mess with my woman.'

She placed them carefully on the coffee table, searched thoroughly for any attached card —a card I had neglected to stipulate.

'Hang on a sec.' I began searching around the room, coming up with a strip of cardboard torn from a discarded tissue box, quickly scribbled a note and stuffed it into the bouquet, announcing, 'Oh, here it is.'

Retrieving it, she would have read: *I'm sorry.*

It turned out that nurse was right. She gave a little smile, and tears actually welled up in her eyes. 'You bastard,' she said, sweetly, and it appeared that I was back in the good books.

Took arrived soon after, wearing full leathers and helmet, his beard and hair protruding all around the World War 1 style flying goggles. We heard the rumble of the classic 1937 Ariel Square Four, 1000cc with sidecar, as he pulled up out front. Dismounting, he pulled a box of beer free from the sidecar, marched up to the front door, rapped twice on the frame and entered, calling out, 'Greetings, fellow human beings!'

He found us out back, the takeaway tucker laid out on the table for casual consumption. Janie and myself shared one of the two bottles of wine I had purchased, out under the verandah in the late afternoon. After consigning a few cans to the refrigerator inside, he emerged.

'How you doin'?' he asked, carefully placing a large, supportive mitt on my shoulder. 'Alive, I see.'

'*Lucky*, is what he is,' Janie answered for me. 'Give me a look. Must be sore.'

'Nothing to see,' I told him. 'Sit down and behave yourself. Grab a plate and eat if you're hungry. Plenty to go round.'

'I will, thanks. Nice facial wounds,' he said, studying the multiple scrapes and gashes resulting from the exploding stonework. 'You needed to add character to that mug of yours. It'll scar up nicely.'

A glance in Janie's direction told me she didn't especially welcome the remark, but, thus far, and bless her heart for her decision, she continued to refrain from criticism.

'I was way too pretty for my own good,' I agreed, keeping it light.

He pushed his ample frame back into the chair, found extra comfort by resting his crossed feet on the next chair along. 'What the hell happened? That Zendell bitch set you up?'

It was time to get to it. Janie had not interrogated me for the fact that she knew I would have to tell it all again when Took arrived. 'It's one possibility,' I said, both of them fully attentive now. 'I have to admit, I haven't concluded anything much, yet.'

'Zendell's daughter,' Took returned, speaking volumes in just two words.

I went through the whole affair from beginning to end, from the time she turned up at the office to the moment I last saw her, disappearing into the crowd on Argyle street. 'You tell me,' I said in finishing.

While they remained silent and thoughtful, I rolled a cigarette and lit up, took a sip of red and watched their faces, enjoying their almost comical expressions: Janie running her finger around the edge of her glass, making it sing, her face giving nothing away, with a blank, poker-face expression. Took was blowing his cheeks up, allowing the air to escape and repeating the process, a scowl invading his countenance.

'I say she set you up, well and truly.' 'Why?'

'Devil's advocate. I expect one of you two to take the opposing view and we can thrash it out.'

'Okay,' Janie obliged, and to me she posed: 'You said she appeared confident, poised when first she appeared in your doorway.'

'I did, and it seemed to me a sham. Practiced, I remember thinking at the time, and the facade began to fade. I think that's what had me doubting myself, my original suspicion. After learning who she was I instantly doubted everything she said, searching for the deceit. The facade wore off, like I say, and underneath there appeared to be a frightened girl who was completely unsure of herself, why she had come to see me.'

'She said you thought you were the only one who might understand,' Took threw in. 'Mother dead, father in prison?'

'Yeah. Kind of believable at the time.'

'I don't buy it,'said Janie. 'Hard to believe,' don't you think so?' 'Honestly,' I replied, 'who's to say?' and we all fell silent again for a moment.

'People are weird,' Took offered. 'The very person who got her dad slammed up. Okay, I guess I can see how she might feel too embarrassed to ever approach anyone else with the letter. Most people would run a mile, right?'

'Right,' Janie and I chorused.

'So she doesn't have to risk you not understanding. The ins and outs, what's at stake.'

'I thought you were the devil's advocate,' Janie point out.

'Why couldn't she talk to someone else? Anyone else but you?' he switched.

'I think her argument is valid,' I told them.

'It is believable,' Janie agreed, and so too Took, after a brief silence.

'Okay,' let's say she passes on that score, for the moment. What next?'

Janie took the initiative: 'You said you believed her at one certain moment. When and why was that?'

Damn, she had a memory like a steel trap, when she wanted. My memory served well enough, but I wasn't terribly keen on answering that question.

'When and why?' she persisted.

'She began to cry when I pressed her about what the hell she was doing in my office with this problem.

She had just told me she didn't know of Cassandra, apart from the Greek seer.'

'How could she not know?' Janie admonished.

'It was an obvious lie,' I replied, 'which she did admit to when I applied the pressure, but I think she was, not inexcusably, trying to separate herself from the dark affair. From blame. From any culpability.'

'She cried and you caved in,' said Janie, accusingly, and Took was shaking his head, I noticed, feeling ridiculous now.

'That's a bit much,' I protested. 'Do you really think so little of me that I would fall for that old chestnut? Do you really?'

After a moment of consideration, she relented. 'I guess not. Sorry. So you came to believe her story at that moment,' she outlined, causing me considerable self-doubt.

'I came to believe she knew the name Cassandra from overhearing a discussion between Guido and her father,' I clarified. 'Of course I could be mistaken on that count. Just. . . I don't know. She was very young at the time. She didn't understand until the shit hit the fan, what she had been semi privy to. I imagine at that impressionable age it would cause problems. Can we agree to that?'

'When I was eleven,' Took chimed in, 'my old man was involved in an armoured car job. It was Christmas. He bought me a trail bike out of the money. It was great. They got over two million bucks, but one of the guys bought a GTHO phase three Ford when he was supposed to be on the dole. He was busted pretty quick, and the coppers rounded up dad and the third guy in no time.'

'Does that mean you agree or disagree that I was right to believe she was traumatized by what her family were involved in?' I asked.

'Didn't you tell us you twigged to her being an actor? Why should I agree about this trauma thing. I was proud of my dad for having the dash to take down an armoured car.'

It was a valid point, and I told him so. 'Fair enough. It was a big deal. She may have felt some pride in the fact that her father and uncle had almost shaken the globe. They certainly succeeded in shaking up global security.'

'She likely shares genetic predisposition, dear. The whole thing could be a thrill. If that's true—

'—she might well have set me up,' I concluded.'

'You say she took off like a rabbit when the shooting started.' Took said, taking up another aspect. 'Was she distancing herself from an attempted hit on you, or on herself, running scared, frightened for her life, hence validating the threat in the note she says was slid under her hotel room door?'

'Describe again for us, the shooting,' Janie asked.

'She asked me to escort her down to street level as we continued talking. When we hit the street we paused for a moment, rounding off the meeting. Come to think of it, there was something. She opened her bag and started rummaging around in it. I don't know what for. That's when the first shot came. I guess the purse rummaging might have been a signal to the gunman on top of the building opposite.'

'It's very possible,' Took agreed.

'It is,' Janie concurred. 'She never retrieved anything from the bag?'

'Not that I remember. Actually, no she didn't, but as I say, the first round was fired at precisely that time. There may have been something she was searching for.'

'Or not,' said Janie. 'It could well have been the signal to open up on you.

'With her standing just a pace away from me? That takes guts if one knows there's a high powered rifle pointed in your general direction. I say it's entirely within the realm of possibility she had no idea what was about to occur.'

Took straightened himself in his chair, putting his feet back on the ground. 'We're getting nowhere, guys. Maybe, could be, possibly. So tell me, what made you wear your life jacket to the meet?'

'Damned if I know,' I responded. 'Don't laugh if I tell you, some kind of sixth sense. I told you the story, years ago. Some kind of sixth sense, I guess. I've lost count how many times it saved my bacon.'

'I remember the stories. My point being, that queer talent you have told you she wasn't to be trusted. Why not admit it? She's a conniving, murderous piece of work.'

Jane pointed out the flaw before I could. 'It only means he felt something was going to happen today, do you see? Not necessarily that she was the one behind it.'

Took was annoyed by this. 'That's technically correct, but I say the feeling came from her. Her malicious intent, you picked up on it, Alex.'

'Maybe. Maybe I just picked up on the approaching danger in general, and took the precaution of slipping the thing on. I don't know. I've never known how it works. Probably never will,' I said with a sigh. 'Damned glad it's still with me.'

He shook his shaggy head in dismay. 'We have solved absolutely nothing. You realise that, don't you? We're not an inch further forward.' He went inside and got himself another beer, leaving Janie and I alone for the moment.

'He's right,' she said. 'This is all but hopeless. We don't even know for sure that the shot that hit you was meant for you.'

'It was meant for me,' I found myself saying. 'Oh, really?'

'I can't conceive of any would-be assassin being so lousy a shot.'

'You say she took off in an awful hurry. If it was meant for you and it was her plan all along to lead you into the crosshairs, wouldn't she take the time to make certain you were property taken care of? You say she didn't linger for a second, didn't you?'

'I'd just stopped a high powered round, dear. I'm not really sure of it, truth be told. By the time I had gathered my wits, enough to look around, she was off and running. I just don't know if she did of not. But I was still breathing. . . well, trying to. . . when she departed. She could have finished the job if she wanted. I was vulnerable for a while there.'

Took returned to his position, fresh beer in hand, 'I was thinking,' he said, wearing a suitably thoughtful expression.

'Always a good sign,' I jibed.

'Thanks, pal. I was thinking that you might employ the same tactic you did the time you didn't know who relieved you of your money in the White Horse Inn that time.'

'What are you talking about? When I went to speak with Guido out at villa Vulgar, find out what he knew?'

'Exactly. What's different this time?' he insisted. 'We're as much in the dark now as then.'

'I hate to put a crimp in a an otherwise wonderful plan, buddy, but Guido is in Holdsworthy maximum security prison.'

'Zendell's the likely man, ain't he?'

'Same problem. What do you suppose we would get from him anyway?'

'Well, I figure the little prick is a man who likes to gloat, don't you?You think he wouldn't love to take credit for this thing, if he's behind it? Watch you squirm when he says there ain't a thing you can do about it?'

'The note was signed by Cassandra, remember?'

'Yeah, but if his daughter wrote the note, which is a decided possibility.'

'True enough,' I told him, seeing the logic. 'He's as easy to read as a book. He couldn't help but gloat.'

'And if it's him behind it, what you got to worry about?'

'Not so much as if this Cassandra person is behind it,' I said, considering.

Janie was following the conversation. 'So if it's Zendell, we've still got to worry about him trying again. If it's not him and it really is this Cassandra fruitcake, we've still got to worry about him trying again. Only this guy is very likely way more resourceful.'

'It's a starting point,' Took pointed out. 'What do we have now?'

I turned from Took to regard Janie. Evaluating it for a moment, she gave a little not, tilted her head as if to say, *he's right.*

'I'm still kind a hoping this'll go away,' I said, distractedly. The whole deal was a major upset to my plans to run a nice little private detective agency, and for Janie and I to live out our lives peacefully. Comfortably even. I had already begun putting down those roots I mentioned earlier. What if I had lost my edge and wasn't up to this kind of thing anymore?'

'It's not going to go away,' Took correctly advised. 'Miss Zendell might disappear from sight, but whoever is playing this game, her, her father or this Cassandra character, there's malice behind it.'

'And intent,' Janie added. 'I agree with Took. There's more to come.

We have to be ready.'

'And counterpunch,' said Took. 'We need to act. You were lucky to have survived today, sixth sense of not. I'm sure it was never considered that you would. It's the only advantage we have right now and we need to make ground on it.'

I noticed the concern in both their faces. It wasn't entirely concern for themselves. I had, with my unguarded, stupid comment of a moment ago revealed a crack in my armour. *Wishing something away?* Where had that come from; another symptom of the ineffable change at work me within me?

'Alright,' I agreed. 'However we work this we had better do it quickly, while they regroup. My surviving, as you say, was not expected and they likely don't have a contingency in place.'

'Identify our opponent,' Janie said.

'I'll try and locate Zendell's daughter tomorrow. See what she has to say for herself. Took, do you think you could try and organise us a prison visit, to talk to Vincent Zendell and Guido Spinoza? Separately, of course.'

'I'll try. Failing that, I have connections in Holdsworthy. Friends of friends sort of thing. We might be able to set up a line of communication, at least.'

'Good enough,' I replied.

'What about me?' Janie asked. 'You don't expect me to sit on my hands, do you?'

In that moment I again found myself self-analysing; how I had so readily slipped into mission mode, deciding to jump, feet first, into the fray, possibly leading my wife and my good friend into all kinds of strife.

'What is it?' she asked, noticing my sudden consternation.

'I have no right dragging you into any of this. Or you, Took—' regarding my friend. 'Whoever this is, their gripe is with me alone.'

'No one is being dragged,' she replied.

'But you are a vet now. That's your life now, one you worked hard for and which you fully deserve. I don't want to take you from it. And concerning you, Took—' regarding him again. 'Round one with these pricks was a different kettle of fish. Circumstances were way less unpredictable. We knew who and what we were up against, and we had certain advantages, unlike now.'

Took responded first. 'He's right, Janie,' and I thought I detected an odd intensity as he regarded her. 'It's a bad idea, you being involved.'

We waited for her response and it's wasn't at all what I expected. Lowering her eyes, she nodded. 'Alright, but I can help from the sidelines. You can't deny me that, she insisted, looking me in the eye now.

I reached over and put my hand on top of hers. 'Thanks, dear. Things have changed, haven't they. I just cannot risk your being in harms way. There will be things I'll need your help with. Just not out in the open, okay?'

'Good,' Took said, himself sounding relieved, 'but don't even consider keeping me sidelined.'

'Why would you want to upset your own peaceful existence?' I asked. 'Look at what you have for *your* self.'

'Give it a rest,' he responded, looking and sounding aggrieved. 'You don't make decisions for me. What's up with you, man? Is there something you ain't letting on about? I ain't letting you take this shit on without backup, and I need to know everything you know.'

SEVEN

Some hours after Took had returned to his own home, Janie lay peacefully asleep beside me while my mind stubbornly continued resisting all attempts of being shut down. Nights like this were common and had been so all my life. As a means of dealing with the condition and affording myself the benefits of exercise, I once used to put on my trainers and go out jogging through the nighttime streets. It was, simultaneously, a peaceful and stimulating solution to the annoying condition: Not a soul on the streets, every dwelling silent, inhabitants deep in undisturbed, somnolent rest after a long, busy day.

It always struck me as I glided, almost spirit-like, through those streets, how only a few hours ago many of those households were filled with noise and sundry strife; bitter arguments between husbands and wives, trouble with unruly kids, perhaps, money problems, unpaid bills and maybe the threat of suspension of services applying extra pressure; any number or manner of human affairs fueling all manner of life's perturbations through the daylight hours. At the end of the day though, when all lay down their heads, with any luck to dream whatever pleasurable dreams emerged from deep within the human psyche, such transformations occur.

The streets, steeped in darkness and shadows as they often are between the widely spaced street lamps, so quiet, the air cool, crisp and still, with only the sound of my runners softly marking the passage of time. I once derived such pleasure from it; the only time the world for me was a sane and amicable place. At my doctor's insistence I had given up running through nocturnal streets when my knees began suffering the strain meted out by the pounding they received from the ubiquitous concrete and bitumen. I tried walking, but being reduced to walking only tended to remind me of how the merciless advance of time had, and continued to erode physical skills and attributes afforded to young men.

Try as I might, the hours oozed by without sleeps intervention. It was pointless continuing to lie here, I realised. Time was far from being an ally. There had to be something I could do. I at least could prepare for the coming day and get a head start on proceedings.

Managing to leave the bed without disturbing Janie, I went out to the kitchen table, grabbing the phone directory on the way through. Matilda Zendell was unlisted, of course. She wasn't a resident of the town, merely renting accommodation. My brain was sluggish for want of sleep.

'Bugger,' I cursed, but was Zendell the name she really went by? I had assumed, which is never a terribly good thing to do, and I had called her miss Zendell to her face without contradiction. Perhaps she had allowed the mistake to slip by, viewing it a convenient mistake.

I recalled asking her to scribble her contact details on a slip of paper at my office. There was then only one thing for it, and I figured it was a good a time to bring *Lullaby* out of retirement. It's the name I secretly adopted for my needle gun. A compact little piece, she fits snugly into the palm of my hand and is capable of spitting fast acting, neurotoxin coated, 20mm needles at ample velocity to drop most human beings at twenty paces. A pneumatic powered defensive weapon of my own invention, I could have patented the design, maybe made some money out of it, but, being a somewhat vain individual, I very much enjoyed being the only person owning so unique a device.

It was already nearing four-thirty in the a.m. as I pulled up in the unlit car park behind my building. I instinctively employed stealth mode, driving in without headlights employed. There was no particular reason for doing so. An impulse. Sneak impulse, I guess, and I've always allowed my impulses free rein where possible.

I used my key to enter via the rear door, entering a hallway at the base of the stairs, where I halted, listening intently for signs of movement within the closed confines of the building. In an empty building, and especially at nighttime, with all entrances and exists closed off, contained silence it complete. Like a drum, any sound becomes amplified, resounding from every hard surface within. If anyone had been moving about, there was every chance of me detecting them.

Without employing the flashlight I had brought along, I negotiated the stairs, emerging across from my office on the top floor, where, again, I silently paused. Nothing.

The slip of paper was where I remembered it, where Matilda had placed near the corned of my desk, and I switched on the desk lamp to read: M Z, 117 Rosetta, Ravenswood. There was a phone number, too, which may of may not prove useful, but why not just drive out there and take a squiz at the place?

Ravenswood is an inner suburb only a couple of miles from my office, on Argyle Street. There was barely a vehicle on the streets, apart from one cop patrol and an interstate bus cutting through the city on its way to Melbourne, I guessed. There was an almost perfect hush as I motored along, the engine purring sweetly as car engines do when cruising in the cool of the night along deserted city streets; and feeling cocooned and snug within I switched on the radio to listen to SYFM, the *Sounds of Yesteryear* station with its propensity for playing tracks Janie and I enjoyed, as the scenery glided smoothly by, lit here and there by the mercury vapour lamps illuminating the intersections along the way.

Information via the computer street navigation system brought me up close to the address I was looking for. It was just ahead now, on a slight slope, so I switched off the headlamps and coasted the remaining distance, coming to a silent halt across the road from one seventeen.

Through the venetians in the front window I noticed there was a light on in a back room. The kitchen, I imagined, lowering the window to catch ambient sounds. A fortunate neighbourhood; not a single, yapping, annoying dog to be heard.

'Since I'm here. . . ' I suggested to myself, and raising the window, I drove into the nearest side street, there parking forty metres from the address. As a precaution, before leaving the vehicle I decided to call Took's home phone, knowing it would be switched to his answering machine, and I left a message telling him what I was up to and where the car was parked. It occurred to me that this was probably not the most prudent thing to be doing, alone. This visit was not terribly well thought out, but experience had taught me well that dead time almost always belonged to the vanquished. We were still very much in the dark and the gathering of intel, as quickly as possible, was the best way I knew of catching up. Whoever was behind this can of worms was already streets ahead, having planned well in advance and putting in place contingencies for all foreseeable counter moves. I could only hope I was correct in thinking they considered me entirely out of the frame.

I moved silently along the sidewalk while keeping to the deeper shadows. I found a low side gate in a break in the hedge along that side of the house. On the driveway alongside the house was parked a dark coloured sedan, the trunk lid up and with a couple of cases packed in the back. I could step over the gate and follow a narrow concrete path leading up to the back door, but just as I moved to do so, the light over the back door came on; wan, yellow illumination emanating from it.

The light was insufficient to pose a problem from where I stood, pressed against the hedge, and as I stood, stock still, I watched Matilda emerge, pulling a travel bag on wheels behind her, which she quickly compacted before lifting it into the trunk with the others.

She returned inside the house, switched off the light. I moved briskly over the path and halted at the back door, to peer within through a narrow opening between cheap, floral curtains.

I watched as she poured water into a kettle at the kitchen sink, set it to boil and began spooning the makings of a cup of coffee in to a mug. On the table remained her handbag and some papers. It all added up to me like she was getting an early start on a trip somewhere.

'Would you mind making one extra?' I asked, casually, from inside the doorway. I indicated with a wave of Lullaby's muzzle, the coffee she was preparing.

She spun with a start, but then quickly regained composure. 'I don't believe it,' she gasped. 'You're alive. What is that thing you have in your hand?'

'You don't need to find out,' I replied, in as conversational tone as she had begun. 'Let's just say, it's precautionary.'

'Oh, I see.' She pulled an extra mug from the cupboard, asking,' how do you take your coffee?'

'Black and two.'

'I have to tell you I'm glad you're okay.' she said, preparing my coffee. 'I'm afraid running felt like the better part of valour, in the moment.'

'I think that's *discretion*, isn't it?'

'Running, discretion. It felt much the same to me at the time' The kettle began to jet steam.

'Well come on in, and close the door behind you, if you're staying.

It gets brisk, this time of day.'

I did as she suggested, and moved to the table. 'I must say I'm a little stumped at your composure right now,' I told her.

'You're not here to do me harm,' Mr Jaeger. 'I know that. You just need to know what's going on and

I'm not surprised. 'But I could have sworn you were hit, yesterday. I'm shocked to see you standing there,' she said, bringing the coffees to the table and sitting. 'Sit down, why don't you?'

I pushed my needle gun into the holster under my arm, and sat at the opposite end of the small table. 'You're leaving?' I asked. 'At five in the morning?'

She glanced at the clock on the wall above my head. 'Ten after six, actually. Yes, and I would have left much sooner, after what happened, but the first available flight to Melbourne wasn't til seven this morning.'

As I processed data, a look of contrition came to her face. 'I'm sorry. I was twenty metres down the street before I realised I had left you alone back there. How on Earth did you-'

'Don't give it a thought,' I interrupted. 'Completely understandable, but tell me this: Is your father still unaware of the threat received in the note?' Another thought occurred: 'And tell me, did you pre-book your flight?'

'I did book the flight, online. Yes. And I managed to get word through to my father by faxing the note through to the prison after the superintendent assured me he would see my father got both my message and the note.' She watched as I considered for a moment.

'Under what name did you book your flight?'

'Matilda Zendell, why?'

'That may well prove foolish, considering someone out there is threatening harm. If that someone is the actual signatory, why would they not be keeping watch on flight bookings? You think someone like that doesn't have such abilities?'

'God, I didn't even think of it,' she replied, wearing a nervous expression. Does that mean I can't leave this morning?'

'I really wouldn't advise it,' I replied, earnestly.

This was difficult. I still had not been able to rule her out as a co-conspirator. After a first attempt of revenge failing, was she continuing the subterfuge, keeping me on the hook as they tried reeling me in yet again? She had until now every reason to consider me dead. Leaving on an early morning flight would be entirely in keeping after a job being completed. I was still no further forward.

If she were indeed an innocent and my being shot was an accident, it meant that she remained very much in danger. I had already agreed to take her on as a client, and deserting her didn't fit with my sense of honour, as warped and as anachronistic a concept it might be in today's world. The other possibility, that she was in league and a part of a plot in retaliation for my role in bringing down the Cassandra conspiracy, the option was still very much alive and well in my racing mind. If I let her disappear, I would be losing an asset; a potential, hopefully unwitting source of information in a game intelligence agencies have played for many decades. The old adage of keeping one's enemies close seemed apt. Without her I had nothing, and having nothing right now was a terrible position to be in as time continued to tick by.

'I have an idea,' I told her.

EIGHT

Took woke typically early. Checking messages on his answering machine was what he did first thing, in hope of picking up missed calls in the evening offering paying jobs for the day. Upon hearing me outline my early morning exploit, he checked his watch before driving over to our house, keen to get the full story of how things had panned out. He was at our home, sitting at the table, eating a cooked breakfast Janie had prepared by the time Matilda and I arrived.

'Morning guys,' I greeted, entering the kitchen with Matilda at my side. 'This is Matilda, Vinnie's daughter. I've invited her to stay with us while I sort out this business.'

Took merely nodded, and got back to his eggs and bacon. Janie gave me a dubious look before turning to Matilda. 'Hello, honey. Are you hungry? I was just preparing breakfast.'

'Hello Misses Jaeger. Pleased to meet you. Perhaps a coffee. I had a bite to eat, earlier.' And acknowledging Took: 'Hi, I'm Matilda Zendell.'

He nodded as he pushed his cleaned plate away. 'Hi, I'm Took.'

Introductions out of the way, we sat.

'Matilda is in a bit of a spot, as you know. She was booked on a flight to Melbourne this morning, but if we really are dealing with Cassandra, it's a sure bet he'll be keeping tabs on miss Zendell, watching air, rail and bus-line booking. I'm sure you agree, we cannot make the mistake of underestimating this guy. Time was short and I figured she would be safe here until we have a better handle on things. If that's okay with you, dear?'

'You're most welcome,' Janie told Matilda. 'I imagine this would be the last place they would look for you. You'll be safe here. We'll make some space for you, later, in the spare room.'

'Thank-you, Misses Jaeger.' 'Janie,' she corrected.

'Let me lay out what we know thus far,' I said, needing to cut to it. 'In a nutshell, very little and not nearly enough. One threatening note, suggesting that Matilda is a target. The attack on the street outside my office building, missing Matilda, and fortunately, only wounding yours truly. Matilda notified her father through the Department of Corrections, faxing through the threatening note accompanied by a personal note written by her, which he will soon be in possession of, and making young Vincent, as strange as it must seem, a possible ally in this instance. So, we know Vinnie is or soon will be more or less in the know. Presuming Cassandra is at the bottom of this, we are all headed for deep and murky waters. So, people, let's keep our wits about us, okay?'

'There's that word again,' said Janie.

'What word?'

'The presumption word,' Took obliged. 'It was you who said it was dangerous to presume anything, only yesterday.'

'True enough. So, what? You're suggesting the author of the threatening note and the attack on Argyle Street might be different parties?'

Took and Janie looked at one another. Janie shook her head. Took merely shrugged, saying, 'It's possible,' but with little conviction in his voice. 'Forget it. Go ahead, man—' and I did.

'It does, on the face of it, appear that Cassandra is the author, and, as I was about to mention, we shouldn't be just accepting that. The only thing we *can* be reasonably certain of is that whoever is responsible has an axe to grind with our old friend, Vincent Zendell, and that, my fellow agents of karma (and I noticed Took's eyes light up at mention of the old appellation he himself had coined the last time we were involved in similar circumstances) *that* could include any one of the disaffected, resentful number Vinnie pissed off over the years.'

'A needle in a haystack,' Took chimed in.

Janie had risen to begin clearing plates, scraping them clean, ready to wash in the sink. 'Are we completely ignoring Guido,' dear?'

The question gave me good reason to pause and consider. 'We can't ignore anything at this stage.'

'I'm not discounting the runt's involvement,' Took remarked, laconically.

Matilda entered the discussion at surprising volume: 'Uncle Guido? *It's an absurdity!*' Then, embarrassed at her own effusiveness, demurred. 'I'm sorry, the idea of uncle Guido being involved is impossible. *Ludicrous.* You don't know him like I do. He would never ever do anything to risk harming me, I assure you. He wouldn't.' She searched our faces then, attempting to gauge our acceptance of this.

'We're throwing around ideas, dear,' Janie explained. 'Nothing more.'

Took seemed amused, a condition not lost on Matilda. 'What's funny?' she demanded.

'We've all grown quite thick hides around here, girly. Is it warm in this kitchen?'

Took's remark briefly puzzled her, but then, retorting with surprising acerbity: 'It's my family we're talking about, *mister*, and *my* life that's on the line.' Noticing Took's continued amusement, she changed tact. 'Oh, I get it. You don't trust me? Looking for chinks in my armour? Well you found one, if that makes you happy.' She stood. 'I wonder if you could show me my room?' she asked of Janie. 'I would like to bring in my few possessions, and, if you don't mind, retreat for a while. Maybe take a nap. I'm quite weary. It'll give you a chance to talk freely in my absence.'

Janie assisted with her belongings, finding drawer or hanging space as needed, while Took and I moved our discussion out to the yard.

'Someone had to do it,' he replied, without my having to ask.'

I pulled a pre-rolled quirly from my shirt pocket. Lit up. 'What did you get?'

'Seems reasonably genuine. Tense, nervous, skittish. What one might expect, but the *"my life on the line"* line? Still, she *is* a woman. Clarity and logic aren't their strong suits.'

'Making allowance for excessive emotion boiling over?' I weighed in. 'She looks the goods—' but the moment the words left my lips, I remembered her performance at our initial meeting.

'If she's not, she's dangerous,' Took determined.

NINE

Holdsworthy maximum security prison has an inmate population of two thousand, give or take. It houses what are regarded as the country's most able, adept and therefore more dangerous criminals. Its fully up to date security designed construction and operating measures had not once been breached in the twenty one years since its inauguration; boasting available education in most areas, trades workshops where those looking to improve themselves can enter apprenticeships under expert tutelage. Psychiatric and psychological facilities are also present, with qualified staff. Among other things there is a fully equipped gym and exceptional hospital facilities where battery and stabbing wounds are tended to on pretty much a daily basis.

Vincent Zendell, with aid and leverage provided by his lawyers, underworld contacts and business associates, had managed to make his confinement less restrictive than most other inmates. His allotted accommodation at the end of the upper tier of C-Division included four regular size cells, their dividing walls modified to provide ample living space within which expensive furnishings had been installed.

At seven o'clock in the evening, as he lay on his bed, hands behind his head while watching a movie on his wall-mounted, large screen television, a guard tapped on his unlocked cell door before pushing it open, to be regarded speculatively by Vincent's thick set body guard, standing sentry at the threshold.

'The super wants to see you,' said the prison guard to Vincent. 'What about?'

'How would I know,' replied the guard. 'You think he tells me what about?'

Vincent sighed in annoyance, paused the movie and moved to sit on the side of his bed, regarding himself in the mirror placed against the wall. He had been here thirteen years. At thirty eight years of age his short, slicked back black hair had begun greying at the temples. His lean, predatory and hawklike features, with piercing, dark eyes and aquiline nose reminded him of his proud Mediterranean heritage. Over his perfectly fitting green prison uniform, which contacts in the tailor shop had cut and modified to perfectly fit his slender frame, he wore a silk smoking jacket, which he slipped off to lay on top of the bed as he stood to comply.

On the way out he retrieved his felt jacket, also tailored perfectly to size, and with a distinguishing pleats stitched at the rear.

'No one enters 'til I'm back,' he instructed his protection.

He is led down through the tiers via metal stairs, at the bottom the C-Block door is unlocked and he is led across the courtyard in the chill of the night to the Superintendent's office, told to stand while the officer taps on the door and announces their arrival.

'Thank-you, McIntyre. Have him come in, and wait outside, ' said Commander Morris Babcock, the aging, uniformed Super; a big man of military bearing, his pale blue eyes sharp, intelligent and focused.

McIntyre held open the door for Vincent, closed it firmly behind him. Babcock extended a hand towards the chair in front of his desk. 'Have a seat—' and as he settled, Babcock got to it.

'Your daughter telephoned. Something to do with a possible threat to her person. She insisted you be made aware.'

'*Possible* threat?' Zendell emphasized. 'From who?'

Babcock unlocked his desk drawer, withdrew a brown envelope and rounded his desk to hand it to the prisoner. 'Open it.'

He did so, from the envelope retrieving the faxed threat his daughter had sent, accompanied by her handwritten message:

Father...

The last thing I want to do is to give you cause for concern while you are in that place. I didn't know what to do when the (enclosed) note was pushed under my door recently. I only know that you have a right to know, but please, do not worry too much. It is very possibly some crank finding perverse pleasure in doing this. I have engaged the services of a private detective.

Your loving daughter,
Matilda

Superintendent Babcock watched closely as Vincent's brow furrowed ever deeper, his face darkening with anger. At last he lifted his gaze to regard the watchful jailer.

'This arrived when?'

'I found it in my tray, today, but I didn't want you seen by the general population, coming here to my office. I waited until after lockup. You understand. Best for both of us that you not be seen coming here.'

Babcock remained watchful as Zendell grimly regarded the fax again.

'I've done my part,' he told Vincent. 'What you choose to do is your business, but I do not want the smooth running of this facility upset. Is that clear?'

When Vincent remained silent, he called, '*McIntyre!*' When the escorting guard entered the office, he was told, 'You can return the prisoner to his cell.'

TEN

On the ground floor of B-Division, similar living arrangements as had been made for Zendell had been made for another prisoner, Zendell's uncle, Guido Spinoza. For Spinoza, the end of the hallway had been sectioned off; a partition fabricated out of half inch steel bars, floor to ceiling, with a locked gate at its centre. The barred partition rendered the end of the wing inaccessible to anyone other than Guido, certain prison guards, and his selected group of trusted inmates with proven histories of fealty to organised crime. The contained cells provided Guido Spinoza, as with his nephew, Vincent, several cells, their walls breached to augment living space and combining with the central hallway to avail even more personal space than his nephew had been afforded.

Guido, a dwarf, standing at three feet nine inches and of stocky build, had developed a considerable paunch since commencement of his sentence. As with his nephew, Guido's outside connections to captains of industry, heads of organised crime and powerful political figures, national and international, afforded him all the leverage required to live very comfortably during his term of internment.

His ability to operate beyond prison walls was no less extensive than it had been before his arrest and sentencing. Only his location had changed. His onetime residence, the one I call *Villa Vulgar*, since being seized by the Commonwealth in retribution and repayment of unpaid taxes, had been his castle—his self-bestowed, vainglorious tribute to himself and his warped self-perception. Its loss, I imagined, constantly gnawed at him.

McIntyre wasted no time in reporting Guido's nephew's nocturnal *tete-à-tete* with Gerald Babcock, the prison superintendent. At ten o'clock McIntyre opened the gate of the steel barricade and made his way to Guido's sleeping quarters, tapping on the heavy steel door with his night stick.

Like Zendell, Guido has a sentry standing within. The large, heavily tattooed sentry pulled back the door as Guido's peevish voice asked, 'Who disturbs me at this late hour?'

McIntyre was given leave to enter by the doorman. 'I thought you might want to know,' he uttered apprehensively.

Guido sat at his desk in the corner of his room, where a window had been excavated to provide extra light during the day and to allow him to watch activities in six yard, where occasional sporting events were held.

He twisted around in his chair, pulled a large cigar from his mouth. His hair was in the process of receding backwards over his pate in recent years, leaving a horseshoe shaped, partial cover. His dark and beady eyes glistened, surrounded by his chubby round face, puffed up and ruddy, with a network of fine purple veins spreading from his nose into his cheeks.

'Know what?' he quizzed McIntyre, who had halted two paces inside the domain. 'I hope it is important to be disturbing me. I was about to turn in.'

'I think it may be, Mr Spinoza. I escorted Vincent to see the keeper, moments ago. Something about his daughter, is what I heard. I was told to wait outside and couldn't much of it, but your nephew received a letter, handed to him, personally, by Mr Babcock. It upset him terribly, I could tell.'

'From his daughter, did you say?'

'That's right, sir. From his daughter. I did catch that much.'

Guido smiled, his teeth clamped around the enormous cigar, and puffed a cloud of smoke into the air. Removing it, he gave a short laugh. 'Very good. I'm glad you told me of this. I would like to see this letter, George. I want you to copy, word for word, the contents. Bring it to me.'

'Tonight?' McIntyre asked, anxiously.

'Of course not tonight. Wait until morning parade. Can you do that?' 'I'm on yard duty in the morning, Mr Spinoza.'

'Lunchtime then,' Guido told him, 'while everyone's in the mess hall.'

Guido giggled amusedly to himself as McIntyre's receding footsteps echoed along the hallway. *'Te-he*he—'* a high pitched, irritating emanation. Like that of a tittering schoolgirl, and oddly disturbing.

ELEVEN

In relating further events it is unnecessary to include the less pertinent occurrences during the time immediately following. It may be worth mentioning that incidents within the prison were assembled piecemeal from layers' recordings and written notes, trial transcripts and what I recall of verbal accounts given in open court by the many witnesses called to testify on behalf of both defense and prosecution.

Since I cannot claim to have perfect recall, and since it's impossible to fill in every detail of events happening throughout the relevant time period, I am rendering this written account as I might when writing a story, using personal knowledge and witness accounts, as well as my understanding of the characters involved in order to fill any gaps; some small, some large but easily predicable enough that I am able to maintain sufficient continuity in offering a clearer account than if I were to omit portions not offered as testimony and witnessed first hand.

I also need remind myself that this situation arose purely from me trying my hand at the private detective caper. I had figured it an easy transition, given my passing experiences with military intelligence, and, later, my years of living on my wits as a freelance bandit and chancer, needing always to stay two jumps ahead of those in pursuit if I were going to enjoy the fruits of my labour.

Trouble was, even at this early stage, it wasn't turning out quite the way I had imagined. Janie had her veterinary skills and her love of working with animals. After various law enforcement branches of government had forced me into retirement, I tried to make the most of all I had; my freedom for one, a wife I adored, a nice place to live on ten acres beautiful countryside, income, enough that I need not worry much about the kinds of things so many others are faced with. From anyone's point of view, I was a lucky man.

And then, goddamn it, I began to envy her; my wife, Janie, with her rushed, early morning starts, the belonging to a team thing, as they pulled together in healing and saving the lives of people's pets, strays and farm animals. The sense of fulfilment in her; the renewed passion she had discovered after dragging herself up by her bootstraps, from the nightmare existence of her early years. Despite the weariness at the end of a long day she would relate to me the excitement, the life and death urgencies, as I sat, listening, smiling, sympathising at the appropriate moments. I guess it began to wear on me.

God forbid she would ask, 'How was your day, dear?' After losing my other, much preferred mode of existence through government intervention, I was at a loss and came to a total impasse. But, hey, it had to end some day, right? It wasn't as if it could go on forever. Truth is, I think, that I was forced to grow up. From the outside looking in, my previous life may have looked exciting and attractive. Fast living, money to burn, women, fast cars, risking it all on a job because ego said no one else could do it, or if they could then not as well. The military thing, too. For me it was little more than ego, even though there were plenty of good reasons to be trading led with the military arm of radical despots, fascist dictators and the many other assorted scumbags. The initial ideals which put me in the situation I was in fell away soon enough (and, let's face it, there's little attraction in sleeping in muddy trenches and dining from a tin can) leaving ego alone to drive the organism, and with, perhaps, the added attraction of the chance of my stumbling across a huge stash of ill-gotten gains, loot left behind by a fleeing warlord, or wrenched from the fist of some high powered political demagogue.

I don't believe the direction this narrative has taken here. I'll probably edit this stuff out, but it must be serving some purpose, if only in exorcising sundry demons.

I was saying how trying my hand at private eyeing was probably a mistake; how I only took this route out of a need to find a new mode of existence, something catering to the altered, more thoughtful human being I felt emerging. *Hugh. . .* If I didn't know better I would never admit that words like this could possibly come from someone like me. Live and learn, I guess; and I have to admit that had this emergence not come, the thought of having to live to the end of my days as the person I formerly was? The end would not have been pretty. The old adage of, *Live fast, die young, leave a pretty corpse?* It was one many young men I knew lived by, and *literally* died by.

Young men are not as crazy as many regard them to be. Many of them see the world way too clearly. Their sense of honour and camaraderie is fiercely upheld when they see the surrounding world as a rat-race, a dog-eat-dog battle, a world where the wealthiest and most privileged exist on the backs of those inheriting nothing much more than a life of toil filled with pain and injustice. Live fast, die young and leave a pretty corpse? Hell, it's not as crazy as it sounds, and society can count itself lucky that these people don't opt to get even, as some do.

Over the following couple of days Matilda made use of her family connections, going through formal channels to arrange meetings, first, with her father, Vincent Zendell, followed by an audience with the little big man. . . that puffed up pipsqueak, Guido Spinoza.

TWELVE

Holdsworthy prison was across the border, in New South Wales, thirteen kilometres from the town of Grafton. I had intended for Matilda and myself to do the trip by ourselves, but Took would not have it. Apparently some of *"the brothers"* —members of affiliated motorcycle fraternities— whom he had not seen in many years were doing time at Holdsworthy, and he would not miss the possibility of visiting them, catching up and giving them news from the outside.

We drove down to Adelaide in a hire car in order to board a domestic, interstate flight. Matilda took the precaution of using an alias. We left at seven-thirty in the morning, arriving in Ballina NSW two hours later. From there we drove the remaining distance in a hired Ford Mustang, arriving at Grafton, a ten minutes drive from Holdsworthy prison, with an hour remaining before we were due at the prison.

The Mustang we hired at Took's insistence. The moment he saw the advertising at the Ballina airport terminal, he went to the counter while neither Matilda or I were watching, coming back to us at the baggage collection point with the hire contract in hand and a smile on his face, saying, 'Bags I get to drive.'

We paused at a service station and café after passing through Grafton. It was on the main road, a mile out of town; a way point truck stop and refuelling depot where we were able to take a breather, sample the cuisine, reboot the travel addled brain and take stock of things.

It was a bright, hot morning and already the mercury was pushing up toward the mid thirties. There was a grassed area outside; a semi arid patch of under-watered couch grass scattered with umbrellas beneath which were placed metal tables and chairs. I remember that every time the wind gusted, anyone taking a bite of their sandwich at the time got a mouthful of dust and grit as garnish.

I had just returned to the table with a second round of soft drinks when, from up the road in the distance, we detected the rumble of big-bore motorcycles approaching. Took was able to distinguish make and model of several by the sound they made, and before long maybe twenty of the brethren had rumbled up to the edge of the *'picnic area'* where we sat, and dismounted.

On their backs, patches denoted, *'Finks'*, a club I was familiar with. I had spent a brief amount of time in Adelaide Gaol with three of their members, while on remand for a firearms violation and illegal possession of a bag of money I couldn't account for to the full satisfaction of the officer concerned. This after the ungrateful bastard declined my generous cash offer to get in his patrol car, drive away and leave me in peace. It was three in the morning and I was parked out back of an establishment called *The Bijoux,* a pub, cathouse and gambling establishment owned by Omar the Greek. It was Omar who came to my aid, testifying that I was transporting the night's takings for him at the time the copper stumbled upon me relieving myself against a wall in the unlit car park. . . but I have digressed. It's surprising what the mind will dredge up, given a chance. I find more and more memories rising from the depths as this account continues. Perhaps I could try my hand at novel writing sometime. It's what some people do in their latter years, isn't it? I wonder if there's any money in it?

In the knowledge that he might catch up with old pals while visiting, Took had donned his old colours; a raggedly, sleeveless denim jacket over a lightweight leather jacket; embroidered on the denim, an emblem denoting crossed spanners under a scull wearing a motorcycle helmet, and beneath this the words Spanner Heads MCC. The colours he wore over a blue singlet, the remainder of him covered by those olive-drab, multi pocketed trousers I've never learned the name of, but which are much favoured by the armed forces. With six foot seven inches of brawn, his long, shaggy mop of hair and beard stretching down over his chest, when he strolled over to talk to the group who had parked and dismounted near us, the moment he joined the congregation he was indistinguishable from the rest, but for his head protruding above the most of them.

Matilda and I sipped our sodas, chatting, occasionally keeping an eye on Took lest his presence be misconstrued. I had taken my own advice since the day Matilda had turned up at my office, and I began carrying

Lullaby, snug in her holster under my arm and hidden from view by a light sports jacket.

Bikers are a cautious lot; cherishing their right to privacy and freedom of movement, and defending them as best they can, as any of us would, given the recent spate of additional prejudices. Their freedom of movement in this state, and right to reasonable privacy were being eroded by politicians being pressured in turn by public opinion driven by television and the print media. Endless mileage had been discovered by the media, in vilifying the boys and girls, branding them all as drug pushers, organised crime members, or uncouth and generally unsavoury individuals the police were directed to be ever suspicious of. Across the border in Queensland they had been outlawed almost entirely.

I was enlightening Matilda to their plight when Took emerged from the pack and returned to our table.

'How about that?' he said, sitting. 'Some of these guys are stopping by Holdsworthy on their way through. It's Spike's birthday. His old lady is bringing him a cake, to celebrate.'

'Spike,' I repeated. I had heard his name mentioned from time to time over the years.

'Yeah. He's fifty. Still got a couple of years to cut out, but these guys look after him pretty good.'

'That's heartwarming,' Matilda chimed in, but Took would not be baited.

'I asked them about Guido and Vinnie. They say that between the two of them, they about run the place.'

I laughed at that. 'Why am I not surprised? Anything else?'

'Not really. Guido is top dog. Vinnie. . . Your father,' he amended, regarding Matilda and wearing a friendly grin, 'runs the smaller enterprises in the population. But Guido is *the pin*.'

'Okay, well. . .' I checked my wristwatch. 'Let us press on, troops.'

Took hesitated at this. 'Gecko says I can ride with him. He's got a thirty-nine Indian and sidecar. I'm going to go the rest of the way with him and his missus, and meet you guys there. Okay?'

It was like watching a five-year-old asking to go on a carnival ride. His crazy eyes, the one blue and the other brown, couldn't have opened wider.

'Sure, son,' I told him, laughing. Just don't tell your mother I let you,' The comment brought a chagrined expression to his face, giving Matilda reason to laugh, outright, and me, reason to immediately regret saying it. He raised a mock-threatening finger, accompanied by an appropriate scowl, saying:

'That's one I owe you, Dad.'

I left Took in the company with his new friends while Matilda and I climbed into the black, now dust covered Mustang, and took off. We had not far to go now. Maybe a fifteen minute drive at an easy pace.

I remember thinking at the time, as Matilda and I cruised sedately along the class-A link road toward the prison, how capricious were the winds of change. It was at that moment the true implausibility of life's whimsy struck me: That I would be driving in a car, and a five litre Mustang thoroughbred at that, twelve hundred miles from home, with Vincent Zendell's daughter beside me, while going to meet her father and her uncle Guido, who were in prison, on this hot, blue-sky day twenty years after playing a major role in their being where they were now? Is life unpredictable, or what?

My mobile rang then, and it was Janie on the other end. A certain Detective Sergeant Carruthers had dropped by the house. Carruthers was the police detective who had failed to attain a conviction against me some years back. He told Janie he was in the area and dropped by to see how I was getting on. Not a chance. There may have been something happening around town which had some small connection to what happened back then. My guess was he had never really gotten over losing the opportunity of gaining my scalp in court, when the opportunity was closest to him. Very likely, on an impulse he had dropped by just to annoy me. It's the sort of man he was: unforgiving, holding grudges, still pissed over the missed opportunity and thinking he could unsettle me all these years later. At least that was what I told myself as we whittled down the miles to Holdsworthy.

I told Janie, 'Don't worry. The man is a sore loser and a bastard. He won't be back. I'll see you in a couple of days.'

I drove on in silence, with a scowl on my face as I remembered DS Carruthers only too well.

'What's the problem?' Matilda asked, having studied my altered demeanour for a moment.

'A ghost from the past,' I answered, hoping she would take the hint and leave the subject alone.

Holdsworthy prison sat at the end of a mile long private road. Imposing and anachronistic, it struck me as looking like something out of the Dark Ages: built of massive bluestone blocks, thirty foot high, crenellated battlements stretched between turret like watch houses positioned at every corner, where armed guards hung out—very bored armed guards, it should be noted, shouldering automatic weapons. I know the types.

They spend half their life pacing their little strip, trying to ignore the dragging hours of their day until they can punch the clock and go home to the wives and kids. Most are married; the thinking being that a married man will endure greater discomfort and lower wages for the sake of financial security for their family. A single, unencumbered man won't. Not unless he's getting his kicks lording it over the prisoners. Some do quite well, having some shady enterprise in operation, supplying contraband or trading information. I've heard of cases where infiltrating neerdowells, put in place by organised crime, would change out of uniform after hours and get to work at night, dealing out retribution and mayhem, practising extortion on wealthy families wanting to keep under wraps information of their disgraced family members.

The run of the mill guys are cutting out harder time than the criminals themselves, I shouldn't wonder; and there are some who would love nothing more than be given an opportunity, if only to relieve the crushing tedium, to take a shot at a desperate, fleeing inmate. Such is the mentality of some of these guys that they see their job as being employed to inflict ongoing punishment on society's discards. Happily the trend was discovered and moves were made to better test applicants for these positions. Implementation of psychological testing acts to filter out the more obvious psychos and misanthropes. The clever ones, however, remain. To me, the basic rule stands: Give a man a uniform and watch the changes occur.

The roar of approaching motorcycles brought me out of my reverie, as we stood in the sun, leaning against the vehicle, waiting for the girls and boys to arrive with the third member of our group.

They backed up and parked their bikes along the wall. Took climbed out of the sidecar, returned his borrowed helmet and gave a parting wave before walking over to us, a wide smile buried somewhere within his plentiful beard.

'We're invited,' he said, propping before us. 'They're setting up camp at a reserve, just up the road a piece. Making the return trip in the morning.'

'Invited to what?' I enquired.

'A blowout, you know. There's another chapter coming down to meet these guys. They'll be at it for days, but we're invited to come along and enjoy ourselves tonight. What do you say?'

'No chance,' Matilda responded, adamant.

Took refused to acknowledge her. 'It'll be a blast, and we ain't flying out till tomorrow arvo anyway.

Checking my watch, I saw that it was time to line up at the visiting office. 'How about we discuss it later?' I deferred. 'Let's get our game face on and get this thing done.' And turning to Matilda, 'You ready for this?'

THIRTEEN

We went in through the visitors' entrance and were directed to a window where we explained why we were here.

'One visit a day,' the guy told us. 'If you want to see two prisoners, come back tomorrow for the second.'

We stepped out of line to consult, deciding we would talk to Guido today, Vincent tomorrow. Matilda wasn't at all happy but acquiesced because there was nothing else for it.

The visiting building, we discovered as we came through the main gate holding a brass disc with a number imprinted on it, was a weatherboard building placed at the centre of the yard. Within was a long, central bench divided by a glass panel to separate visitor and visited.

A guard came up to the three of us who were standing in a bunch, asking: 'You people here for Spinoza?' Answering in the affirmative, he responded, 'Follow me.'

We did. We followed him out of there, across the yard to a steel door allowing entry the solid stone, three tier cell block denoting C-Division. We followed him up the wide, steel staircase to the top tier, then down a long corridor until we came up to a wall to floor barred barrier with a locked entrance door made of more steel bars.

Standing inside the locked door was another guard, to which our escort said, 'Spinoza's visitors.'

The guy looked us up and down, had us turn out our pockets, the contents of which he placed on the little table beside him. Only then did he turn a key in the lock and allow us entry.

'I'll take 'em from here, Sid,' he told our escort, and we followed him down the broad passageway, where he halted at the third door on our left and knocked twice.

A musclebound inmate with shaved head and scorpion tattoo on it, and who must have measured 28 inches around the neck, stepped out to look us over. 'You Matilda?' he enquired.

She nodded. 'And these are my companions, Alex and Took. Uncle Guido is expecting us, I believe.'

Her voice must have carried beyond the heavy cell door. Guido's unmistakable vocal tone issued from within; a rasping, peevish emanation I would recognise anywhere.

'Matty, my dear girl. Come in and let me have a look at you!'

The gorilla stepped aside and we entered, though our watcher made sure to impart a threatening scowl as we did so, no doubt meant to convey that Took and I were not especially welcome and would be under continuing scrutiny while there.

Guido had aged significantly. He came out from behind his desk, sliding his three feet nine inch self down to the carpeted floor from his plush, leather upholstered, swivel chair. His girth had increased and his hair had greyed, receding halfway back across his round head, although what remained was perfectly clipped, oiled down into place with something smelling, even from where I stood, like vanilla essence mixed with cheap aftershave. His face was florid, as though suffering the heat, but I had a hunch it was more to do with a dodgy heart, a condition not helped by the fat cigar he pulled from his fat lips and placed in the ashtray on his desk, before waddling over to his niece.

'How marvellous to see you, young lady.' Matilda had to bend low in returning the hug he wanted. 'You came all this way to see your old uncle Guido. It is so marvellous of you.'

Took and I watched from three paces away, as meathead watched us watching the display of deep family affection, which, I for one, was not buying for a second.

'And Alex, my boy—' releasing his niece to regard me, his arms wide in a gesture of acceptance. 'I am glad you came to see me. And Mr Took, too. *Marvellous.*'

I swear I though he was about to begin jumping up and down with excitement. Understandable, perhaps. I doubted he got many visits from the outside world. Well, not from actual human beings. Crime bosses and underlings, maybe, but, even then, underworld figures and underlings would do well to avoid the scrutiny a visit with Guido would surely attract.'

'It's so nice to see you again,' Matilda almost crooned. 'It's been so long.'

Both Took and I were distractedly eyeing the accommodation and obviously expensive decor.

'Yes, yes. . . Do come in and be comfortable,' he enthused.

There was a long couch, scattered armchairs, floral printed curtains over barred windows but which had been widened to allow extra light and air into the space.

'You like my little room?' Guido asked, noticing our incredulity, and he began to giggle. 'Punishment, bah! This is nothing, as you can see. How can I be angry at you boys? I like it here. Besides, my legal team say I might not be here very much longer. Good news, eh? We will be able to chat under more appropriate surroundings, God willing.'

We arranged the chairs, making a rough circle, and sat. 'Refreshments anybody?' he asked, and before long we were sipping cappuccinos.

'Don't look so concerned,' Guido said, leaning back into his recliner, coffee in one hand and cigar in the other. He had correctly read the expression on my face. He should have been annoyed at mine and Took's presence, to say the least, seeing as how we had instigated his fall from his previously lofty height.

I could only shrug in replying. 'You could be forgiven for holding a grudge, Guido.'

He turned to his niece, sitting in the chair beside him. 'You probably don't realise what a strange coincidence it is to have approached Alex here to help.'

'I do, actually. I remembered his name, and how he was involved. He seemed to me to be the only one in a position to fully understand the problem.'

'Yes.' Guido replied, sighing. 'The problem. How unfortunate to upset our gathering with something so alarming as this.

'Dom,' he called to his minder, 'would you retrieve the letter for me from my desk?'

'The big guy did as he asked and obediently trotted over with the fax Matilda had sent to her father. He scanned it, briefly, before waving it in the air. 'You are well acquainted with this mischief, Alex?'

I nodded. 'A little disturbing, isn't it. Who the hell *is* Cassandra, I asked, point blank.'

'The sixty-four-dollar question,' he answered, chuckling. 'You're telling me you don't know?'

'Why would you assume I would, Alex? A man in his position. Why would he allow it? He would be. . . how do you say it? Not very clever to reveal himself so easily.'

'How did you come across him,' Took asked. 'It was a big operation and you're a careful kind of guy. You took him at trust?'

Again he chuckled. 'I took him at his money, Mr Took. Is that right, Mr Took?'

'Just Took,' he answered, sitting with legs stretched out in front of him and looking comfortable with hands clasped behind his head. 'Don't ask me how it got started. They just started calling me it when I first grew this.' He ran his fingers through the thick, long beard covering his chest.

'But your first ever communication with Cassandra,' I persisted. 'How, and where, through what channels?'

Guido was dismissive of my question. 'Is this important? *The sins of the father,*' he quoted from the note. 'To be visited upon the children. This is so not good and so unfair. There is not good reasons for threatening like this, and for what?' He turned to Matilda. 'Your father did nothing for this to happen to you, my dear girl.'

He was upset, I saw. Whenever his English began to fail I knew he was feeling something. A condition not frequently observed in the little troll.

He moved to reach over to his niece, intending to place a consoling hand on hers but found it wouldn't reach the distance.

Matilda reciprocated, and reached to make contact. 'It's why I took the chance of contacting My Jaeger.'

'Do you remember?' he asked, turning back to me. 'I once asked you to come and work for me.'

'I remember, Guido. And where would I be now if I had accepted *that* offer?'

Why was he trying to elicit this *auld langsyne* bullshit from me? I remember thinking at the time. He was trying to draw me in close, as he always did. Blowing smoke up my arse, and I was instantly on my guard. I mean, even more on my guard, since I came here full of suspicion and wariness to begin with. The fact that he appeared to be putting animosities aside, was, to me, not a sign of setting aside grievances between us for the benefit of clearing a path towards eliminating the threat to Matilda. I've never witness true fondness in or from him, despite it being the impression being served up to his niece now. The man was a lizard; a chameleon, able to approximate an outward appearance of emotion when it suited him. He was adept at this and other deceptions, I had long observed over the years. Of what I was observing today with his niece I could not be sure. It might well have been authentic. His Greek heritage would suggest very strong family bonds, ordinarily, but this was Guido Spinoza I was watching. I had to hand it to the squirt. He was one person I always had trouble with in getting a good read on.

He was watching me intently. Maybe he was making the same analysis of me as I was him. We even smiled at one another; a small, knowing, amused smile, in recognition and perhaps even mutual respect, acknowledging the never ending contest which is never decided by just one game, and putting me in mind of two chess players who, over the years had pitted wit, skill and cunning against one another without final victory over the other. I definitely got the feeling as I sat there in the moment, that he did not accept his capture and imprisonment as being the final round of a larger tournament.

'I do *well* remember,' I told him, in answer to the question.

'You might be living high on the pig,' he replied, incorrectly citing the metaphor; but he had done it on purpose, eliciting an authentic laugh from everyone present.

'I am so pleased you are all here,' he said, still chuckling. 'The people I must deal with. In this place is only common criminals and stupid persons. But you know. Took, you have experience. . . places like this?'

'I've done my apprenticeship,' he answered.

'Yes. I know—' and the corners of his mouth curled upward. 'I had you explored. Back when you and Alex first were team. Little stuff, mainly. You punched the policemen?'

Took looked uncomfortable. The first time I had seen him that way. 'A long time ago,' he said in answer to the charge. 'I was just a kid.'

'Yes, but it is always interesting for me to know. Whatever is the child, becomes the man. Do you see?'

'But we're wasting time,' I interrupted. 'Can we focus on the problem at hand, do you think?'

'Cassandra?' asked Guido.

Matilda had been sitting, quietly observing the conversation with studied interest. 'You must know something about this person, uncle. You're a student of life and an observer of people. I know that about you. You must have talked over the phone with the man? Sent messages via email? Something which offered a clue. Didn't you form an impression of this person who was able to control and organise from a distance, without once being identified?

'I did,' he answered, focussing at last. 'I will tell you.' He raised a pointed finger in the air. 'I always picture the man in my mind. You know, how you do when you talk on the telephone? He sounded like a general. A military man, sitting at a big desk, wearing a military uniform, medals, very smart. It was how his voice sounded. American, a big man who is used to having his orders done quickly.'

'American, are you sure?' Matilda pressed. 'Like from where? There are several American accents, uncle.'

'I am not expert, dear, but to me he sounded like. . . do you remember a television show where soldier was always doing stupid? An idiot. *Mmm*. . . private *Gome* something, maybe?'

'Gomer Pile?' Took chimed in. Do you mean Gomer Pyle? I remember that show.'

'Yes, yes. *Gomer* Pile. Funny voice. I remember thinking of *Private Gomer*, which was not very good thing to be thinking for this big boss-man, eh?'

'What accent *is* that then?' I wondered aloud. 'Southern? Alabama, maybe?'

'Jim Neighbours played the role,' Took informed us, 'and he was from Alabama, as was private Pyle.'

'A possible high ranking military man from *The South*,' I muttered, unimpressed. 'That should narrow it down to thousands. Anything else?'

Guido sipped his coffee. Dissatisfied with it he put it aside with a disapproving look. 'You seek a man who does not want to be found, Alex. What do you expect? A smart man, capable of much. It is like the wolf barking at the moon, yes?' Guido reached out in demonstration. There, in the sky so close, shining. Impossible to reach.'

He was taunting me. He knew more than he was telling us, and still, despite possible harm coming to his niece, he didn't seem disposed to doing so. I was about to remind him and press him on just that point when Matilda took up the challenge.

'Uncle—' reaching across and taking hold of his hand '—there must be something more. Anything. I'm frightened. This awful man. What he said in that ghastly letter. Do you think it's merely a hoax from someone like him?'

He appeared to me to be reassessing, albeit briefly. 'Why not? The message was to your father, remember? Why not would he want to make Vincent feel threatened and vulnerable? A little slap. Teach Vincent so he knows never to make mistake again.'

He was smiling as he said this, I noticed. What was there to smile about?

'The boy had it all in his hands,' he continued, 'and I let it go because of mistakes he make. I think maybe you are not in so much danger, dear girl—' releasing her hand with a final shake. 'This is on Vincent. It is his responsibility to worry about. Not yours. Tell him that when you see him. Tell him that, from me.'

We spent time going over the few facts we were privy to, inventing hypotheses, imagining possible means of carrying out the presumed threat, reexamining previous presumptions needing attention with Guido becoming increasingly annoyed and wanting the available time used more for his amusement, taking us back to where we began and which was nowhere terribly useful, although Matilda was satisfied for having visited and seen how *"at home"* he appeared to be.

An announcement came over the public address, making known that visiting time was over. It was lunchtime, evidently, and prisoners were to begin making their way to the mess.

Guido's words regarding Vincent stuck in my head. As expected, the mysterious Cassandra's identity was and remained well concealed, although the possibility of his being a high-ranking officer in the US military seemed valid. Probably a Southerner, too. It was more than we had before coming here, and it made alarming sense. Someone in this position had innumerable, high level avenues of operation by which to pull strings, undetected. I knew that the higher the rank the less scrutiny one faced, especially if one had a chestful of medals, a solid war reputation and one was respected by surrounding, equally high-ranked officers. The thought of a five-star general surrounded by a cadre of like-minded, war weary and jaded generals who saw the world as being full of unworthy, uneducated, non-contributing heathens who did nothing but tax depleting resources gave me reason to shudder. These guys were battered, uncompromising proponents of some imagined, idealized new world order capable of putting the world back to rights. Many were, and to my mind understandably so, alcohol and drug dependant. Regardless of this, and with the sanction of those around them dependant on their expertise, they were necessarily protected individuals even as high functioning wrecks—high functioning wrecks who had their hands on enormous firepower. They were skilled tacticians and manipulators, well able to influence, or, if needed, squeeze politicians until they caved in to imagined superior intellect, all the while keeping everything compartmentalised so that the left hand had no idea what the right hand was doing. Christ, how many wars had been launched this way? Iraq and the so called weapons of mass destruction perfectly illustrated how— *when the lies and propaganda begin*— how easily and how rapidly things can go to hell in a handbasket. The trilonite conspiracy we had stumbled on, back when, might well have been hatched and initiated through military channels in exactly this way.

FOURTEEN

That the trilonite conspiracy may well have been hatched within the ranks of the most powerful military organisation on the planet, with the possible exception of China, I suppose, stuck in my mind; the germ of an idea unobtrusive and dormant for a time. I had plenty of other concerns to occupy the old noodle with.

One of these concerns was Took's desire to party with his motorcycle brothers and sisters. The pair who had given him a ride had sketched a map denoting a reserve not too far along the main road from where we were at the prison. At the reserve was a track running North, used by local farmers and terminating at a chestnut grove, beyond which a gully provided shelter and a broad, flat area where everyone intended congregating for the shindig.

'First things first,' I suggested. 'There's a motel about three miles back along the way we came. Why don't we grab a room, a meal and a shower, or whatever. Freshen up a bit after our travels. If we're going to trip the light fantastic, I don't know about you guys but I could use a nap. I ain't as young as I once was, I told them,' admitting that I was already quite weary. If I was going to have a night out, there was no way I was going to hold up without getting some downtime, namely, at least a couple hours of sleep.

It's true. I didn't much like admitting this to myself, let alone telling Took and Matilda. Took most of all. Since we had first met, becoming fast friends, there had always been a quiet, undeclared competition going on between us. One of those stupid macho things. I guess most guys do it, in their way. Especially those who pride themselves on their physical fitness and athletic prowess. It didn't much matter what it was; chopping wood, digging a ditch or maybe just pulling on a joint. That *I-can-do-it-better-faster-longer-than-you* thing creeps into the equation, and before you know it we're grunting and sweating, with wood chips flying in all directions, digging like demons or pulling as much tetrahydrocannabinol saturated smoke into our lungs as humanly possible, just to prove superiority. Superior stupidity.

We one day confided in each other that neither of us much enjoyed the weed anymore. This, after the great hairy galoot had bet me a hundred dollars that he could smoke more cannabis from the biggest hookah either of us had ever seen, on the night previous. Javanese tripping grass, too. We both nearly blew our brains out. Janie twigged that something was wrong with me the moment I arrived home at seven the next morning, taking undue, cruel pleasure in teasing me; first by speaking gibberish, mocking me when I couldn't understand; and then moving her lips without speaking, making me think I had gone deaf. I was still hallucinating, too, seeing miniature dragons and gremlins and things. The girl for sure has an evil streak. When I told her

I was hallucinating she sneakily dug out one of those golly-wog dolls, one she found in an op shop months previous, and from behind a curtain she made it appear as if it was dancing on the table while saying, in a nasty little voice, "I've cast a spell, I cannot tell, a spell from Hell a spell from Hell I will not tell." It really freaked me out, and *she* thought it was hilarious. She's a bad girl sometimes, and everyone thinks she's so sweet.

So we did just that. We went back to the motel we had passed on the way here, and got a room. Two rooms. Matilda would not share with Took and I. Can't imagine why not. After a good, long, hot shower I laid down and tried to nod off while Took and Matilda amused themselves in whatever way they could find, but it was futile. I was body tired, the mind, after so long travelling, was still revved up and whizzing through all the information I had been trying to assimilate these past few days.

At six in the evening we went to the restaurant to order a meal. Not great but edible, and filling. With some prodding and cajoling while sitting, sipping our beverages in attempt to wash down the charred mixed grills we had consumed, Took and I convinced Matilda that it would be no fun at all being left there at the motel on her own for the duration of the evening; that she ought to come along, broaden her horizons and see how the other half lived.

'I have a good idea how the other half live,' she said, somewhat crustily. 'A bunch of drunken bikers and their bitches, isn't that what they're called? All drunk, standing around a bonfire or rolling in the dirt like animals.'

Took shook his head, woeful. 'Lady, you got one hell of a poor opinion of us, don't you.'

'You count yourself as one of them?'

'Sure. I guess I'm not what you might call an active member anymore, but. . .' He shrugged. 'Those people. People *like* them. . . they were my family when I was young, when my real family didn't give a damn about me. I'm sure you won't believe this, but I was headed for a life in and out of *the slammer* when a lady by the name of Gail, *Big Momma* to all who knew her, a motorcycle bitch according to you, took me in and straightened me out. There wasn't a damn thing I went without if she had anything to do with it. Including an education. She put me through night school when I was old enough, where I got my papers as a mechanic. So yeah, I count myself as one of them, and proud of it.'

Matilda had listened to every word, looking more embarrassed as Took went on. By the end she could scarce look the big guy in the eye, and a poignant silence descended over our table.

'I'm sorry,' she said, now meeting his only mildly reproachful gaze. 'I guess I'm guilty of swallowing popularised public perception.'

He shrugged, telling her, 'Don't sweat it, girl. Them one's rolling around in the dirt? They're out there too. But these we're meeting tonight, the Finks? I'd vouch for any one of them.'

'The *Finks*, she repeated,' smiling. 'I like the name. It sounds to me like they have a sense of humour. Not what one might expect, is it?'

We followed the directions given us earlier, and parked the vehicle beside a grove of chestnut trees at the end of the narrow track. Each of us had brought coats or jackets with us to fend of the cooler temperatures of the night. Took remained dressed as he had been during the day; olive drabs, blue singlet and leather lined colours, but with the added accessory of a thick, black beanie pushed over his head for extra warmth.

Lamps had been hung from trees leading through the grove, illuminating the narrow trail leading towards a fiercely glowing bonfire further down the slope in a sheltered gully. In the firelight, where everyone had congregated in a natural alcove sheltered on three sides by the steep landscape, the gully appeared as a picturesque dell, like something out of a children's storybook.

Matilda was so taken with it, she let out a squeal of delight. 'Oh, my goodness. It's beautiful down here.'

I had to agree. It was that, and around one hundred folk milled about, talking, playing with their children in some cases, where a makeshift stage had been put together.

I noticed equipment being carted down on wheeled sled type apparatuses: sound equipment, a couple of generators, amplifiers and cases containing what looked to be drum kit, guitars and other instruments.

'What do you think of this?' Took said, turning to us. 'Surprising,' I told him.

'I'm going to mingle,' he said, casting his eyes over the crowd.'I want to see if I can find Ted and his missus from this afternoon.'

'Sure. We can meet up here, later on, under this tree, if we lose one another. Enjoy,' I said to his back, as he strolled off toward the densest part of the crowd.

This left Matilda and myself standing at the edge of the throng and wondering what to do with ourselves, but we needn't have worried. In a moment a woman approached us. She was dressed like most of the women here tonight. Jeans, thick leggings, windcheater under a heavy coat, and, like Took, with a knitted beany on top. She had a pale, smiling face surrounded by long, dark hair as she came up close to address we two.

'Hello, I'm Missy. I heard you might be coming tonight. I saw you at the roadhouse today. Took told me you might feel left out, so I've come over to bring you to meet my friends.'

Matilda stayed close, looking somewhat nervous and out of her comfort zone, although she was obviously fascinated by the goings on. The sound system started up, playing the *Allman Brothers'* Rambling Man, immediately appreciated by all. Took swung by with beers for us both and departed back into the heart of the gathering. Missy brought us to a group of four, rough looking individuals accompanied by three women.

'This is Alex and Matilda,' she said, presenting us. Obviously Took had informed her. As one they raised their drinks in greeting, and Missy pointed to each of them in turn, presenting Jason, Tilly, Aaron, Zee, Bessie, Sab and Lena.

'What are you guys doin' in these parts?' the tall, lean Zee asked. 'We're visiting Matilda's uncle,' I told him. 'This is some gig. Is it a frequent event?'

'We meet up annually, around time of year,' he informed us. 'Since the club was inaugurated back in the seventies, members have drifted around the country and we all get together somewhere once a year. This year it's here, and we're also celebrating a departed brother.'

'That's too bad,' I obliged, and decided to avoid the loss of their friend, seeing as it was really none of my business. 'It's a great spot,' I responded. And again, 'A great gig.'

One of the guys in the group, Aaron, a big fellah wearing a leather skullcap, asked Matilda, 'Visiting your uncle? You're in that red Mustang, aren't you? Is your uncle sloughed up back there?'

'Sloughed up? I don't understand.'

'Is he an inmate at Holdsworthy, I mean.'

I watched as Matilda appeared beset by indecision, but eventually nodded.

'It's okay,' Aaron consoled. 'I get it. Just because he's slammed up doesn't mean he's a bad guy. I have a friend in there. Prisons are like small towns. A village, you know? I probably know of him. What's his name?'

Now she was in trouble, but I had to admit to being caught up in the small drama that must have been occupying her mind right then. I was surprised to hear her respond as quickly as she did, although there was a certain amount of defiance involved, I remember thinking.

'Guido Spinoza,' she said, and plenty loud enough that all present heard the name clearly over top of the music.

At the mention, all adopted expressions of casual interest, but the masks of blithe indifference that they were, seemed stuck, frozen to their faces, and the reaction was not lost on Matilda, I noticed.

It was Bessie, the stout, cheerful looking girl who responded with, 'Guido Spinoza? The organised crime boss from Monarto? Wow. What's it like being his niece, Matilda? I bet it's a blast, right?'

'Not so much as one might expect,' she demurred. 'It has it's drawbacks.'

They appreciated the response, a few of them nodding, inferring that they understood what it must be like to be a member of the Spinoza family. I'm certain Matilda concluded the same, deciding in the moment to spell it out for them.

'My Uncle Guido. I sued to stay with him when I was little. My parents were educated professionals, well off, but they had no idea of what it was to be a parent. After I was nearly taken from them by child services, my uncle made a point of keeping an eye on me. He even had *"his people"* follow me to and from school, making sure I didn't stop off anywhere I could spend time with my friends. Eventually I spent way more time at his house than anywhere else. Cloistered, monitored, lonely. I guess he thought he was doing what he could, but he had no idea either. I lived in what amounted to a prison until I came of age to cut out my own life. By then the damage had been done. I had no idea about a *normal life.*

Zee, a wiry guy covered in tattoos, bandana tied over his head and with several teeth missing, ventured: 'That's fucked up, girl. About as fucked up as any of us here.' He smiled pleasantly, accentuating the missing teeth. 'People are fucked up. We all just put our shit behind us and live the way we choose. That what you're doing?'

She shrugged, a sad look emerging. 'Maybe.'

The band had gotten themselves organised. The master of ceremonies rode up onto the stage on a Harley pan head chopper, revving the thing so that it roared like some wild, metal beast, echoing from the surrounding hills. With everyone's attention gained he killed the motor and dismounted, took possession of the microphone to address the assembled kith and kin.

'Yo guys! Hey! So glad you all could be here tonight to mourn Bear's passing, and to celebrate the man that he was. We're going to miss you, big fellah,' he said, raising a hand to the dark sky. 'You were a rock, brother. Ever dependable and always there when there was need, either for action or restraint, confrontation or commonsense. You were the voice of reason. You always had a way of turning life's adversities into a philosophical learning experience. I remember once you said to me, 'This life is a proving ground. What we learn here is not lost. It will be carried over, either back here into the next life, or, if we get it right, into the next, higher plain of existence, where we will continue the process, and just maybe earn our wings.

'Man, you really made me think. Well, I hope you earned your wings, brother. You deserve them. Now, everyone, if you please. . . A minutes silence for our departed brother, Bear.'

We all observed a minute's silence for their departed comrade, a moment I have duplicated more times than I care to think about, remembering fallen comrades in arms throughout the years. Everyone attending fell silent. A calmness descended; a kind of palpable hush over the landscape, the variety of which can cause tingles up and down the spine; and in the moment I recall hearing the screech of unidentified night birds coming to us, way off in the distance. When the minute was up, the emcee pronounced:

'Let the celebration begin!' and with that the band ploughed into a powerful rendition of *Black Sabbath's* Child In Time.

The place was really rockin' from then on. All were there to give Bear a respectful send-off and to make one great night of it. Those who had brought their kids along gathered them together and put them to bed in an old, converted bus parked back at the grove. Taking it turn about, sentries were posted to keep watch over them, lest any wander off and get lost, or maybe find mischief for themselves while the adults were otherwise occupied.

I had wondered off into the copse, to find a suitable place to water a tree in privacy, when my phone began to vibrate in my pocket.

Unidentified caller, my phone revealed. I might not have bothered but for remembering Janie had told me that the noisome detective sergeant Carruthers had dropped by the house earlier.

'Yes?' I answered.

With the band playing in the background I thought I heard someone say, 'Hobbit.'

'I'm sorry, can you speak up a bit? There's a party going on and it's difficult to hear you.'

'I said, *drop it .*'

'Drop what? Who is this?'

'I do not advise to go on with investigation, Mr Jaeger,' the strange voice said, and I noted an unusual accent. The *Boris and Natasha* kind. It was thick with something akin to a Northern European cant, enunciation coming with some difficulty, suggesting to me that English was not their preferred language.

'I am always open to friendly advice,' I told whoever this was. 'Is this *friendly* advice?'

'Drop it,' he repeated, though more forcefully this time, 'or be sorry, I promise.'

'And I have advice for you, Boris,' I told him. 'Destroy your phone. It's being traced. I'll be able to call you back in a moment. Another twelve seconds and I can knock on your door.'

There was no reply. He had promptly hung up. I had an electronics whiz buddy of mine rig my phone when I was working, so I could record *all calls* instead of only the last call, as they do these days. Although that was before this private-eye gig, it was plenty useful. The phone trace thing was a lie, and I wondered, amusedly, if I had spooked Boris into destroying his own phone.

This was a development. An interesting one. Someone had become nervous, but who and why? If it was anything to do with the illusive C, I could be sure that the message had been delivered with plenty of forethought behind it. Smart buggers like Cassandra never did anything without thinking it through. Especially European smart buggers, for some reason. Something to do with heritage; being connected to an old civilization, all that culture and sophistication. It alters how these guys think and how they see themselves. Still, an old civilisation meant having survived centuries of war, with lots of machinating and outwitting going on. Best be careful, I warned myself.

Someone was trying to manipulate me from a distance, and, in truth it could have been one of several likely candidates, beginning with that twirp, Carruthers, who apparently was still nettled over his courtroom defeat when trying to tie me in to the unfortunate demise of Mr Draganov, of the *Deciples*. The only other likely candidates were, of course, Guido and his snot-nosed nephew. Yep, that about accounted for them.

I returned to the shindig and began searching for Took. I hadn't seen much of him during the course of the night. Now and again I caught sight of him cavorting with his biker buddies; a beer sculling competition using those enormous German steins; a kind of dance-off, I think, where I saw his bunch doing that Russian thing of squatting, throwing one leg out in front, then the other, in that thing the Cossacks do; and, if I'm not mistaken, later in the night I think I spotted him up a tree, where someone's boot had lodged high in a branch and he had gone up after it.

I found him beyond the fringe, stretched out in the shadows on an embankment, talking to a girl.

'Hey, brother,' he greeted, 'enjoying yourself? Wanda here has some A-1 hooch, if you're interested.'

'It's cool. I've been in the thick of it,' I told him, pointing to where a huge cloud of smoke lingered over a group who had congregated in a natural depression in the landscape. 'A miasma of altered states,' I clarified. 'Spend a minute in there and you'll come out different than when you went in.'

'Yeah, I know. Oh, hey, this is Wanda,' he informed me for the second time already. Then, 'Oh, I said that already didn't I? Where's Matilda?'

'No idea. I thought she might have been with you.' I scanned the area. Most were on the ground, but there was a crowd in the centre of the throng who were still standing, appearing to be circling, watching something going on at the centre.

'I was thinking, we've got things to do tomorrow. How about we make tracks, try and get enough sleep so we're able to function properly?'

He nodded, in slow, exaggerate fashion. '*Y-e-a-h*, we should—' and turning to Wanda, 'I gotta go, Wanda. Thanks for the taste. It's a buzz.'

'Do you have my number, safe?' she asked.

'Right here. I'll give you a call next time I'm in the area.'

'Even if you're not,' she replied, coyly, and coming on all coquettish like.

'You old dog,' I commented, as we wandered about, trying to find our lost girl, Matilda.

'Not so much of the *old*, buddy. And nothing of the sort, I assure you.'

'Assure her,' I told him. 'I get the impression she wants to do more than chat on the phone.'

We found Matilda. It was her at the heart of the commotion I had spied a moment ago; her and another girl, dancing. Exotic dancing, it might be described. She had stripped off and donned a veil, tied about the waist, and with other light materials waved around her, she performed what might have been the fabled *dance of the seven veils*, together with the other girl who was similarly clad. . . or *unclad*, as the case may be.

She was making a good job of it, too. The way she moved and spun and cartwheeled, maybe she had been a dancer in her time, or an athlete, judging by her well toned, athletic physique.

Took and I allowed her and her new friend finish the routine, found the clothes she had arrived in and led her back to the car.

'You can dance, girl,' Took was telling her, while helping her into the back seat of the Mustang. 'Where'd you lean to dance like that?'

'I was a professional nightclub dancer,' she declared with pride. 'I earned good money, too. Enough to pay my uni tuition and to live on.

Are we going home? Already? I'm having such a good time, guys.' 'You sure are, but we've got another important day coming up tomorrow.' I put her street clothes on her lap, and smiled. 'We're going to visit you father tomorrow, young lady. You need your beauty sleep so you're at your best, right? By the way, what have you taken tonight? You really got into the spirit of things, didn't you.'

'Something called *excee*, eccy-see?' she mispronounced. It's wonderful. It makes me feel all warm and lovely. What a great bunch of people and what a wonderful night, tonight is. Hey, look at the stars.'

Took and I made a silent pact as we looked to one another in amusement. Neither of us would make fun of her in the morning. Even if she remembered everything. She had a good time, met and enjoyed the company of people she never would have ordinarily. Best not spoil things by making a joke out of it, and after having apparently conquered established biases.

FIFTEEN

It was something of an odd night. Whatever Took had imbibed caused him to lapse into periods of deep dreams, where he irritatingly chatted away to dream people. From what I could gather, as I lay awake in the darkness, mulling over recent events, he was on some kind of magical mystery bus ride with people he knew from out of his past. Snippets of conversation included, '. . . *Yvette!* . . . you doing here? . . .dead, aren't you?. . .Robbie Bobby-dazzler . . .spooky, and . . .*this is the wrong bus.'*

I've had to listen in on several gabby dreamers, and it's nearly always amusing. I say nearly always amusing because, in an FOP (forward observation post) first, and strictly speaking, in a time of war sleeping on duty in an FOP is a crime punishable by execution by firing squad. Still, it happens. Using the buddy system it's not so uncommon over long periods of time while hunkered down in a hole in the ground, to let one guy rest while the other keeps watch. And secondly? Listening to someone prattling on as they dream can be unnerving. There's no filter, and all kinds of weird stuff can emerge. I remember listening to a young corporal Preston's rant one night. A pale, nervous looking recruit who was pushed up to the front line by mistake. The first night he began mumbling stuff that curled the ears: Satan, virgin sacrifice, beating hearts being cut of the chest. We never closed our own eyes while that guy was around, and more than a few were relieved when a ricocheting round hit him dead between the eyes before the week was out.

Matilda, who had originally insisted on a separate room, now insisted she bunk with us. That or none of us were going to get any sleep. Unfortunately this put Took and I in one bed, reverse about, head and feet, if you understand, while Matilda slept in my borrowed bed. Took slept like the proverbial log, no problem at all, and chatting away like a parrot. Matilda, though, she was still excited by her *awakening*, if I can call it that, and had way too much going on in her head to give sleep a chance. . . *all we are saying, is*. . . Yeah, I even used that line on her, to no avail. She did, by around three-thirty, consent to climbing between the covers and allowing me to try and talk her to sleep. You know, like a hypnotist using a steady, low voice. Like telling a small child a bedtime story, using my voice to coax sleep into her overactive mind, I began telling her the story of Took's, Janie's and my adventures during the Monarto riots many years ago. But, infuriatingly, she kept asking questions during my telling the tale. In the end it was I who fell to sleep first, and when I awoke there was no sign of Matilda anywhere.

It was already after ten o'clock when I woke. Took was still sleeping soundly. I guess I had gotten around five, maybe six hours sleep, which I couldn't really complain about, but upon opening my eyes there was only Matilda's empty bed across from me.

Took did not stir until after I had returned from the motel office with sandwiches from a machine.

'Make yourself useful and make some coffee,' I suggested, and perhaps a little more forcefully than I had intended.

'Keep ya shirt on,' he responded. Then, noticing our missing third member, and with no sound coming from the bathroom: 'Where's the queen of the dance?'

'Gone.'

'What do you mean, gone?'

I was in no mood to repeat myself and allowed him to work on it while he dragged his arse out of bed, scratching his head, then his crotch before pulling on his trousers.

'Gone?' he repeated. 'You look in her room?'

No I hadn't. I hadn't even thought of it, which pretty well summed up how sharp my mind was after a less than refreshing night's sleep.

'I'll go get her,' he volunteered.

She seemed fine, if a tad lethargic as she entered, following Took, grabbing a sandwich and a cup of coffee to take to the tiny, motel sized table against the wall, where she sat to begin consumption of her tuna and onion sandwich.

'Good morning,' I offered. 'Sleep well?'

'I could use six more hours,' she answered, 'but okay, considering, I guess.'

'Good. We're already behind schedule,' I informed them both. 'If we rush we can about make the morning visiting session. Or we can-'

'Wait for the afternoon session,' they answered in unison. 'I won't argue. I've got a sleep deprivation headache.'

'Bullshit,' said Took. 'I saw you drinking tequilas like water last night, pal. Admit it, you're hung over like the rest of us.'

I had, as accused, quaffed several plastic cups of the entertaining spirit, and was undoubtedly paying the price this morning.

'I'm not as young as I once was,' I argued. 'What's your excuse?'

'I don't know what I drank last night,' Matilda volunteered. 'I'm not exactly hung over. I feel as if I ran hurdles last night. And what's with the veils and things I discovered in my room this morning?'

She had no sooner posed the question when a look of sudden realization hit her. 'Oh, God. I remember,' she said with a moan, and covered her face with her hands. 'Tell me it isn't true.'

'What isn't true?' Took replied, munching on egg and lettuce with mayonnaise.

She lowered her hands, revealing a pained expression as she turned to me. 'Alex?'

I shrugged. 'All I know is, you enjoyed yourself. Nothing wrong with that, is there?'

She let her hands fall to her lap, the look of one resigned to the truth dominating her face. 'Fuck it,' she said, surprising Took and myself. 'I did have a good time. What was that stuff Trog gave me?'

'That was ecstasy, young lady,' I told her. 'How do you feel this morning?'

'Considering? Actually, beside feeling tired, and having, I think, overdone the physical activity. . . Not so bad.'

We finished breakfast and lazed around for a few hours, nodding off sporadically until wakefulness took command of the faculties. Matilda seemed okay with the fact she had let her hair down and gotten into the spirit of things. After each of us had taken a good, long hot shower to reinvigorate mind and body, we were all in good spirits once more and ready, by one o'clock in the afternoon, to reapply ourselves to the task at hand.

Filing through the visitors' gate we were led across the yard, on this occasion up to a three tiered cellblock building designated B-Division, where the guard unlocked the ground floor barrier into Vincent Zendell's end of the wing, where he had been similarly accommodated as his uncle. Though less spacious, consisting of only two cells adjoining on either side of a wide central corridor, as opposed to Guido's three cells on either side, when admitted into the Vincent's enclave through the barred barrier, the guard called out, 'Three visitors, Zendell,' and left us standing, waiting. In a moment the man I remembered emerged from the farthest cell and came strolling toward us.

Vincent Zendell, maybe five ten in the old scale, slight of build, although he looked to have gained some weight about the middle since last I saw him. Still that hawklike face with dark eyes and short, slicked back hair reminiscent of the fifties. He wore a kind of a robe, possibly described as a smoking jacket. Lightweight, printed with palm trees, parrots and such and coming down to his knees. As he moved stealthily towards us his face displayed recognition of his daughter, then focussing on Took and I, he said:

'What are you doing with these guys?'

'If you know of a safer place than being in our company right now, I'd be glad to know of it,' I told him. 'I only took this job to provide protection for your daughter, Vinnie.'

'Perhaps I can arrange something. This girl is my one bright light as I rot in this hole.' And turning to Matilda, 'Hello Angel. It's good to see you again.'

'Hello dad,' Matilda warmly greeted, and the two embraced for a moment. 'It's wonderful to see you again too.'

'You look well, my dear—' his voice affected by emotion as he held her at arms length in viewing her. Then, regarding us once more: 'Come on down to my hole in the wall, and let us talk.'

As Took and I followed Vinnie and Matilda, who were holding hands, I considered the initial changes I saw in the man. There were as yet no traces of grey in his hair; he seemed barely to have aged at all, yet there was a new quality in his voice which had struck me immediately he and spoken. There had always been what sounded to me like restrained hostility. It wasn't there as he greeted us, which was odd.

We followed him to the last cell on the left, which, as it was with Guido's quarters, had the dividing wall removed to provide greater space of two adjoining cells. It was furnished, in fact *over furnished:* a couch beneath a remodelled, wider window, a coffee table, writing desk, one recliner chair and three other, standard lounge chairs. There was a large screen television up on one wall, landscape paintings on two others, a coffee machine had been installed along with a small fridge, rugs on the floor, a tall reading lamp and oversized book shelf housing an array of publications listing from *Art* through to *Zoology*. With so much filling the room it was in danger of being a clutter, but it was actually served to give it a cozy feel.

'It's nice in here,' Matilda told he father.

'It serves, I suppose. Sit,' he invited. 'Can I offer refreshments? Tea, coffee, soft drink?'

We settled for sodas, sated our thirst and made ourselves comfortable, with Vinnie and Matilda sitting side by side on the couch while Took and myself sat adjacent, in comfortable lounge chairs.

'The length of visiting can be unpredictable around here,' he informed us. 'Can we get to the situation at hand? This letter,' he began, and reaching down beside the couch he produced a copy. 'It's disturbing—' and he placed a consoling hand on his daughter's shoulder. 'What do you make of it, Alex?'

'It's difficult to pin down. It might be anything from a hoax, a red herring, something instigated solely for the purpose of making you sweat, to an authentic threat on your daughters life, in retribution. If it's the last, with that note the perpetrator is serving multiple functions at once.'

'And if it's authentic,' he correctly pointed out, 'my precious Matilda is in danger.' He turned to face her. 'I'm sorry dear, no one is going to let anything happen, but we must speak frankly. Why on Earth did you agree to take this on, Jaeger? Oops, I mean Alex,' and he laughed at the slip. 'How odd a turn of events this is.'

'Jaeger is fine. It's weird alright, I have to admit. But I already told you why. Also, I've always hated loose ends, but to get back to it, my guess is that retribution is the motivating factor. It's my best guess, at least, so I have to ask the question. If it really is this Cassandra nut job, how did you incur his wrath?'

'We failed.'

That was it, of course, but I was digging for anything else pertinent. Something hidden from view. Someone like Vincent would have rubbed a lot of people the wrong way. Someone close to him; someone in the know, there might be many who could be masquerading behind the name Cassandra. We paused in silence for a moment, until Took chimed in.

'I don't buy it. I mean, any plan can come undone. Doesn't matter how well it's pieced together. And, Christ, don't be forgetting that Alex took a bullet the very morning he took on this cockeyed job. How suspicious is that?'

Matilda was nodding her head in agreement. 'So brave. I am indebted.'

'But, no. It's obvious that the bullet was meant for my daughter.' 'Was it?' Took countered.

'Moot point,' I cut in. 'Vinnie, we've come a long way to talk to you. What are you not telling us? This whole thing is like something out of a cheap detective novel. Personally, I find it preposterous to think any would-be assassin can miss his mark from an elevated perch right across the street. Following the logic, *I* was the target, and the only reasonable explanation is, you sent your daughter to set me up, in retribution for, shall we say, hindrance?'

'*Really,*' Matilda huffed, angered.

'It's alright,' Vinnie responded, patting Matilda's arm. 'I understand we are here to clear the air. Accusations are expected in getting to the truth, but you are quite wrong, I assure you, Mr Jaeger.' Matilda, I noted at the time, was having difficulty containing her displeasure as Vinnie continued.

'We cannot dismiss this note,' and he waved it in the air between us. 'This person has every reason to express anger after his plan of International proportion was unravelled in Monarto. Monarto is our city. Guido and I were responsible for stage one, and we failed.'

'Then why was I the one in the crosshairs?'

'Look, perhaps that's it,' Took enjoined. 'He's got you both suspicious of one another and-'

'*Yes, of course!*' Matilda blurted out, interrupting. 'Don't you see? Uncle Guido and my father failed him due to your intervention. The expensive, meticulous, time consuming planning and doing of it. Surely that's what's going on here. He is after you all, and toying with you all at the same time. You're almost certain to turn on each other, saving him from having to reach out across the globe and mess with you himself. It makes perfect sense.'

It wasn't bad, I had to admit. It had everyone in the room stumped for a rejoinder, as we sat, metaphorically scratching our heads. In Took's case though, he really was scratching his head. . . also his long bushy beard, and combing his fingers through it as he does when cogitating.

'You don't got lice in this joint, do you?' he asked seriously. When no one answered: 'Are we going with this theory? It seems to fit.'

'It fits,' I echoed, weakly, though for no reason I could identify and experiencing deep misgivings about the proposal. Maybe because It was so obvious and I hadn't thought of it myself. If that was it, what was I doing playing private detective when the stakes were so high?

'I agree,' added Vinnie. 'We're being set against one another for the amusement of the mysterious man at the top. Maybe he thinks we will tear one another apart? Would that not be a perfect outcome for such a person? He is watching, being amused enormously at our expense, as we grope for answers, begin flinching at shadows around us until we begin with reprisals at one another?'

I did not answer. I had just remembered the mysterious phone call of last night and I was caught, distracted in reckoning it into the equation. What point was there in warning me off?

When I snapped out of it, Vinnie was admiring the locket around Matilda's neck, letting it lie on the palm of his hand as he inspected it.

'Pretty. A delicate design,' he commented. 'The craftsmanship is superb and I just had to buy it for her. Did you think I wouldn't recognise it, Mattie?' he invited, smiling knowingly. 'You mother's. I bought it for my Adelia the first week I met her.'

Matilda had a curious expression on her face as Vinnie let it fall back against her chest, returning his attention to other matters.

'Are we agreed? We are being played? Alex. It is obvious now. Well done, my girl. You were always the clever one.'

Humbug, a voice jeered from deep in my skull. As far as I was concerned, the question was not resolved. Why? You might well ask, but the reason will not much impress. Try it this way. . .

Some people, when they do mental arithmetic, will come at a problem from all different angles. Some might round figures up or down for convenience, deal with the multiples of ten and apply the stragglers at the end. Some might make an educated guess to begin with and tackle the problem in bits at a time, and if, in the final reckoning the answer is close to the guestimate, they feel confident in the answer they have calculated. My thought process are about as tangled, relying as much on logic as instinct. Nevertheless, I have come to rely on my cockamamie process, especially since they have so often proved trustworthy.

The supposition that we were all being played was a perfectly good idea. It held water pretty damn well, but. . . I don't know, it just didn't get me there. As with recognising the successful manipulation of numbers, of getting to that *Yes! that's the answer!* That all important certainty was missing. I was sure that somewhere within the old noodle the reason for this doubt remained, waiting to be discovered or to emerge in its own time. It would surface, I told myself. It had to. Just keep working the problem. It will come.

There was some further discussion as I baited and probed Vinnie to reveal anything of further relevance, however minor it might be. Did he know where whoever was at the centre of this might be gaining their intelligence from? Had he or Guido had dealings with anyone else who might conceivably be connected? Did he have connections outside this country? Europe for example, and Northern Europe especially. I studied his bird of prey countenance for any indication of being misleading or outright lying. Vincent Zendell had always been difficult to read. I had always suspected him of being psychopathic, a condition making it near impossible for anyone but a trained professional to detect differences between when he was fabricating a story and when he was telling it straight. Psychopaths, I figured, were so messed up that they believed their own lies, making detection all the more difficult.

I excused Took and myself. Matilda had come a long way to see her father and I had already used up much of the available time. We left them to it, walked up to the barricade where a guard let us exit, then out into the open air where we leaned against the exterior wall of B-Division, there to wait until Matilda rejoined us.

'What do you think?' I asked Took, rolling a cigarette while we waited.

'What do I think? I think I didn't trust him before we came here, and I don't trust him even more now.'

'I can't argue with that,' I answered, and lit up.

In a moment he continued. 'He's changed. Maybe it's all those books. He seems less Vinnie and a little more Guido, you know? More controlled, for one thing. I always used tho think he seemed to be on the verge of lashing out at someone or something.'

'Naturally vicious,' I suggested.

'Yeah, that. Always on the edge of violence. But today? Not so much. More in control of himself, don't you think?'

'More cunning?'

'*Crafty*,' he suggested, and I agreed. Crafty fit perfectly well and I was sure that he was lying through his teeth.

'It is interesting, the change in our Vinnie,' I processed aloud. 'I wonder what that's about.'

'They do have psychiatrists in these places, you know. It's not unthinkable he took advantage of that fact.'

'Not something I would image he'd do of his own volition,' I said in answer to the questionable suggestion. 'Although, there would be brownie points in it for him, when it came to the question of parole. Maybe that's it?'

'Maybe it is.' He chuckled after a moment's contemplation. 'Vinnie talking to a shrink. I'd love to listen in on that.'

When I pulled a small notepad out from under my shirt, Took asked, 'What you got there?'

'His scribble pad,' I told him, and I began flicking through the pages, searching for anything remotely useful. 'I snaffled it from his desk on the way in when no one was looking.'

'This place is full of thieves,' Took quipped. 'Can't trust no one.'

I noticed someone dallying some yards along the wall we had propped against. An elderly inmate, and he was sidling up, nonchalant like, appearing ambivalent about whether or not to come up to us.

'What's up, old-timer?' Took asked. 'You after a smoke, perhaps?'

He was at least seventy, not out, frail looking, as if he had been in this place far too long a time.

'Don't mind,' he said, his voice sounding as rickety as he looked.

He made his way over and I handed him my pouch. 'You been visiting Mr Vinnie?—' to which we nodded.

'You friends of his? Work for him, maybe?'

'Maybe,' I responded, wondering if opportunity might be knocking here. 'Why do you ask?'

He looked us over, carefully, as if attempting to decide something.'Pah!' he expressed derisively. 'You ain't no friends of his. I don't like him neither,' he told us, making a face as if having swallowed something nasty. 'Johnny-come-lately. One of them millennials don't know nothin'. Things he's big stuff, but he ain't. Not like them came before him. You're old-school, I can tell.'

The description brought a smile to our faces.

'You've got that right,' Took replied. 'Same goes for his uncle, the little squirt.'

Took was on the same page as me. The old fellah passed back my pouch and I gave him a light from my own cigarette. A small gesture, but in this place, one translating as trust—trust or a shortage of matches.

'I don't know Mr Guido,' he continued (and pulled on the very fat cigarette he had rolled for himself. I should have rationed the old goat). 'Him I'm not sure of, but he does look after people. That much I know. But I ain't no suck. He's got plenty people doing for him, you bet.

'I could keep an eye out for you fellas, if you wanted,' he said, scanning the yard cautiously, as if demonstrating the meaning of keeping and eye out.

'An eye on who? Mr Vinnie?'

'I clean in Mr Vinnie's wing, you know. All over. I clean his rooms, too. Nobody but me is allowed,' he told us, perfectly explaining his offer.

'Yeah? Maybe you *could* be of help,' I replied. 'Tell me, do you have telephone phone privileges? Can you get to an unmonitored phone?'

'Are you kidding? Sure I do. I been here twenty six years. Ain't no one got more run of the place than old Willy Banks, I tell you.'

I tore off a strip of paper from the purloined notepad and scribbled my number. Slipping it to old Willy Banks, I told him, 'Can you tell me when he gets other visitors. And, if you can, who they are? Maybe the same for Guido?'

'Him I don't know so well, but—' Willy giggled conspiratorially, a mischievous light shining in his old eyes— 'I can with the other, if. . . you know.' he waited for the metaphorical penny to drop.

'Of course, Willy. I'll put a few dollars into your property for you. You can buy what you need from the prison shop. Do we have a deal?'

Willy drove a hard bargain. I ended by handing over what tobacco remained in my pouch, but a deal was struck. We now had eyes inside these walls, and a bargain at twice the price.

SIXTEEN

We returned the rented Mustang and flew home the next morning. The flight was difficult. Why? Because I was perplexed and annoyed; *more* than annoyed, and worst of all? I was perplexed and annoyed with myself. Sitting, trapped in an aircraft passenger seat, travelling at over five hundred miles per hour and having to stay put until we reached our destination, all I could think of was how little I had achieved. Had I lost my touch? There was a time I would have beaten the bushes, hard, threatened, banged heads where necessary and generally raised hell to come away with as many answers as I required to wrap this thing up by now. My frustration was excruciating.

Instead of making use of the flying time to work on solving the problem, I found myself distractedly ruminating on things I observed regarding myself, and the fact that I began losing focus irritated me even more. I had collected several pieces of intel, but they remained only as pieces, refusing to meld, to reveal in what manner they related to one another in any significant way.

Was it because I was growing older? because my mind was losing its once razor sharp edge? because, God forbid, my usually reliable instincts were fading in recent years? This thought at that time, as I recall, was the first time I really contemplated mortality. *My* mortality. Sure I had been in many firefights, been surrounded by death and myself come close to death on many occasions, but when adrenalin is coursing through one's body and shrapnel is flying all around, who has time to think? Even after these events one did all in their power to avoid considering the possibility that they might be lying out there in the field with the fallen. Young men believe they're invincible, and for good reason. Nature has a way of protecting homicidal, suicidal fools such as we were. Being dumb was one of those ways, I suspected; being all macho and gung-ho while wiping the reality of possible death from one's mind was necessary inoculation and allowed us to keep on doing what we were trained for, contracted and oaths given to do.

But that was the past and the river of time had flowed on. Lately I had been reviewing my life, the devil may care attitude I had employed for so long, up until Janie and I had tied the knot. We had recently discussed the possibility of children, raising a family. Was that what had started this insidious decline? Quite likely.

Now I was thinking how fortunate I had been to survive all I had experienced, and in reviewing the facts I began thinking maybe I ought to be more careful in future. If we were going to raise a family there would need be the two of us, not one of us and a burial plot in the municipal cemetery. I had to wonder if our beginning to plan for the future hadn't caused this sudden onset of self analysis and pathetic examination of the faculties which, at least within my own mind, had always separated me from the most of humanity.

Now I was watching as my inability to find answers and solve puzzles began to manifest right in the middle of my first commission. I had never before dealt with such a bout of self doubt, and I don't mind saying it scared me. I was growing older and the corrosive forces at work were slowly, irresistibly seeing me lose my edge and fill my mind with clutter. The universal constant, entropy. Everything in creation was subject to it, albeit at varying rates. There was no escaping it. Human beings unravelled at a faster rate than many, and that I had reached this juncture where the process began accelerating? and for someone like myself? It didn't get any worse than that. That's where I was at by the time the plane landed back in Adelaide.

Janie drove from home and collected us from the passenger terminal. She was concerned about the unexpected visit she had from detective sergeant Carruthers. He had called on the telephone only hours ago, wanting to come and talk with me. She had managed to convince him that I was out of town, but he insisted I contact him upon returning. "Something of a concerning nature," he had insisted, nothing more, and the fact that he was being less than forthcoming caused me added anxiety, augmenting my already sour disposition.

We dropped Took at his property and drove on home. Janie set out cups and plates, switched the kettle on to boil as she prepared sandwiches to fill our empty bellies.

Matilda dropped her travel bag in her room and came back out to ask if she could listen to the late afternoon news report on the television. She returned to sit at the kitchen table, watching; also watching through the opening into the lounge room where I mooned around between the furniture, attempting to gather my wits.

'Grubs up,' Janie called. 'Come and get it before you wear tracks in the carpet. What's the matter, dear. Trip not go so well?'

She had held off asking about the trip until now. In the years we had been together we had learned much about one another. Raising the subject during the drive home, she had observed, was not the time to do so; not while I presented so moody a countenance, sitting there beside her in the front passenger seat.

'Not as revealing as it might have been,' I told her, coming out to join them. I reached for a sandwich as Janie poured the drinks.

She left it at that, turned instead to Matilda. 'How was your father, dear?'

'He looks well. It was a great relief to see him again, after all this time,' and turning to me, 'Thank-you for the trip, Alex. I do appreciate your taking me. I feel much better for it, although. . .'

'Although?' I prompted.

'Other than my seeing dad again, I don't think we got anything much in the way of answers.'

'Time will tell, Matilda. Or should I call you Mattie?'

'Oh, that. As a little girl I was always called Mattie. I actually prefer it. So, yes, by all means. Mattie is fine.'

'Then Mattie it is.'

Under the girls talking, from the television set issued a voice which gave me reason to listen intently. With the Russian, Ukrainian war still in full swing, soldiers, common folk under siege, diplomats and assorted types in Russian uniform were being interviewed and asked for comment. A foot soldier was being asked about the looting, rapes and murders being discovered in wake of Russian withdrawals from towns and villages they had taken. So much had been pulverised by artillery, forcing many either to flee or hold on, scrounging a meagre existence amid the ruins or taking their chances on the lamb. But it was the soldier being interviewed; the accent I recognized and could not identify.

'*Hush-yer-din*, ladies' I asked, raising a finger skyward and turning toward the tv. 'That soldier, what nationality is he?'

He spoke in a mixture of broken English and his native tongue, with subtitles clarifying his meaning. We all listened as the he recited Putin's pernicious propaganda of a threatening political and cultural contamination of mother Russia, but what nationality was he?

The accent. It was a dead ringer for the one I had listened to on m y mobile just one night ago, at the Finks' big biker bash send-off for their beloved brother, Bear.

I moved to the lounge room and pressed *record* on the remote. When the interview was over I replayed it, asking the girls to try and identify his native tongue.

After replaying it a couple of times, it was clear that none of us had a clue. It always sounded Russian to them. I had a little more exposure to the ethnic languages of Northern Europe, but deciphering which tongue or dialect it might be was far beyond my capability.

I brought my phone to the kitchen table, searched out the audio file I had recorded at the Finks' bash. I replayed the soldier from the tv interview, followed by my phone file. Again and again. Heads were nodding now, and, at last I felt that long lost spark of optimism.

'I'm going to need a professional's advice on this,' I told the girls.

'Any ideas where I can find a language boffin—' I consulted my watch— 'on a Sunday afternoon at five-twenty in the p.m.?'

Not a chance, of course. I would have to wait until Monday, but Mattie, as we now called her, and Janie were still baffled by the *"Drop It"* message I had recorded on my phone, so I replayed the complete conversation from two nights ago:

ME: 'Yes? I'm sorry, can you speak up a bit? There's a party going on and it's difficult to hear you.'
UNKNOWN: 'I said, *drop it .*' ME: 'Drop what? Who is this?'
UNKNOWN: 'I do not advise to go on with investigation, Mr Jaeger,' ME: 'I am always open to friendly advice. Is this *friendly* advice?' UNKNOWN: 'Drop it or be sorry, I promise.'
ME: 'And I have advice for you, Boris,' I told him. 'Destroy your phone. It's being traced.'

I detected a flicker of agitation in Mattie's face, the first time I had played it through.

'Not at all,' Mattie replied to my asking if ever she recognised the voice.

'That's a shame,' I told her. 'I was seriously hoping you might have heard it in connection with either your uncle or your father. 'It's not Cassandra's voice?'

'Such a long time ago. How would I possibly remember? I was a child.'

'Yes, of course,' I expressed, only slightly discouraged.

There was little to be done until Monday. More dead time, exactly what I did not need, but that evening, and not entirely unexpectedly, there came a knock at the door.

On the front step stood my old foe, Detective Sergeant Carruthers; six feet of misery and trouble combined, wearing a trilby hat, dressed in a grey suit, cop blue shirt and navy tie. The bugger had aged. I remember thinking in that moment of seeing him after going on twenty years, and thinking he resembled Prune Face, from the Dick Tracy comic book, though he looked healthy, sporting a tan suggesting he might have just come back from six weeks in Hawaii.

We stood facing each other, I suspect while both of us mentally catalogued the changes in appearance we had both suffered since the last time we faced one another, much like this.

'Carruthers,' I acknowledging.

'Jaeger, you slippery bastard. God, you've hardly changed at all. 'Married life. What can I tell you? The same can be said for you,' I told him, wondering if he knew it was a lie. 'You had better come in and explain what this is all about.'

I brought him through to the kitchen and closed the door leading into the lounge room, where the girls were watching tv, so that we had some privacy.

'Be seated,' I told him, and I did likewise, so that we were facing each other across the table. 'Well, what's up? Don't tell me you've unearthed fresh evidence from that ridiculous Draganov thing. How did you find me, anyway?'

He pulled one of my fliers from his pocket and unfolded it. 'I'm a detective, remember?' He let that sink in for a moment before answering the first question. 'Nothin' to do with your previous life, Jaeger. It's more to do with what you've been up to recently.'

'Oh?' What the hell would he know of it, I was wondering.

'It shouldn't surprise you to learn that you have made some enemies over the years. It *will* surprise you to know that I am not one of them.'

This did surprise me. 'Oh?' I said again, ruing how trite it sounded.

He appeared to be having some difficulty now, but he took a breath and began anew. 'I was an alcoholic for many years, Jaeger. *Am,*' he amended. 'It doesn't go away, but I've taken measures. You've heard of the twelve steps?'

I nodded. This was getting weird. 'Yeah, sure I have. It's a program, right? Alcoholics Anonymous?'

'That's right. One of the steps, the ninth step, is to apologise and to make amends to anyone you might have offended, wronged or harmed while in the clutches of addiction.'

'I've heard that, and you're here because?'

'I'm here to apologise, Jaeger. To make amends for any wrongs I may have done you.'

'Wow,' I responded, not at all meaning to. 'This come's as a shock, I gotta tell you.'

I was having a difficult time believing a word of it, until I noticed how he couldn't hold my gaze and seemed to be very uncomfortable, shying away as he restively let his attention fall on random items around the room.

'It's a tough gig,' I finally told him. 'Alcoholism. I know a lot of you guys have trouble. Divorces, alcohol. I suppose you know I used to be a soldier?'

'I do know that about you,' he replied, beginning to focus.

'I saw a lot of good guys crash and burn. The stress. Soldier, cop, parameds, fire fighters, too, I guess. Any job where you come up against the worst. It takes its toll. I get it.'

'Yeah,' he mumbled. 'Humanity.' He then appeared to remember why he had come, sitting up, squaring himself in his chair. 'I'm sorry for hounding you the way I did, Jaeger. Messin' with you when you were obviously tryin' to get on a new track and all. I'm supposed to ask your forgiveness now, I think.'

I laughed. I know I shouldn't have, but I couldn't help it, seeing the bastard sitting there the way he was. He looked as uncomfortable as it was possible for a man to be.

'I'm sorry, but. . . Shit, this is really one for the book. You coming to me, asking forgiveness? It took some guts to come here. I'm not discounting' it, but you really fucked with me, Carruthers. You would have seen me slammed up back then. Fuck that, and fuck you for being such a prick.'

'That was my job,' he responded, at last finding his feet. 'I ain't apologising for that anyway. The investigation was clean. I'm apologising for pullin' strings to try and stop you being a private dick. Shit, I know you killed Draganov. The courts acquitted you but I know you did it. Regardless of what an animal he was, it's against the law to go around popping bad guys willy nilly. That was our job.'

When he realised what he had said, he returned to his former, less assertive self. 'You know what I mean. There's a systems in place for a reason. The justice system, law and order, it's a fragile mechanism. We cops are authorised to do the dirty work and deal with the likes of him.' He checked himself then, realising things were not going as planned. 'I'm apologising for the extra I went, okay? That's all I'm here for.'

He was about to take his bat and ball and go home. I didn't want that. It had just occurred to me that he might prove useful somehow, if it wasn't too late already. I had to try it on. I needed any and every possible ally, not knowing yet the full extent of what I was up against. A cop wanting my forgiveness. There were possibilities here.

'Okay,' I said, appeasingly. 'I know what you're saying, and I guess I even agree. I agree with what you just said. Does that help?'

'Mmm,'he expressed, mumpish now, and he was looking at me with much more meaning in his eyes than a moment ago. 'Why won't you admit it, Alex? There's only you and me here right now. It would mean a lot, you know?'

Goddamned if he wasn't playing me, I realised. I had to keep my calm and not let him know I had twigged to his game. 'Would it really make any difference?' I asked, assuming an expression I hoped conveyed I was considering the request.

'A guy comes to a point in life where he begins questioning himself,' he told me, now feigning vulnerability. 'Decisions made. Actions taken. Getting further down the road of life and lookin' back, doubting himself and the things he believed in all those years ago. It plays on the mind, especially in the night, when sleep won't come and the demons come out. That's when it's the worst—when a drink is what you want most, just to help you sleep. Don't tell me you don't understand it. I know you do, being what you are. It has taken me a log time to realise this, Alex, but, hell, in some ways you and I are more alike than you might imagine.'

I couldn't believe what I was hearing. More clearly, I did not believe a word. What was going one here? Was I meant to say, *Fair cop, I killed the son-of-a-bitch?* What then? Was he taping our conversation, waiting for those very words?

My thoughts shifted then, as instinct alerted me to something out of left field. Too many strange things had recently been happening to and around me to ignore the possibility that they were all connected to one thing.

I noticed how closely he was watching me. As if reading my thoughts he broke eye contact, small yet distinct traces of tension expressing in his countenance. Was he taping this conversation as my sudden onset of paranoia suggested? Or was there something lurking deeper in the shadows, and should I go with niggling suspicion, test these nebulous slivers of evidence?

'This is between you and me, Jaeger,' he encouraged. 'I've been retired six months. I guess I'm looking for closure, you know? For piece of mind.'

'Motherfucker,' I growled, deep in my throat.

'What?' His eyes widened, then darted about, shifty again.

His right hand was already moving steadily towards something under his jacket, exactly where a cop holster containing a cop thirty-eight Smith and Wesson would be snugly strapped under his left arm.

Janie had chosen the exact moment to enter the kitchen, I noticed, as I lunged across the table, pinning his hand and whatever it clutched beneath his jacket against him. He went backward in his chair, crashing into the sideboard behind him with me on top of him, as quickly as I could spinning him flat against the floor, my full weight on top of him and holding his arms spread, keeping him from reaching for anything else mischievous he might be carrying.

Janie had frozen in the doorway, with Matilda now behind her, peering over her shoulder as I rolled him onto his stomach, looking for something to bind his hands. His handcuffs, clipped inside the leather pouch on his belt presented as the perfect item, and in a moment I had him secured, repositioned in his chair, the thirty-eight and his cuff keys safely in my possession. Also the micro-recorder I had suspected. It was running inside his jacket, in the inside breast pocket.

'Shall we start over?' I suggested, puffing from the exertion; and it was yet another thing that would not have been happening just a few short years ago.

To the girls I explained, 'There's no problem here. Can you grab whatever you came out here for and go back to your tv show?'

'But-' Janie began.

'I'll explain latter. I need to talk to my friend a moment longer.'

She pulled the chocolate *Boom Boom* biscuits from the cupboard where she had secretly stashed them, before both returned to the lounge room. I had been looking for chocolate only hours ago, and she had told me she didn't think there were any. The sneak. I would mention it later.

Carruthers had not said a word, and remained silent as I repaired to my previous position, across the table from him.

'You cop bastard, pretending you're here seeking forgiveness. Imitating an actual human being. I mean, I know some of you are, but, *Christ on a Tuesday!*' He looked shattered, and I was surprised by that.

'*Sonofabitch.* What are you playing at?' I asked, conversationally. He shook his head kind of mournfully, looking woeful. 'My family. I had to.'

'Had to what? Kill me or catch me admitting to a crime?'

'Either. They want you dead, but locked up where I figure they can get to you easily would have done.'

Now we were getting somewhere. 'They?' I prompted.

He looked genuinely scared. 'They threatened my daughter and my grandkids. I can't, Jaeger.'

'Okay, maybe we'll come back to it in a moment. How and when were you approached?'

'A couple weeks back. I started getting messages. Notes, disturbing phone calls. A guy even spoke in my ear as I queued for a train. He was gone before I could react. Into the crowd.'

'Saying what?'

'They knew about how you slipped a conviction. Knew there was bad blood between us, and, I guess, figured I was perfect for their purpose. Carrot and stick. I was promised twenty grand.'

Well that made sense, I judged. 'You were really going to *off me* for a mere twenty gees, here in my own home, with my wife in the next room?'

He didn't answer at first, but I waited. 'My daughter and the kids. Look, I didn't know what I was going to do, okay? Jesus, Jaeger. Time was running short and I had no handle on it. I couldn't think straight.'

'Straight enough to reach for this,' I reminded him, brandishing his snub-nosed revolver.

They were threatening his family, which I didn't even know he had. No mention of a wife, but I believed him. Maybe he was a widower.

'Listen to me Carruthers,' I began, 'I will assist with keeping your daughter and grandchildren safe, but you have to tell me what you know of whoever was threatening you. Did you say you're recently retired?'

He nodded. 'Six months.'

I shook my head, emulating dismay. 'After how many years on the force?'

'Forty goddamned years.'

'Forty. It's a long time. You not think about legacy? After forty years faithful service you were going to let this be how you would be remembered? A hell of a thing, guy.'

I appeared to have touched a nerve. I had never witnessed a cop tear-up before, but his eyes began to glisten, betraying emotion.

'What the fuck, Jaeger. What do you not understand about family?'

Truth was, there was a time I would not have understood the depth of a man's devotion to family. That had changed when, only recently, Janie and I had begun talking about starting one of our own.

'I get it,' I said, understanding perfectly well. He had been put between a rock and a hard place. I could accept that his family came before anything else.

'That stuff about booze, getting straight?' 'It's true, he said, and I believed him.

'Look, fellah. You had an option before you came through my door tonight. Not much of one, but still. . . Right now you have none, so get your head on straight. What is there you can tell me about the people jamming you up like this? I don't care how small and insignificant a detail it might be. Think, *goddamnit.*'

He looked distraught, desperately searching his memory for anything of possible use. After a full minute he was shaking his head, looking as though he had given up.

'It's not much, but the first time they contacted me was by phone. I still have connections I used to use when I was a cop. I had it traced, not all the way back to the caller. It was blocked. Impossible for my contact to discover anyway. But I was surprised to learn it didn't originate here Australia.

'How is that helpful?' I replied, disappointed.

'The prefix code was 375. The call came from Belarus.'

'Belarus?' I repeated. It fit. I still had to find a language expert who could identify my mysterious caller's lingo, bet we were definitely zeroing in on the right part of the world.

'Where are your daughter and grandkids right now?' I asked.

'Not far away,' he replied, somewhat reluctantly.

'Get them out, to somewhere safe, and I mean *safe*. Don't call them, go to them. Your calls will be traced. Destroy your phone. You'll need cash money. Don't be using traceable plastic. Do you understand what I'm saying to you?'

'You're releasing me?'

'What, I'm supposed to kill you? In my home? Nobody dies in my home, fellah. It's a rule, and as far as keeping you. . . Why would I want to keep you? So again, do you understand?'

'I do, but how will I know if it's ever safe to return?'

Not my problem. There's a long way to go yet.' I shrugged, thinking briefly on it. 'Okay, scan the classifieds, the public notices in the Sunday Review, every week. If you see *Come home Agamemnon, all is forgiven*, you'll know the danger has passed.'

He seemed to grasp what was going on, so I hurried him out the front door, emptying his revolver of cartridges before returning it to his possession.

'*Sayonara*,' I told him, hoping never to lay eyes on the man again.

It was time to explain to the girls what had just occurred.

SEVENTEEN

I had, until now, neglected the notebook I had swiped from Vinnie's desk. The three of us sat, scrutinizing pages of doodling, laundry lists, and even a list of collections and payouts to and from inmates who had placed bets on the ponies, with Vinnie running the book. One page in particular did grab our collective attention. On the reverse side of a dog-eared page were these numbers numbers: 375 (17)! and with a tiny sketch of what looked to be a guy on a tiny horse, holding a lance, and next to it were ten digits: ••

'I know those first four numbers,' I told the girls. 'Carruthers told me three seven five is the phone prefix for Belarus.'

'And this is?' Janie asked.

'Areas code, I guess. Grab your phone and we'll search online.' In thrice she had it: 'Area code one seven is Minsk,' she told us.

'And these ten digits here, complete the connection,' Matilda, summed up.

'Should we dial it?'

It was a good question. I had a hunch that the number might put us in touch with either the diabolical Cassandra himself, or someone close to him.

'What if we're asked to identify ourselves?' Janie asked, just as I was about to say those very same words. 'A code or password or something. Coded question and answer?'

'Suspicion would be instantaneous,' I answered. 'They might well disconnect and use another number, or worse, somehow trace back to our phone.'

'Can they do that?' Janie asked.

I shrugged. 'Maybe. I don't know, but should we risk it right now?' 'Call it,' said Matilda, sounding unsure, and now biting her lower lip.

'To what end, exactly?' I asked. 'What purpose would it serve, besides tipping a possibly very security conscious someone at the other end that an unauthorized someone else has access?'

'No, this number could prove valuable at a latter date. In fact,' I said, paused and turned to Janie. 'Do you remember those military brass and ASIO stiffs who decided our fate after I got out of hospital that time?'

'How could I forget?'

Matilda looked at a loss. 'What?'

'After the big ruckus here in Monarto. Janie, Took and myself ran foul of the National Security bods. We were privy to matters deemed secret. We had to sign documents promising never to reveal what we knew. That or God knows what. But I was thinking those guys ought to be let in on this about now, don't you think?'

'No,' Matilda instantly blurted out, then scrambled for an excuse for doing so. 'I mean, do you think that's wise? ASIO? What about my father and uncle Guido?'

Here it was. I was wondering when this was going to become a problem. We had a crime family member, here, right amongst us, and she was always going to be protective of them, no matter what.

'You're going to have to choose, Matty,' I told her. 'You're here for your protection, but now Guido and your father are implicated.'

'Not in the attempt on my life, they're not!' she said, loud and petulant.

I was still far from convinced that she had been the target. Something told me I had been the bunny, and that I was damned lucky to be alive. She was holding my gaze as my cogs whirred, processing all I had learned. I was thinking she could well be in it up to her neck, with her father and her uncle pulling the strings, meaning she was nothing but a liability to have around.

'Call the number,' she demanded. 'And tip them off? Not a chance.'

'You intend calling the authorities then?'

'If that number leads to who I think it does, Matty, it's a whole new ball game. Yes, that bastard Cassandra could be out to settle an old score against everyone, me and therefore Janie included. You might have nothing to do with it, but then Guido and your father may be in the firing line, vengeance for failure to complete their end of the operation. Do you want him to get at them?' Before she could answer, I continued: 'I have a strong suspicion that number will either lead to, or lead us very close to, that psychopath, and I'm not tipping our hand. If that's the number I think it is, what in hell is Vincent doing with it? I'm all for making this situation go away, quickly and with as little personal involvement as possible, but there's one added problem. . . You.'

'Me? Why me, a problem?'

'For one, I took the job of getting to the bottom of who is possibly targeting you.'

'*Possibly?*' she repeated, immediately picking up on my meaning.

I had made the mistake of letting slip my unrelenting suspicion. I had brought her here as much to keep a possible enemy close as I had to keep her out of harm's way, if there really was any danger to her. As to the question of her being in any danger, I was beginning to think there was none, and that I and those around me, my family, *we* were the one's who were in danger.

'Possibly,' I said, confirming my doubt about her.

To this, she sat quietly, staring at me with a look of injured disappointment beginning to grow on her face. Janie seemed surprised and disappointed, too. Boy, what an idiot I was, saying it to her face, but then Janie broke the uncomfortable pause.

'Don't worry dear,' she said to Matilda. 'He says things he doesn't mean when he's under pressure. 'You're staying here with us, where you belong and where you're safe. He's angry because he doesn't know what to do, that's all.'

I kept my mouth shut, lest I make things worse. I didn't really want her packing up her bag and leaving, but if she stayed? And, hell, she was my client after all. What a shemozzle.

'Janie's right,' I apologised. I'm sorry, I shouldn't have said that. It's obviously not true,' I told her, hoping she didn't detect the whopper. 'I'm angry for not knowing what's going on, is all. I'm sorry.'

'It's getting late, she said, glancing at the wall mounted clock in our living room.'

'Perhaps we all should turn in and get some rest,' Janie suggested, despite the early hour, and we left it at that.

I shaved while Janie showered, and showered as Janie pulled on her pee-jays and climbed into bed before me. It was darkening out side the window as I joined her, but we did not immediately lay back to sleep. Instead, we puffed up the pillows, drew up close to one another with my arm about her shoulders; a custom we had fallen into whenever we had something needing to be talked over, and I explained all that had occurred during the trip, and how irked I was at the lack of any real progress.

'Don't worry, it'll come,'

'Things don't just come, dear,' I replied, wondering how she could be so unmoved by my plight. 'I have to sort this out quickly.'

'You will,' she said, dismissive of my mounting anxiety. 'You've put many contingencies in place. You can only wait and see what turns up.'

'Monday I need to find a language expert. Someone who might recognise that accent on the recording?'

'Why does it matter so much? Bulgaria, Belarus, Russian, why does it matter?'

'I've decided to connect with ASIO, and I would feel better if I had precise information to go to them with. It's important. We've got to narrow it down. Northern Europe, it's easy for someone to disappear into space like that. Especially someone of Cassandra's wiliness, and he has the whole world to fade away into. I don't want that *son-of-a-bitch* slipping away again. He's obviously still on the loose and up to no good. How on Earth he was allowed to remain at large after the last time, I'll never know.'

'Going to ASIO is a good idea, sweetheart. Let me look after discovering the nationality of the person on the recording. I'll contact the university on Monday, and do what it takes. Okay?'

'That would be great,' I responded, glad of the offer, and I gave her a peck on the cheek in appreciation.

'So what else is bugging you, and don't—' 'Nothing.'

'—say nothing,' she finished, and twisted herself around to look at me with those simmering, clear, brown eyes which had captivated me all those years ago, at a place called The Old Coach, a caravan park on the outskirt of town, where I had found her holed up with a two-bit drug dealer I ever only knew as Stocky. Stocky's face had been blown off that night, by Guido's goons, during a drug takings rip-off attempt, leaving her defenceless and about to suffer much the same fate as her companion, had I not intervened. She had done the near impossible and kicked the angel wings habit which had made her all but a possession and a slave within the trade. What strength there was behind those eyes, I reminded myself, and how lucky had I been to find her?

'I know there's something worrying you, Alex,' she stated with certainty. 'Something I don't think is connected to what's going on around us. I'm right, aren't I?'

Anything but the truth at that moment would have been wrong and instantly recognized.

Janie had snuggled up to me, with her head resting on my chest. 'What is it?' she persisted, and realising that this was a perfect time to try and resolve the niggling concern, with a quiet sigh, I relented.

'It's not anything specific. Something I can nail down. I thought with this private eye gig it would be something which would, I don't really know. . . fill a hole maybe, you know? And I thought it was perfect, considering my background, and that I'd take to it like a duck to water. But look where we are, and it's not the same and that's the problem, I think.'

'It's not the same as what?' she asked. 'As it used to be.'

To this I felt her give a small nod. 'It's not fulfilling enough?' 'No, it's not that.'

'I was going to say I find it hard to believe. You've always lived for this kind of thing. Out there surrounded by uncertainty and with nothing but your wits guiding you. It's who you are, dear,' and she gave me a reassuring little squeeze.

Maybe I sighed in that moment, or it was because I didn't immediately respond with something smart-arse to say, as I normally would. Whatever it was, it was clue enough for her to sit forward, twist around again and regard me with a serious look on her face, saying, 'It's not who you are *anymore?*'

Bang, Janie had said it, and I had no response other than to sit there under the covers with a blank look on my dial. I may have shrugged, thinking back on it, but, for the most part I remember feeling totally defenceless under the glaring light of the truth.

'That *is* it,' she said, and after scrutinising a moment longer she smiled a knowing smile, resumed her position pressed up against me. 'It's about time. I was wondering if ever you might. . . mellow.'

'Must you use that word?' I complained, and elicited a giggle from her. 'Mellow, really? It's just another word meaning old.'

Her giggle turned to laughter then, and she pinched me, hard, so that I let out a yelp. 'I love you,' she told me, 'and you can't go around being the lone avenger, grabbing the devil by the tail for all of your life without eventually it loses its luster. I've been watching the changes since this first began. You're afraid that you're slowing down, losing your edge or whatever you call it. It's how you think.

'But it's not that at all,' she continued, her hand stroking my neck now. 'There's so much more to life, and, I think, that fact is dawning on you at last. You're not losing anything, darling. You're tired, fed up and over it, and that for you that kind of existence has lost it's appeal, that's all.'

I was listening to what she was saying, to her logic, and damned if it didn't add up and make perfect sense. I was so relieved to hear I wasn't falling apart, and I didn't much care right then if it was true or merely an excuse for me to cease driving myself. I figured she was right, that no one can go through life being the same person for all of the time. People grow, and in my case they *grow up*. That was just the way of it and no body's fault, least of all mine. I could live with that, and suddenly everything didn't seem half as bad as I was imagining it to be. I had been through much worse and come out smiling. And fuck it, I decided, I didn't have to carry the load all by myself, feeling responsible and at fault if my thinking had changed and I no longer saw how the onus was on me to solve the problems of the world. Let someone else handle it for a change. I had done my bit for the forces of good. This *agent of karma*, as Took had amusingly once described us, was going to stop worrying so much and take a back seat.

'*Kemo Sabe*,' she intoned, softly, her eyes wresting me from my thoughts and seductively gaining my attention; and whatever happened after that is no body's business, but Janie's and mine.

EIGHTEEN

The next morning, Sunday, we discovered that Matilda had left sometime during the night. It was a Sunday ritual that Took would come over at around nine to enjoy one of Janie's fabulous Sunday breakfasts of bacon, eggs, sausages or lambs fry, with an abundance of fried tomatoes which came from our garden, fried with butter and dill, and with plenty of buttered toast on the side to mop up the juices. The ritual of a hearty Sunday breakfast together was a part of the new life we had all grown into and so much appreciated. We had all grown exceedingly close since our coming together in the days of crisis which had rocked the city of Monarto some twenty years ago. We were family, something we had all lost early in our lives, and, though no one had actually said so, I knew each of us felt privileged and lucky to have rediscovered the feeling in later years.

Took noted Matilda's absence as we sat down to eat, but he wasn't overly surprised by the development. Over ample coffee, the second and third rounds taken outdoors on the back verandah, we contemplated our options while watching the cat stalking anything that moved in the grass and thick vegetation of the garden.

'Where do you suppose she's gone?' Took asked, stretched out in a lazy-boy chair with his mug of coffee?

I had just lit the first cigarette of the day, and was sitting beside Janie at the outdoor table, taking in the vista and enjoying the warmth of the sun.

'That will depend on her part in it all,' I replied. 'My thinking is, if she's an innocent party she defiantly wouldn't be returning to her rental in Monarto, or back where she came from. She's too smart to do that, I would hope. But if she was merely playing a role directed by Vincent or Guido, I guess it doesn't much matter.'

'I'm worried about her,' Janie told us. 'She seemed quite authentic, to me. I hope she's got somewhere safe in mind to go to.'

'That's the problem,' came Matilda's voice from behind the flywire screen door in the kitchen. 'I don't.'

'Matty,' Janie responded. 'Are you alright? Where have you been, dear?—' and she rose to greet the girl, opening the screen door and reaching out her hand to bring her outside with us.

'I realised I had nowhere safe to go,' she said, sounding miserable. 'I hope you don't mind that I've come back here.'

'No, of course not. We want you here, safe, with us,' and Janie embraced her in reassurance. 'Come sit down. Are you hungry? You just missed breakfast, but there's plenty left over if you want some?'

She nodded. 'Sounds lovely, thank-you.'

Janie attended to bringing a plate outside for Matilda while Took and I were left to make conversation with her.

'Why'd you do a runner?' Took asked, as she looked for somewhere to sit, eventually propping on the low brick wall separating the edge of the verandah with the rose garden.

She shrugged, a sideways glance in my direction making the answer clear to me at least.

'I was hoping you would forget my inappropriate remark from last night,' I told her.

'What remark?' Took asked, but neither of us answered.

'Not just that,' she replied. 'It made me think, Alex. My being here, it could be dangerous for you and Janie and I—'

'Don't be silly, Matty,' Janie called from the kitchen, where she had been listening. 'You think Alex didn't think it through when he invited you to come and stay? I told you last night why he said what he did. You mustn't take seriously what he says in the moment. I've leaned that much over the years.'

Took and I exchanged looks, with him wondering what it was I might have said, though obviously amused by the way I had been taken out of the discussion, and with me looking very much like a man who had been taken out of the discussion. When women do that, there's little to be done but accept it.

'What remark?' Took tried again.

'Never you mind,' Janie told him, appearing from the kitchen with Matilda's breakfast on a try. 'I don't want you stirring up trouble the way you do.'

Now Took wore the expression I had just a moment ago, negated by my wife.

'Here you are, dear, said Janie, setting the breakfast tray down at the table for our runaway, and as far as I was concerned, our still under suspicion guest.

'It's nice out here, Matilda observed, sitting to eat. 'You're lucky to have such a lovely home.'

'We like it,' Janie replied. 'There was a time I could only dream of something like this. Life is unpredictable, Matty. We'll get through this little upset, you'll see, and you can find whatever it is you're looking for.'

'I hope so.' She was about to take a first sample of her breakfast when she returned her knife and fork to the plate with a *plonk*. A squeak escaped her throat, and her shoulders shuddered as tears spilled from her eyes.

Took and I could only watch, but Janie came around beside her and gave the girl a gentle hug.

'I feel lost,' she said between sobs. 'I shouldn't have come back to burden you nice people. It's not fair on you at all.'

'It's okay, Matty,' Janie consoled. 'Everything will turn out fine. We need a bit of excitement in our lives. We were getting way far too complacent around here. Besides, this is Alex's idea of fun, and me and Took, too.'

'Yeah,' Took chimed in. 'This is normal, for us. If you hadn't happened along I'd be cleaning gutters or some dreary thing. Janie would be pushing thermometers up a dogs' backsides and Alex would be going out of his tiny mind for things to do to get him through the day. Why do you think he took up private eyeing? The man is obviously going through mid-life crisis. I was expecting to see him buy a red sports car any day now. That or start writing his memoir. You saved us all from that, thank Christ,' he said with a chuckle.

Matilda managed to raise a smile. Janie began to laugh. I, on the other had, and of all things felt exposed and embarrassed. Hearing Took say that about me came as a shock. Mid-life crisis? Me? That sort of thing only happened to boring arseholes who had spent their lives pushing a pencil, didn't it? To someone who wakes one morning realising they had wasted their lives doing nothing they could look back on coming close to adventurous, worthwhile or as fun. The idea hit me like a brick in the head. Mid-life crisis? God, was it true? Had I been the only one unaware of what malady had been gnawing at me these past months?

It was true, I realised, and the revelation brought me crashing down to earth. I was no different to all those billions of other men in the world subject to so pathetic a condition? The idea that I, Alex Jaeger, soldier of fortune, righter or wrongs, professional thief and co-member of Agents of Karma inc. could be subject to so banal a predicament as this was not, for me, reason for levity, but my reluctance to join in my wife's and Took's levity seemed only to induce greater jocularity. Even Matilda seemed to find it amusing.

'Okay guys. Not that funny. And what do *you* find so entertaining?' I aimed at Took. 'Your time will come. And what's wrong with writing a memoir, anyway? It's actually not a bad idea. I might just do that.'

'You couldn't write about half the things you've done,' he replied. 'Not unless you want to go to jail.'

He had me there. All of my good stories were things I couldn't mention without taking a huge risk. Half of the half were matters of national security for several countries, with a penalty of twenty fife years incarceration attached. The things I had done after quitting the military, if one wanted to be pedantic about it, were outright criminal; but, then, being criminal against criminals made it a good thing, to my way of thinking. It's a simple enough equation. Two negatives make a positive. The universe I live in has a great deal to do with equations. It makes the place much easier to understand. Ask any scientist. The whole deal can be explained as one gigantic equation, including both physical and behavioural rules. The meaningful ones anyway. The mathematics of it actually differentiates between bogus, manmade rules of behaviour and the more expansive, universal kind.

A memoir was something to be carefully thought about, and screw Took's sarcasm. Perhaps I could disguise the truth as a fictional account, change a few place and people's names ? I would definitely examine the possibilities in time to come, I determined.

*

Everything returned to the way it was without much upset, and by the time Monday rolled around I was chaffing at the bit to get on with things. In the morning, Janie headed off into the city, with a copy of the voice file from my phone. Took, refusing the offer of being excused from further involvement, and seeing the offer as nothing other than being dropped from the team, insisted on accompanying me to the city of Monarto's edifice known to most as *The Federal Building*. The general population was under the assumption that it housed blue collar pen-pushers, and that maybe it was in some way connected to general functions of the Federal Government. I knew it housed national and international telecommunications relay services, clandestine services linked globally as well as being a state branch nexus for ASIO and other similarly disposed organisations. From within it's maze of hallways, highly protected and surveiled alcoves and offices, were able to be initiated all manner of secretive endeavours, with grey men and women given decision-making abilities in the areas of State, Federal and International arenas, and in cooperation with most other well known, international security services, barring, of course, those with a leaning toward the less democratic methods of leadership. Even then, back doors and secret technology gave access to many of those countries as well.

Monarto had been designed and built with Federal money, the idea being to decentralise the way the State of South Australia operated in all sections of government and major commerce. It had started out well, until organised crime saw the possibilities here and got their greedy hook into it. Then the grand design went tits-up, and the place lots its charm. The Federal Building was a legacy of that original plan, continuing to serve perfectly well in its designed function as being a technological hub and information storage and relay station for many commonly connected facilities around the globe.

Took and I walked up the wide concrete steps impregnated with granite chips leading to the entranceway at the front of the building, aware that we were already being monitored from many angles, visually as well as being scanned from a distance for firearms and other concealed devices, all of which were to be handed over at the security gate on the ground floor.

A pair of security guys had us empty our pockets and submit to a hand scanner being waved around, while being observed, I had no doubt, by armed guards in their station behind a fake mirror to out right. The briefcase I carried, containing all the information I had on the case was rifled, scanned and eventually returned. I then presented the card I had been issued with long ago by the Feds. Took likewise had a similar card and we were admitted, asked to wait in a room we were led to by our escort.

I had called ahead, naturally. Walking into a place like this unannounced is not the way things are done in situation like this, and in a moment a be-suited, nondescript elderly man entered the room.

'Mr Alex Jaeger,' he greeted, 'and Mr. . . ?' he inquired. 'Took,' he responded.

'Your full name, please. For the record, you understand. We have your friend's history, but you, I'm afraid, are not well documented.'

In response Took handed over his passport, which our inquisitor flipped open to read, 'Adrian Aristotle Jones.'

'Took,' my tall, amply bearded friend insisted, but he was ignored as the man jotted down details from Took's passport before handing it back to him.

He left the room, returning again in a few minutes. 'I'm sorry for the delay. This way, gentlemen, if you would?'

He escorted us to the lifts, rode up with us to the twenty-third floor and led us to an office at the end of a long corridor, where he tapped twice on the wooden door.

From within issues a tenor voice: 'Come on in.' The escort pushed open the door and bade us enter. Once in, he closed it quietly behind us and departed.

We stood facing three grey suited individuals. Two men, middle aged, ex military looking types. The other was a woman in her late forties or so and dressed in one of those drab, female suits; and once attractive, I imagined, but a life in an environment of too little sunlight and fresh air had jaded her appearance, making her much like her male counterparts.

'Do come in, boys,' she said, her voice sounding as nondescript as the rest of her. 'Take a seat.' Two available chairs had been placed in front of the panel of three, which we availed ourselves of. 'My colleagues here are Mr Tidswell and Mr McCormack. My name is Phillipa Cromwell, but you are expected not to remember this the moment you exit this building.'

I was pretty certain these were bullshit names but I simply nodded in compliance. The sooner this was over with, the better I was going to like it.

'So, gentlemen,' the guy at the far left of Phillipa Cromwell began, 'you have something to tell us, in relation to a character known to us as Cassandra, I believe. Is that correct?'

'It's correct,' I responded, and when no further response came from any of these stiffs, I took a breath and launched into it. I was, however, not about to be influenced by this bizarre, pantomime of *we are powerful people, feel our presence.*

'I won't ask if you know anything of our previous, end game connection to the scumbag, Cassandra. I'm sure you all are well briefed.

'I took on a client, the daughter of one Vincent Zendell, some weeks ago. She seemed to be under threat of harm. A note warning as much, and signed Cassandra.

It wasn't long before someone took a potshot at one or maybe both us as we stood outside the building in which my office is situated, on the very day I took her on. The day after our first meeting.

'My investigation led me to discover that Vincent Zendell, Guido Spinoza's nephew had a contact number I suspect has the potential to lead to this Cassandra person, a number connecting to the city of Minsk. That's Minsk, Belarus, if you're wondering. My investigation was originally to verify whether or not there really is a threat to my client, and if so, to take measures to ensure her safety. That's what I'm being paid for. But I have reason to believe that the Cassandra who identified themselves on the threatening note is very possibly the same slimeball Cassandra who tried to kill thousands of people in Monarto, and across the globe, for that matter, several years ago.

'As far as I'm concerned, I've gone as far as I can in this matter. I'm handing over all the information I have, plus a written summary and personal thoughts and insights, all of which should go a long way toward capturing the giant toad, a man who is an international threat, a known criminal and still a danger to global security.'

The three suits remained placid for a moment. 'What have you there?' the middle guy asked.

'Notes, documents, voice recordings. Everything I have on the case, on Spinoza and Zendell and their likely continuing connection with the man you guys have been hunting for the past twenty years.'

'Would you pass it over, please, Mr Jaeger?' Phillipa Cromwell directed. I rose and took it to her, returned to my seat beside Took, who was already becoming distracted and making funny faces, trying to crack me up. I managed to stick my elbow into his ribs, undetected, as I sat back down alongside him.

The panel inspected the contents of my briefcase, passed the documents I had spent hours compiling between one another, quietly commenting, head-nodding, glancing occasionally at the two of us, who were becoming a little cheesed off by their behaviour.

The guy on the far left, Tidswell, finally broke up the whispering discussion. 'Thank-you, Mr Jaeger. Good work. We will take it from here.'

Great, I thought, I'm out of here, but there was a question I wanted to ask: 'What will you do now?'

'That is to be decided,' McCormack answered. 'Yeah, but you're going after the bastard, right?'

There was silence, and a couple of sly looks passing between them before McCormack responded with, 'We did discuss a contingency before you and your friend's arrival. Can I ask you, er. . . Mr Jones. Adrian.'

'Took,' my comrade corrected.

'Yes. Mr Jones. You worked closely with your friend the first time around, did you not?'

'You mean when we saved the city? Yeah, I did.'

'We at the, um, agency. . . we work under restrictions. International boundaries of law, standing agreements and the like. There's much red tape to be negotiated during investigative stages, but especially concerning deployment. Permission, first of all, but then who will do what. Who will direct the exercise. Things of that nature. Do you understand?'

We understood, and nodded to convey as much.

'It might be many months. Years might pass before all contingencies are in place, access is granted, and then funding might suddenly dry up before we can physically act. Anything could occur to get in the way of a rapid and decisive conclusion.'

Cromwell took up the telling. 'Mr Jaeger, with your experience in highly classified military operations, you would understand that someone like Cassandra might have positioned themselves within the more shadowy network of International business and politics that he could be considered by many, Middle Eastern and Northern European Government alliances included, as playing an indispensable role, particularly as a source of intelligence.'

At this point I began to guess what was coming. 'You're not going to tell me the bastard is untouchable, I hope?'

'I'm not going to tell you that, no.' Cromwell answered, a tiny smile forming at the corner of her mouth. 'To do so would tend to be counterproductive.' She turned to her colleague on the left. 'Director Tidswell?'

Tidswell, a stern faced individual who until now had little to say, nodded. 'Gentlemen. Understand that what I am about to say to you may not be repeated outside this room. Your assurances, please, before I continue.'

I turned to Took, saying, 'This could lead anywhere. You see what's going on here, don't you?'

'We're going deeper into the rabbit hole,' he answered. 'I'm up for it. Are you? I mean with your mid-life crisis and all. Me? I just want this thing resolved, finally, once and for all. That bastard is still out there in the world after everything that went down. It ain't right.'

'You have them,' I said, turning back to the panel, and Tidswell picked up the thread.

'If you have been following what my colleague has been telling you, you might guess that normal avenues are not our most advantageous in this matter. We cannot deploy a team of hotshots from the military without attracting attention. What we propose would never get off the ground, not through channels, and leaving a paper trail is not something we can countenance.'

Even as Tidswell spoke, I felt my hopes of handing everything over to authorities fade into the sunset and vanish completely. What the hell was I doing? But to have brought Cassandra to the attention of International law enforcement twenty years ago only to learn that he was still operating, and even thriving, it outraged me—my basic sense of right and wrong.

'What we need,' Tidswell continued, 'is a small contingent of determined people to find Cassandra, and to eliminate any threat. Their placement will be known to no one other than a back-up team of professionals, who, like yourself, are no longer employed by the military. Retired personnel who still car about the world we live in, enough that they wish to continue serving the cause.'

This was getting serious, I noted with rising excitement. 'I might point out to you guys that we're not exactly in prime physical condition,' I felt compelled to say.

'Some physical fitness will be required, but your backup team will do the heavy lifting, so to speak. Both of you, if you agree to this, will be assisted in gaining the required fitness standard needed. You were once considered sharpshooter material, Mr Jaeger, he said, flicking through what must have been my résumé. Ample skill for what we expect of you.

'And Mr Jones. . .'

'*Took*,' my stubborn friend insisted.

'. . . I see that you are not without knowledge of firearms. I have also discovered records marking your intelligence quotient. Tested quite some time ago, I see. Juvenile court, in fact. You've been hiding your light under a bushel, Took. One hundred ten. Or under a bushel of marijuana, perhaps?'

A subdued growl escape my friend. Commendable, by Took's standard. He wasn't normally one to hold his tongue if someone had the temerity to criticise his character, manner, skill set or intelligence, and I suspected that Tidswell was, in the moment, testing his self-control.

'What do you say we train the two of you? Shooter and flanker. I would like to see you pitting the bull within five days. You will then be deployed to where you are needed. Is that satisfactory?'

'It's a bit of an ask,' I replied. Are you seriously asking us to train to standard in five days, to go out and put an end to this bastard?'

'If you are available,' he replied. 'There's no one else I can think of who is as available and motivated.'

Took thumped me on the shoulder. 'Come on, man. It'll be a blast. Let's get the *sonofabitch*. In a week's time it can be done and over with. Unless. . .'

'Unless what?' 'Well, you know.'

He was going back to the mid-life crisis thing, which he had been bugging me with on the way over here;

hinting that I was past it, goading and generally taking the piss. It was his way of challenging me to get over it, I knew, but no less annoying for the good intentions.

'Fuck it,' I told him. 'We owe it to ourselves, and to the world, to end this guy.'

He affected a wide, ingenuous grin, punching me on the arm in gratitude.

'Yeah, sure. We're in, dudes, ' he told the three stuffed shirts. 'So when do we start?'

NINETEEN

We started immediately. With the seven day window things moved rapidly after I got off the phone with Janie to tell her I would be back after a week.

From the room we had been interviewed we were taken downstairs, issued with identification cards and ushered out of the back door and into a waiting limousine. From there Took and I were driven out to an old aerodrome, about an hour's drive and fifty miles from the city. I had seen the place on maps, marked as a disused World War two training facility, but as we drew near, at the front gate there was a guard standing sentry, in a guard box, who inspected everyone's pass before allowing us to proceed by raising the boom.

Old aerodromes of this sort are the same all over, with billeting quarters looking much like very large, halved, corrugated iron drums laying on their sides, with a door at the front and windows along the sides. I remembered how they used the same kind of quarters for immigrants who arreived in the sixties and early seventies, cramming assisted passage arrivals from all around the world into these things. Whole families sharing not enough space for two people.

There was a barracks officer's office sitting prominently amid the accommodation buildings, steel constructed workshops and brick storage buildings, and at the far end, a massive hangar, the huge doors of which were pulled closed. The limousine pulled up outside the office building, where we disembarked and went inside to be greeted by a tall, fit looking individual of indeterminable age but certainly somewhere in his thirties. He wore captain's bars on the collar of his olive drab jumpsuit. He stood about the same height as Took, around six and a half feet or so, with short black hair, blue eyes sharply focused, suggesting sagacity. He filled the jumpsuit he wore with broad shoulders and a large frame, but it was the beret he wore which told me all of what I needed to know. On it was stitched the Royal Australian Parachute Regiment badge.

'Gentlemen,' he acknowledged, putting aside the paperwork he had been working on and looking up. 'Come forward and let's have a look at you.'

We neared his desk and stood, waiting, as he came around his desk with hand outstretched. 'No names here, chaps. You will refer to me as *Number One*,' he explained, grabbing my hand in a steely grip and shaking vigorously.

'Jaeger,' I replied.

'Not anymore,' he told me, shaking hands with Took in the same manner. 'As I said, my name is Number 1. Anything else you want to call me you will keep between yourselves,' he said, smiling now.

'The name of this *non* mission,' he said, emphasizing the word *non*,' is *Operation Come Together*. You,' he said, meaning Took, 'are henceforth known only as *Joker*. And you, meaning me, 'are *Walrus*. Got it?'

We nodded.

'Yes sir, Number 1, I believe is the correct response, gentlemen. Why don't you try it on for size?'

'Yes sir, Number 1,' I complied, but heard nothing coming from Took. What was coming from my friend was a distinct feeling of obstinacy.

Our Cee-Oh gave him a visual once-over, smiled. 'Maybe we can work on it,' he responded pleasantly enough, I thought. 'Let's get you squared away as quickly as possible. Daylight is going to waste. The quartermaster is waiting for you in the green building directly across the way,' he pointed. 'Go see him, grab your kit and make your way over to your billets, Hut-A. The Green one with the sign saying Hut-A on it. Dismissed.'

It brought back memories, meeting this guy. I had to remind myself how deceiving first impressions could be. Chances were we would be contemplating murder before these six days were done.

From the quartermaster we collected a large, green, canvas duffel, two sets of green military shirts and cargo pants, the kind with umpteen pockets located everywhere, a camo field jacket, a heavy camo parka and two olive drab jumpsuits, olive drab underwear, grey berets, two pair of olive drab socks, boots (black), shaving equipment, hair brush and comb, soap, toothbrush, toothpaste, towels, a tin of boot black and, finally, a pair of field glasses each, and all of which we stuffed into our canvas duffel bags and carried over to Hut A.

Our billets turned out to be, I guessed, the unmarried officers quarters, and not bad. Hut-A had been quartered; plasterboard walls partitioning four reasonably sized rooms with a somewhat basic bathroom attached. The iron frame beds were not meant to be and were far from being luxurious. A large cupboard with hanging space, a writing desk and lamp, a small dressing table with mirror beside a wide open window, and apart from electrical sockets, that was about all. Blankets and pillows were piled on a bare bedframe.

We barely had time to stow our gear before Number 1 came striding into out hut. 'Alright men. Let's go. I have introductions to make. You are about to meet your new best friend.'

We were marched over to a hut without any signage on it, and which was secured with two heavy padlocks. Once inside Took and myself stood at ease while, from a large, locked trunk, Number 1 retrieved a piece of kit I recognised immediately.

He hauled it out and sat the instrument of death on the bench, beginning his introduction:

'Gentlemen, this is the bolt-action 7.62×51mm M24 Sniper Weapon System. It is capable of 0.5 MOA accuracy to maximal effective range of around 800 metres. The M24 served as the United States Army standard-issue sniper rifle from 1988 to 2010. The Australian armed forces have been issued the upgrade, but this, being a decommissioned weapon whose serial number has been deleted, and thus rendering the weapon untraceable, is your weapon of choice. Any questions?'

Took spoke up, asking, 'Let's go shoot this thing,'

'Not so fast, Joker.' He bent to the trunk and withdrew two other items. 'Rangefinder and atmospheric conditions profiler. ACP, which you will use in ascertaining humidity, wind speed, range, naturally, and air density. These instruments will enable you to calculate range efficiency and drift. I'm assuming that someone with your IQ would be handy with numbers. It's why you're here and not on your couch at home, packing and pulling bongs.'

That crack made no sense to me. Was he trying to get his head knocked off? Because I felt the electrically in the air surrounding Took at that moment. He was slow to anger, but a force to be reckoned with once riled to the point of combustion, and already I sensed a dangerous level had been reached.

To his credit he did no more than to pick up one of the devices and study it. 'You got the handbook that goes with it?'

He did better than that. The remainder of the day we spent out on the target range, with Took calculating wind drift, resistance pressures according to atmospheric conditions, and giving me corrective instructions as he viewed the result of each round fired. We began at three hundred metres, gradually working through distances up to seven hundred and eight hundred metres. I had forgotten about technique, my own little quirks and methods I used, when, more years ago than I cared to remember, I was considered an expert at firing at and hitting a target from a long ways off.

Late in the day we quit what we were doing and returned to barracks, showered, dressed and went over to the mess for an evening meal. It was only Took and myself, sitting on our own in the mess capable of seating around hundred fifty people. Us and the cook, a rotund, baldheaded man of maybe fifty years, dressed in the appropriate white livery who cut thick slices of roast pork as he filled our plates with meat and vegetables covered in thick gravy.

It was after six-thirty in the evening by the time we finished eating and had returned to the hut; and, with some hours remaining before lights out, we considered what we might do with the intervening time.

'I've got some light reading to do,' Took informed me, brandishing the manual which came with the instruments he had been issued.

'A lot of fun, you are,' I grumbled. There wasn't even a radio to listen to. My phone had been taken from me and there was not a television set on the entire base.

I rose from my bed, where I had been sitting on its edge, thinking I might go for an unescorted wander around.

'Give me forty minutes,' Took said, apparently having reconsidered my plight, 'and we'll see what we can scare up in the way of entertainment in this godforsaken place.'

After strolling about for a bit, taking in our new surroundings with some added interest, I wandered over to the CO's office, expecting to find Number 1 behind his desk. Negative on that. The building was vacant, but unlocked, so I helped myself to the telephone sitting on his desk.

Janie picked up just before I replaced the receiver, thinking she was out or otherwise engaged.

'Hi, doll-face. What's cookin'? I asked.

'Oh, not much. It's kind of quiet here without you. What have you been doing?'

'Can't say, hon. You know, hush-hush, but it has been an interesting day.'

'Hey, before I forget,' she piped up. 'Someone rang here today.

Someone from Holdsworthy prison.' 'No shit! Who?' 'Someone called Willy.'

'Really. I'm surprised to hear it. So what did he say?'

'He insisted I tell you thanks for the money in his property. And he said a policemen had visited Zendell, today. He said he knows he was a *copper* because he overheard part of the conversation between the two.'

'He didn't get a name?' I inquired, sure that the answer to that would be *No*.

'Aa-huh. . . '

I waited but she was playing a game with me. 'Are you going to tell me?' I asked, and made an effort to laugh along with her playfulness, despite the fact that I was weary and really not in the mood for much beyond a chat with Took after this before getting a good night's sleep.

'Your visitor from the other night, dear.'

'Carruthers? Unbelievable. And after I let him off the hook, too. Some people are unfathomable. But what the hell is going on?' I said, thinking aloud. 'There's a tightknit little ensemble of no-goods conniving in relation to I have no idea what. What can they be up to?'

'Don't get your blain in a knot over it, darling,' she crooned, trying to calm me. 'You sound tired. Why don't you get a good night's sleep, wherever you are. Tomorrow's another day. Have you eaten?'

'Yeah. Pretty good meal, too. Okay, well, I was just calling to see if everything is all right.'

'We're fine, dear, Don't be worrying. You go and rest.' 'Alright. Good-night, hon. See you in a few days.' 'Bye. I love you.'

'Me too,' I ended, and replaced the receiver.

By the time I returned to our lodging I found Took asleep with the instruction manual open, lying on his chest. I woke him so he could undress and climb into bed, following suit myself. The next few days, I knew, would be testing ones, and I did not intend being found wanting.

TWENTY

The following day we commenced early. To assess our fitness we were required to cover five miles in as short a time as possible, without causing a coronary. The course was an inner perimeter road around the reconditioned runway that we covered by either walking, jogging or running. Running was pointless and would have seen Took and I both lying on the ground gasping after a quarter mile. We jogged for a hundred yards and walked for a hundred alternating. After the second round of jogging, I was done and completed the course by walking. Took, being a non smoker but partial to his marijuana, came in first, having done one extra jogging stint. I don't know what they expected from a pair on the wrong side of forty, but the fact that we completed the circuit at all impressed the hell out of me.

After showering and consuming a breakfast of cereal topped with yoghurt, a boiled egg and disgusting decaffeinated coffee, although juice was on offer, we were given a half hour to relax before continuing. Number One unfurled a detailed map of Minsk, Belarus, on a wide table, as Took, or should I say *Joker* and myself, *Walrus*, stood over it.

'Minsk,' he said as he placed weights on the map's corners, 'Capital of Belarus. Age, about 960 years, founded in ten seven, a population of around two million and a metro population of one and a half million.

He pointed to a section of the map where the borders of three countries, Poland, Lithuania and Belarus converged. Just inside the Belarus corner he placed a red pin, saying 'Ibal, a small village where it has been reported our target is occasionally seen on weekends, protected by body guards as he walks the streets, stopping for coffee and cake, buying odds and ends. And here,' he placed a red pin, 'sits castle Orbach, his main residence when in his home country, about one kilometre from the village. I must stress that this intelligence is hearsay and may not be reliable. It is, however, all we have. The only thing we do know with anything approaching certainty is that castle Orbach is his, he inherited from a long family line, and he is there now and, with any sort of luck he will be there in a week's time when we go for him. Questions?'

'Where did you get your information from?' Took asked.

'We placed a spotter and someone to gather intel only twenty four hours ago, almost immediately after you came to us with your story.'

'You've had someone wandering around quizzing the locals?' I posed, incredulous. 'Was that wise?'

'Not my call,' he replied, looking a tad embarrassed. 'I admit it's not ideal, but—' He shrugged. 'Yeah, I know. Not my call.'

He then produced photographs of the castle and surrounding countryside. 'It's a typically well designed defensive enclave from almost a thousand years ago. Upgraded with electronic surveillance, movement detectors, cameras and the like. We have someone studying satellite and ariel shots for us now. I'll be able to update you both in a couple of days. But for now, we've identified cameras, here and here, two approaching the drawbridge, two on the exterior of the gatehouse, at least one on each corner of the square defensive wall, and inside the baily? Yet to be determined, but there's bound to be many movement, infrared and standard motion guided video cameras throughout the interior.'

'A fly couldn't move in that place without detection,' Took observed. How the hell do we, one, get in, two move without detection, and most importantly to me, get the fuck out again? Why not drop a bomb on the place and have done?'

'It's a thousand year-old historical treasure in itself, Joker, and no one must ever know we visited the place.'

'Knockout gas,' Took suggested.

'A little heavy handed,' One responded, with an eyebrow cocked. 'We don't know who else might be inside. Occasional visitors. Dignitaries, politicians, members of surrounding countries' royal families? If one of them got so much as a scratch, what do you think the fallout might be? We are not to leave a trace. Not so much as an eyelash. Got it? Now, moving on.'

He pulled the bottom most map out of the bundle and laid it over the last. 'The approach. We'll drop you in here.' He pointed to a patch of grassland; an opening in the surrounding forest.

'Drop us in? Took queried.

'Parachute, Joker. Have you ever done any parachute training?'

He looked at me in an accusing manner. 'Why did I ever take up with you? Look at where we are, and we're going to jump out of an aeroplane?'

'At night,' number one added, very much appearing to enjoy Took's apprehension. 'You'll be fine. We have skydiving scheduled for this afternoon. You'll love it.'

Took was shaking his head. '*Skydiving*. It sounds even worse. Diving into the sky. Do you know how mad it sounds?'

'Walrus,' our CO addressed me. 'You're an old hand, aren't you? You can hold his hand on the way down, perhaps. We might have some incontinence pads around here, somewhere, if you think you might need them,' he told Took.

Again Took's blood pressure was seen to rise, effected by the colour in his face; and, to his credit, I watched for the second time as he resisted the impulse to respond.

'These are copies of what I have shown you here.' He opened a drawer in the cabinet behind him, withdrawing two folders and handing one to each of us. 'I want you to study the maps and photographs every chance you get, between now and departure time. Upgrades, as I said, will be supplied asap. Any more questions?'

'I been thinking,' Took responded. 'There hasn't been a single mention of remuneration for services rendered.'

'Yes?' Number one replied, waiting. 'Why not?' Took wanted to know.

'I don't know. Probably because there isn't any? In any case, it's not my department. My job is to get you boys ready. . . as ready as I can for the mission ahead. I could pass your enquiry on to the proper department, I suppose?'

'Do that,' Took replied. 'I can't say I'm overly impressed with the way I see the planning. If we're going to be taking orders from the likes of you and intel gatherers walking around Cassandra's home town asking questions. . . Hell, we ought at least to be getting paid for it. Frankly, I could be feeling more confident about this thing. Come to think of it, I do have a question.'

'Which is?' One waited.

'The extraction plan. Where is it?'

'We're still working on the extraction plan, Joker. Don't worry, we wouldn't think of leaving you behind.'

'I think I would like to see it as soon as it's completed,' I enjoined. 'It's kind of important, don't you think?'

'Sure,' he replied. 'I'll be filling you in on it the moment I have it. Meantime, go find somewhere to quiet study those files I gave you. I'll meet you both back here,' he consulted his watch, 'in one hour, to test your weapons and allied technology knowledge. So bring the appropriate equipment, gentlemen. Okay? We done with question time?'

We left to study the photos and maps we had been given, finding a spot under a tree outside our billet. The photos were good quality, hi resolution, probably taken using drones, which bothered me some. Those things made an awful buzzing noise that even birds didn't like, with the larger birds of prey often attacking, succeeding to down the things. They tend to gain attention, is my point, and anyone detecting one buzzing around castle Orbach was bound to mention it. In a small village and among the agrarian community it would be hot gossip, meaning there might well be a hostile greeting committee awaiting us by the time we arrived. The remaining photographs taken from orbit suggested there was considerable money already going into the mission, meaning that a wider circle of people were therefore involved. This was another cause for concern for me. This was meant to be a very hush-hush enterprise and widening the pool of participants was not an entirely well considered situation. There was a time with operations like this, when I knew everyone in the loop and I knew I could trust the intel and the people involved. With this? Maybe I was being paranoid again. Whether I liked it or not I simply had to extend my trust to people I did not know.

Weapons and allied technology; the M24 Sniper Weapon System. Took was quizzed over and over on technical points of interest while I was instructed in breaking the thing down and restoring it to operational proficiency in as short a time as possible. Boring, dry stuff and we were glad each day when the hourlong instruction and exercise came to an end.

After lunch it was Took's favourite thing to do. The words "sky" and "diving", in any order or standing alone, were stuck off from my list of allowable words to say, under threat of my partner thumping me so hard on the shoulder that I could scarce use it afterwards, and leaving a large, unattractive bruise to boot. The poor bugga really was *"anxious"* (frightened, another banned word) regarding jumping from an aircraft from ten thousand feet. Later jumps went to fifteen and eighteen thousand feet. For that we had to bring in turbine aircraft and use oxygen masks until jump time, else the air began to thin, making breathing difficult, and small, naturally aspirated aircraft were unable to cope without a supercharger.

The first jump, as I say, was ten thousand feet. It took the little Cessna Shyhawk forever to climb to altitude, and from it, with the door removed, our target, a two hundred fifty square metres of chalk covered ground bordered by bales of hay, was barely able to be seen. We had a safety officer with us, assisting us in dressing and making sure everything about our equipment was in order. At ten thousand feet the pilot idled the motor and it was time, and although I had done this countless times in the past, the butterflies in my stomach were rife.

Took, being the novice, was sent to the open door in the side of the aircraft first. 'On the count of three,' the instructor called out, 'and remember to bend and roll on landing. One. . . two. . . ' and he was already gone.

I followed immediately after him, not waiting for any count. By the time I drew level with him he was already in good shape, limbs outstretched and falling in a controlled manner. The beard had parted in the middle, his face framed by the long, flailing, black mass, and the look on his face said it all. His eyes behind the goggles were as large as could be, the one blue and one brown one, his face was overtaken by an enormous grin, and as if he had done this a thousand times already, he adjusted his extremities so that be began to circle around me in a wide circle. Then leaning forward into a nosedive, he plunged away toward the fast approaching terra firma. To see any novice do this is terrifying. I've seen it before. They become so infatuated with the feeling of flying that they forget about immediate concerns as they fall at around 120 miles an hour, their altitude rapidly decreasing at terminal velocity. I need not have worried about the big galoot though.

At precisely the altitude instructed, he tugged at the ripcord, his chute deploying cleanly and opening wide. I had almost forgotten to open my own in time, so concerned had I been in the moment. But there we were, hanging from numerous nylon cords, suspended, looking, I recall thinking at the time, much like washing on a clothesline. Took looked especially incongruous in that situation, and brought to mind the idea of a yeti parachuting gently to earth with an enormous, ear to ear, wide smile.

We landed in good order, although Took found himself a good way off target; a problem he managed to correct the next time around. No knee damage, which, because of our vintage, was of particular concern, and as I approached he let out a loud whoop of joy, calling, 'We gotta do that again soon, brother. Man, that was really something, wasn't it?'

Over the remaining five days these things became routine: Morning walk or jog followed by shower and change into clean fatigues; breakfast, followed by map reading and orientation, weapons and target practice; one hour for lunch, followed by mission definition saturation and intel upgrade. This took us to middle afternoon or later, when occasionally a doctor was brought in to give us a once-over and report to number

One our condition, which we were not once given feedback on. The sharp end of the mission was the pulling of the trigger, and to that end we were often to be found out at the range, fine-tuning our skills at that time.

Belarus for us would be a strange land, the people, language and customs of which would have us feeling very much like fish out of water. Given the small amount of time available to us, attempting to learn the language was a complete waste of time. Beyond the few possibly useful phrases we did learn, we would have to wing it as any western tourist would have to do. We would also be given clothing, helping us to blend in, including headwear which would partially conceal our faces when confronting anyone. The idea was to stay low until we were called upon to act by our handler. A hunting plan would have to be devised on the fly and carried out swiftly. After our job was done it only remained for us to get the hell out of there without being spotted or otherwise traced.

Apart from a couple of training bumps and scrapes the both of us were doing fine. I was only able to sneak one other after hours call through to Janie before our CO caught on and locked the phone in his safe when he knocked off at night. He quizzed me over it, and accepted my excuse, revealing to me that the calls had been monitored by a security section some miles distant.

It was on Saturday evening, the end of the fifth day of training. Took and I had returned from the showers and were lazing on our beds, chatting about nothing in particular, when number One entered the billet and stood in the middle of the floor regarding us.

'Congratulations, men. You've made the grade.'

'Was there ever a way of us *not* qualifying?' Took replied, reclined, with hands supporting his head.

The CO regarded him a moment before responding. 'In truth? This is a mission no one would touch with a ten foot pole. So, no, you failing to make it would have taken both of you losing a leg and an eye. As it turns out, you both exceeded my expectations by a country mile. I'm truly impressed.'

'And that's not you continuing to blow smoke up our arse? Fuck it, dude. Boy scout training camp is over. You can level with us now. I've been hearing nothing but bullshit coming from you since day one.'

'That's some attitude you got there, Joker. What's your problem?'

'Problem? What, you mean apart from the fact that me and my buddy here are to be dropped into some hornets nest to take out public enemy number one while everyone else stands back a thousand miles in case of political blowback, or the mission going all to hell, leaving us hung out to dry in a foreign country where Vlad the Impaler is their Ned Kelly?' He pouted his bottom lip, shrugged— 'Nope, no problem here. Why would I have a problem.'

Number One remained silent for a time. 'Yeah,' he finally spoke up. 'What do I tell you? They said you were smart.' he turned to me then. 'I'm going to drop protocol for a minute.'

'Fine by me,' I told him.

'You've been through this kind of thing before, Jaeger. I know you have. We're soldiers. A soldiers place is not to think outside the parameters of the mission. It's to obey orders. Think only where it concerns winning the contest, keeping his men alive for one more day and to do whatever it takes to succeed. That's what a soldier is,' he told Took. 'I know you're about to be put out on a limb. *Plausible deniability* will be what everyone back in the ivory tower will be paying attention to. If we come unglued, we'll be cut lose, our existence denied and we will be forgotten as quickly as it's humanly possible to do so. Am I anywhere near the mark?' he asked of Took.

'You're bang on the money. Or would be, if there were any money in it for us,' he joked.

Number One asked, 'Do you mind if I sit?'

'Go ahead,' I told him, and there was a cane stool in the corner which he made use of.

'I hope you will excuse my own attitude,' he began anew. Took, I pushed you because I thought that by challenging you, you might respond by wanting to prove you were every bit capable of what was required, and by doing so, vastly improving your chances of returning at the end of it.'

'Why do you think I let you get away with it, dude?' he responded, smiling. 'It's cool. I get it.'

'I'm glad,' he replied. 'If anyone can pull this off, you guys can. That is, if you are still prepared to do this thing.'

We consulted with one another with no more than a glance. 'We didn't come here for nothing. You probably don't know, but this thing started twenty odd years ago. Unfinished business.'

He nodded. 'I can understand that. So, you guys ready?'

'We were born ready, soldier boy, ' replied Took, bringing a smile to the CO's previously grave countenance.

He pointed to us each in turn. 'Walrus. Joker. Get used to using the names. It's for your own protection. The cook has laid on a special meal for us tonight, if you don't mind me joining you? After we eat, make sure the tools of your trade are in order and safely packed for travel. Anything else you want, warm clothing essential. Pack your bag light. There will be time for a couple of hours nap after dinner. Our aircraft arrives at 20.00hrs. We're on a tight schedule, so be ready to board. A jeep will take you from here over to your transport aircraft. I'll be travelling with you.'

'You're coming?'

'Wouldn't miss it for the world,' he said, climbing off of the stool. 'I'll be coordinating. Okay then. See you at dinner? 18:00hrs. You don't want to leave on an empty stomach, I promise you. It's a long flight and warmth could be an issue.'

'He's coming with us,' Took said when he had left. 'Coordinating.'

I resumed the position I was in before he had arrived, lying on my back, eyes closed. 'Seems capable. I guess he knows his job.'

'I didn't know he was coming with us, Alex. Damn, this is going to be awkward,' he insisted, and I began to suspect something was up.

'Took, what have you done?'

'When I went out, earlier, saying I left my folder behind?' he began, already looking contrite. 'I thought we would be leaving and him staying behind.'

'For crying out loud, tell me. There might be time to do something about it. What did you do?'

TWENTY ONE

At just prior to eight o'clock, after we had eaten a big meal in the mess, our transportation arrived. The Boeing C-17 Globemaster came roaring in out of the night sky and landed, taxied onto the apron where a fuelling ranker and crew topped it up before we were allowed to embark.

Within its cavernous body large wooden crates, stencilled as "Military Hardware," had been strapped down in the mid-section. Aft was devoid of cargo, but forward of the secured cargo, uncomfortable looking steel seats with safety belts attached were available along either side. In addition, we were very pleased to note that camper beds had been placed for us, and clamped to the fuselage so that we wouldn't find ourselves sliding about during our sleep.

We deposited our rucksacks and additional luggage into storage bins against the forward bulkhead and wondered what to do next. Number One entered from the tail ramp with his own gear, and after depositing it as we had, climbed up the stairs leading to the cockpit. He returned with one of the flight crew, the navigator, identified by his single wing air force badge sewn onto his flight suit.

'You guys ridden in one of these things before?' he asked.

I raised my hand. 'Something like it, and years ago,' I told him. 'Okay. You will strap yourselves in for take-off.' He pointed to a set of three coloured lights in the ceiling. 'Green means safe. Safe to unbuckle and walk around. Amber means it's safe to unbuckle, but be cautious. It'll probably mean we're flying in unpredictable weather conditions and there might be some turbulence, so keep an eye out for the red light. Red means buckle up, and if it gets rough, hang on.'

'We safe to sleep in these cots?' I asked.

'Yep, but you'll notice there are straps on them too. Use them. You don't want to wake finding yourself being thrown around in here like a rag doll. And there's blankets in this storage locker, down here,' he bent, pulled open a low, wide storage space filled with pillows and blankets. Olive drab, naturally.

'Can I smoke?'

'On a green light, if you must. It's a long haul and we allow the occasional cigarette. There are vapour detectors throughout. You will know if there's flumes back here when the siren sounds. Use common sense.

'There's a toilet and washbasin, here,' he pointed to a set of three steps, leading downward into a cubicle behind him. Keep your jackets and coats handy. We'll be climbing quite high and it can get cold.'

He pointed up the steps where he had come from. 'Halfway up there's a space where we have installed a small kitchen and beverage dispenser. Soup, coffee, tea. You'll find microwave meals and a microwave in there, for when you get hungry.

'I think that's about it,' he said. 'Make yourselves comfortable and we'll be off in a minute.'

'How long is this flight going to take?' Took wanted to know. 'Sixteen to eighteen hours, depending on conditions, to Warsaw. I understand you'll be transferring to a smaller aircraft there. I don't know your destination and I don't need to know. It's our job to get you to Warsaw, along with that cargo.'

'Is that coming with us?' Number One asked.

'No. It's what we were delivering before you guys hitched a ride with us. We've got a load of machinery to bring back to Oz. I've got to get back,' he said then. 'Are you guys about sorted?' We were as sorted as we were going to get. 'Don't forget to dig out your coats,' he called back from the stairwell, as he climbed back towards the cockpit. 'It might get chilly.'

We did just that, and made our heavy coats available at short notice. It was a warm, balmy night where we were presently, but I knew from experience how bone chilling it can get at beyond twenty thousand feet. Higher than that and we would be needing electric blankets and oxygen masks.

We were rolling down the runway in no time, engines screaming as we surged forward, strapped into our uncomfortable, fold-up steel seats against the fuselage framework. Ten minutes before we began levelling off, at which time the green light flashed a few time before holding steady.

'Sixteen to eighteen hours,' Took mumbled, freeing himself from the safety-belt and standing.

'We'll need to amuse ourselves somehow,' said Number One. He freed himself from his own seat and walked over to a small bag he had brought along on the trip. From it he pulled a box of playing cards and chips wrapped in a plastic bag. 'What do you say? Poker?'

Poker it was. We pulled a bunch of blankets from storage and made a comfortable nest to sit on. I went forward and climbed to the kitchen, made coffees for everyone and brought them back down. The lights went down low throughout the space we occupied, and a battery powered lantern was discovered in yet another compartment, serving perfectly well to illuminate our game.

The cards helped us pass the time while the four big jet engines blasted us forward toward our destination. With few creature comforts, a trip like the one we were on can be difficult to endure. I've been among a thousand to fifteen hundred soldiers on such trips as this, and, depending on whether one is flying to a hot zone or coming home for R & R or at the end of a tour of duty, time can pass easily or very slowly indeed. Reading material is essential, and we had all covered that base for ourselves. Sleeping it best, but difficult, and one can only sleep so long before it becomes lost as an option. Cards has ever been an option, but losing a months wages does not add to the enjoyment of a flight like this, and fights are not uncommon when a player appears too lucky, stretching the laws of chance a little too far for the thought of suspicion not to be entertained; the consequence leading to occasional bloodletting or worse, especially when, in the wake of a long campaign, men remain wound-up tight and twitchy, not yet decompressed and free of the survival mode mind set which enabled them to survive long enough to be among those on the return voyage.

The flight reminded me too much of my past. Memories refused to lay dormant during the breaks between our card sessions as I lay on my camp bed, staring up at the curved aluminium shell above. These aircraft were also used to transport the dead from theatres of war, back to Oz; casualties of wars few people at home were ever really cognisant of, and it has always been so. Anyone whose youth had been usurped as mine had been, constantly shipping off to fight over territory in someplace never heard of before, spilling the blood of others whose customs and manner of existence you knew little about, it came to play on one's mind after a time. As the intervening years separated me from those times I grew to despise everything that had conspired to make such actions necessary in the first place. Politics for one. Politicians, especially in the affluent, powerful countries of the world, to me their role grew clearer and more obvious the more I thought on it. They were no more than pawns of those with the real power, the multinationals. Primary industry and more recently the electronics giants who consumed vast quantities of natural resources. When viewed as a hole I saw them as an enormous, conglomerate animal working behind the scenes, their tendrils reaching into every corner of human existence, sucking, manipulating, finding purchase enough to exert sufficient force to send men to war. What irony. Right then I could name three major conflicts responsible for vast numbers of dead and injured, and for what? Not in the name of peace or for any great injustice of a type people justifiably can defend their rights, freedoms and homes. Their thinking had been manipulated by the politicians who came to serve industry and commerce. Politicians, like whores, mouthing propaganda fed to them by those with the real power, with multimedia cashing in and spreading it like a plague until the populace came to believe in a substitute reality not their own; fighting not for themselves, for their freedom, but to further extend the reach and control of already vastly powerful companies commanding ever larger market trends, political, financial clout and swathes of the physical globe—global entities manned by human beings who lost sight of the truth generations ago— destined to so distort the lives of individuals for whom, in centuries yet to come, there will be nothing remaining of once free thinking human beings who were in command of their own destiny.

Awaking with a dry mouth, wrapped in blankets and lying on my anchored camp bed, I twisted about to observe that the others were likewise reposed. The hours had dragged by with nothing but card games intermittently broken by food breaks, hot coffee and occasional trips to the can, all the while with the dull roar of jet engines pushing us forward. We had deemed it prudent to stay awake for one long stretch and to hit our bunks with eight hours remaining in the first leg of the journey. This way we would wake refreshed, we hoped, ready to make the final leg to Belarus.

In Warsaw we touched down at an American military airbase at around ten in the evening. That's 22:00hrs in military speak. We were ahead of schedule and so we had some time, if we so desired, to take a shower, change clothes and to visit the cafeteria, grab a bite of something hot and nourishing for a change. We all took the opportunity to don the garb we had been provided with. Jeans, civilian boots, shirts, caps or hats if we wanted them. It would be cold where we were going, so we rugged up pretty good before climbing aboard an old Fokker F-50 turboprop, converted by the military for use in the deployment of men and assorted goods dropped by parachute. It had been painted red and white, with a blue underbelly to make it less conspicuous from the ground, I suspected. On the tail it sported a painted Polish flag.

We were in the air again before we knew it, and with only seven hundred odd kilometres left to go, translating to a little over one hour's travelling time, it was time to get arses into gear. To that end we sorted and equipped ourselves for any foreseeable contingency. One piece of equipment was an electronic tracker, given to each of us, allowing us to know where each of the others were at all times in case we were separated. A useful device, we agreed.

With ten minutes to go before we jumped, we went over the plan one more time. Deploy, make contact with a waiting ground party, establish digs wherever best suited our needs. Took and I would work as a team of two, naturally, while Number One worked as a solitary *component*, liaising with already installed local components, and relaying necessary information regarding Cassandra, his whereabouts, movements, vulnerabilities and anything else relevant.

The cigar smoking, somewhat dishevelled looking co-pilot rose from his position in the cockpit and came back to us as our target approached. He assisted us with pulling on our chutes, attaching smaller chutes to a webbing net used in deploying our equipment which was to be released immediately before we took the leap. He then removed the door midway along the fuselage.

'Man, I think I left the oven on at home,' Took quipped. I really should go back and check.'

Number One give him a supportive slap on the back. 'You'll be fine, Joker. There's nothing to it. Jump and land. Remember, knees are shock absorbers, rolling will dissipate kinetic energy.'

'There's your standby light,' the co-pilot called over the noise of the engines. He attached our ripcord lines to the wire above us and had us shuffle toward the open door. 'The pilot knows this area well. We should have you right on target tonight. Wait for it,' he called out.

The green light illuminated, and, just like in training, the next thing was a thump on the shoulder and a gentle push for motivation. First the web-net full of equipment, then, one after another we bailed out into the darkness.

TWENTY TWO

We landed without incident and quickly moved to gather our equipment while Number One made contact with the reception party who we hoped would be waiting. He depressed the trigger switch on the walkie three times in rapid succession, and waited. In a moment the walkie clicked three time is response, meaning our arrival had been observed and that they were making their way to us.

In a moment torchlight was seen to emit three short bursts, and Number One replied with the same, resulting in three dark figures emerging from out of the darkness, coming up to us.

'Is blue moon,' said a voice, rich in whatever local dialect it was. 'And clear sky,' Number One correctly replied. 'Are we good to proceed?'

'You come with us. You are Number One?' 'Yes.'

'We take you there. You two,' meaning Took and myself, 'we take to guest house.'

They assisted in gathering and carrying our equipment and we began a cross-country plod through the fields and orchards which, apart from the odd barn and animal holding yards, seemed to dominate the landscape. After perhaps three miles of trudging through the damp, heavy ground, we came upon a stone cottage beside a stream. The moon briefly broke through a low ceiling of cloud, and I remember the place appearing in that moment as a fairytale illustration from a storybook; the cold, crisp and motionless air making everything appear supernatural as moonlight reflected in the stream and glistened from every dew covered blade of grass covering the ground.

Within we were greeted by the cheerful sight of fire burning in a hearth. The single space was furnished with no more than a table and chairs, central, looking as if they had been assembled using scrap wood: *rustic utilitarian*, one might say. On top of the table sat a single oil lamp providing dismal illumination, while over against the wall, four bed rolls lay on four decrepit looking wooden bed frames.

'Delightful,' remarked Took, moving immediately to the warmth of the log fire, with me following closely behind.

'You are here,' announced the group leader to Number One. 'Headquarters.' Then turning to Took and myself: 'She will take you to boarding house. Is already arranged.'

I hadn't realised that one of the party was a woman. They all wore so much heavy clothing, including long, knitted scarves wound about the neck and lower face. Apart from their height they were almost indistinguishable from one another. The girl was detectable only by a lock of blond coloured hair which had escaped between the bound scarf and knitted cap pulled all the way down over her ears.

We were enjoying our brief, warm moment by the fire when she ruined it by saying, 'We go now, please.'

Before leaving we were given an identical pencil-drawn map to Number One's and we left him to the warm fire and the company of his newfound friends, after making sure our tracking devices and radios were functioning. This done, we followed the girl back out into the cold dark night, traipsing a further mile to the edge of the village, the distance approximated by reverting to my military training, counting a thousand paces to the mile. From the village's perimeter she led us to a beaten up building, two storeys of stone and roughly hewn timber: our guesthouse. Taking us to the back door, she knocked three times and waited.

Presently a large woman wrapped in a heavy robe and holding a lantern pulled open the door. Words were exchanged, the door pulled ajar to allow us entry, and we thanked our guide before being led upstairs by our host.

The upstairs room was nothing much more than four walls with some old, framed pictures hung from nails, two cots, a small table, two rickety chairs, and, thank goodness, a fireplace, already stacked with kindling and with split logs stacked alongside.

After pulling blankets from a chest and giving us a box of matches, the woman moved to the door to depart. She hesitated at the threshold and turned back to us, telling us sternly, in broken English, 'You not here. *Not* here—' before disappearing into the passageway.

It had been a long journey and there was nothing in the world more desirable than to get that fire lit, wrap ourselves in blankets and catch as many zees as was possible before dawn. First, though, we checked that we were in radio contact with Number One back at base. This achieved, the fire was lit and made safe before turning in, hopefully allowing a night of deep, dreamless, fully restorative slumber.

I said, *hopefully*. Sleep did eventually arrive, and of the kind mentioned, but not before the mind had expressed its vexation at being reminded of an earlier existence; one I had taken great pains to divorce myself from; memories rejected, buried deep in my skull where I had hoped they might remain, without want for review nor to nettle during the night—the small, silent, perfectly still hours of the night.

I awoke in a void. Intense silence. There was a stillness which felt to encompass eternity itself, and I dared not move, nor breathe too loudly lest I break the delicate, crystalline perfection of it. I have seldom experienced silence of this quality. Such instances are rare, always seemingly portentous, and, for me, never forgotten.

I allowed myself to be absorbed by it so that the silence and I were one. At that point it felt as though I ceased to exist but for being a component part of the ubiquitous stillness; a moment of utter clarity and insightfulness. My entire life was spread out before me in infinite detail. Every defining moment became instantly obvious to me, from childhood and schooling to adulthood and everything up to this precise moment, and the result? The conclusion reached, regarding my life story thus far? One of letdown.

Everything I had ever done; every thought, every decision and move I had made, bringing me to this very location and situation, lying on this cot in an upstairs room thousands of miles from home, with assassination in mind and my most trusted friend lying not ten feet from me, it was in error. I was forced to view it all and to sit in judgment of myself in complete knowledge of every motivation that had brought me here.

In fairness I remembered what my childhood had been like and what had motivated me joining the military. I had, from my earliest days, felt strongly about the forces of good and evil at work. As a child the six o'clock news had daily brought war and conflict and duplicity into our home, impacting heavily on the child who spent every moment of free time wandering the countryside, daydreaming of a better word for human beings to live in. The forces of evil and destruction had to be confronted and beaten down. Joining the armed forces was the only role I could envision for myself if I were going to act on my impulses.

I instantly recognised that decision as the turning point; the pivot on which my entire life became aimed in the direction which had brought me here, to this place. I had never been drawn to violence. Violence inhabited the world I had been born into and the decision to join up had cost me everything. I had entered the chest thumping, macho world of soldiering, and, later, as a mercenary, I was able to choose which theatre of conflict and mayhem, one where I figured I might to the most good, and it had proven addictive. I had lost sight of who I was even before I reached full maturity. So clearly, now I could see that I had embraced this life with all that I had for the simple reason of being scared—scared in the realisation that if I had really thought it all through, I might see how I had already become lost to myself and the world that surrounded me.

I might be forgiven that, I saw then. The world did not allow for young people to develop at their own rate and to be who they were supposed to become, but always pushed them into situations, making them choose long before it was possible for them to know the whole story, too soon committing to one direction or another. It was the major flaw of modern society, that it undereducated the young in it's production line rush to mass produce everything, including its population. Had I developed of my own volition, at my own speed, I would not have been where I was in that moment, looking back, realising with utter clarity that I had, for some thirty years, been on entirely the wrong path.

The sun would rise in a matter of hours; tomorrow when I was expected to draw a bead, pull the trigger on a most dangerous individual and end their life along with their run of evil doings. It was in keeping with my track record, my professional history, and I could see exactly why I had been selected for the task, but I was, for the first time in my life, glimpsing the person I might have been, had circumstances conspired to allow me time to find my way.

I saw my life laid out: the chapters of a book, pages in a story clearly defined and showing every instance where I had gone against my true nature, choosing options diverting me from what, without doubt, would have been far better outcomes and which I ought to have seen, had I the wisdom required.

An unfortunate fact of life. Only after one has made all the mistakes, taken all the wrong turns and dragged one's self through all kinds of hell —only then does perfect clarity visit to show who you really are and what a fool you have been. I might have been a different man; my authentic self, fulfilling whatever inherent and perhaps only small, but honest-to-God real and worthwhile potential I was born with, but never once given the chance to flourish.

I had to rise; so persistent was this vision of myself that I could lie there no longer. The fire had died down, glowing red in the darkness and the air become chill once more, so I piled a couple extra logs atop the coals, pulled one of the rickety chairs over to sit and warm while gazing into the mounting flames. A human activity practiced since the dawn of time; fire gazing, giving the imagination free reign as the flames leap and flicker. A dance, primal, fascinating the eye as the mind opens itself up without the meddlesome processes of thought intervening or interrupting so luxurious a pastime.

Was it too late to change? And to what? Where was my life going anyway? When this was over, should we make it back to Oz unscathed, what then? My want for excitement and my egotistical need for proving myself to everyone around, not least to myself, was at an end. It was foolishness. Did everyone run around through life attempting to prove themselves to everyone else? What a recipe for disaster and madness. Perhaps that was exactly what was going on. It certainly would explain a lot about the human animal. Ego. *Look at me. I can do this. I can do this better than you. Watch me!*

The thought brought a smile to my face as I viewed the whole human race running about, asking, imploring, demanding, *'Look at me, look at me!'* It made me feel not half so bad about myself. I was as nuts as everyone else, and if that wasn't exactly comforting, it did at least allow me to be not quite so self-critical. It was true, I decided. . . . and then just as quickly as it came, the judgement vanished.

Janie—Janie was an exception, and if Janie was an exception the world was full of others. That girl had not an egotistical bone in her body. After a lifetime of struggle she had raised herself up out of the quagmire to survive and become the loving, caring human being she was today, with a love for tending to sick and injured animals. Was that why she came to me? Was I one of those injured animals? Well, so what. Maybe so. All I knew was I was damned glad to have her, and one lucky *sonofabitch* for the fact.

The fire was beginning to roar back to life, with flames reaching out and licking the top of the ingle, causing shadows to jump and flicker around the walls and ceiling. Sitting there, wrapped in a blanket and comfortably warm at last, the room became a haven, insulating from the outside world, making it feel as if time stood still and would stay that way for as long as I needed it to. I didn't much know what the future held in store, not for any of us, but I knew it *could* be as we wanted it to be if we shaped it that way, and as the grey fog of sleep came soothingly upon me to quell my troubled thoughts, I understood in the moment exactly where I wanted the future to take us.

TWENTY THREE

Without the otherwise restrictive influence of male interference to listen in on and steer conversation, I've learned that women like to talk about the men in their lives; a generic trait, I gather, and entirely understandable, with Matilda and Janie being no exception to their kind. With Janie and Matilda left to their own devices while Took and I tended to business, my wife had later related to me how she had done all she could to gain the girl's confidence, and, indeed, Matilda appeared to take my wife into her confidence in short time.

Janie brought Matilda into the veterinary clinic with her each morning, to help out, assisting in caring for a constant influx of sick and injured animals of every description, proving a positive addition, too, to the small, diligent workforce. In the evenings they came to enjoy watching television together after dinner, sometimes sitting up til late, enjoying the occasional glass or two of wine and easy conversation. I was unable to contact home while we were on the job, but hearing that our time of separation had been made easier for Matilda's presence came to me as a definite relief.

She had not dropped her guard though, and had always remained mindful of the possibility that Matilda was playing a duplicitous role in proceedings. One of these cosy evenings Janie had related to me for the interesting topic of conversation had between the pair:

This night they were sitting, relaxed, watching an old black and white spy movie, sipping a *Sauvignon* they both enjoyed after dinner. On this occasion Matilda had sipped more of the stuff than was usual, and had become affected. One of the characters, she had mentioned, reminded her of her Uncle Guido, because of his constant proclivity for wanting to know everything about everybody around him.

'Is that right?' Janie responded. 'I've heard he is a very intelligent man. He would have to be, I suppose. He *has* amassed an enormous fortune. The villa and many other properties, the business empire, and it's telling, don't you think, that they say those who worked for him gave him their complete loyalty? Alex always said about Guido, if it wasn't for his oversized opinion of himself, his lust for power, ruthlessness and lack of human empathy, he might be a pleasant human being.'

It was meant half as a joke, my wife explained to me, but, too, as a means of assaying Matilda's attachment to the pint sized pain in the arse of the human collective. Seeing that Matilda was intoxicated, Janie had taken the chance of baiting her.

'He was always sweet to me,' Matilda had replied, thoughtful, 'but I always suspected a dark side, even as a little girl. 'Between you and me, I can't say I think he is being entirely truthful with me, about this threat.'

'Oh? I can't believe that. Surely, what with the inherent danger to yourself. . . ?'

Matilda's countenance had displayed deeper misgivings in that moment, as she appeared to be sifting through her thoughts, searching to put words to whatever it was causing her concern. 'I've known Uncle Guido all my life, Janie. We were close, once, but. . . It's funny. I somehow get the feeling he's hiding something. Why would he be hiding anything. . . *from me?*

Janie had shrugged, uncommitted in response, leaving it alone lest the girl become suspicious of Janie's interest and spoil the headway the two had made as friends. Matilda's uncertainty in this instance, did, however vague and difficult to appraise it may have been, proved to be well-founded, and had I known of the conversation between the girls on this night, I might have pieced things together much earlier. Although, if I *had* known, I see no way the knowledge would have changed my mind about what I was about to do. Everything was set in place, the deadly plan already in motion.

TWENTY FOUR

Took had woken in the predawn darkness. Not entirely refreshed after my restless night, I was woken when the mobile transceiver crackled into life. Number One's voice came through, telling us that we had to get moving.

An informer had alerted the team that, a little later in the morning Cassandra would be fishing for trout, in a stream just over the hill from the cottage we had visited the previous evening. The stream was well illustrated on the pencil drawn map provided to us; a small footbridge across the stream, too, upstream of which, on a quiet bend, was the spot where our quarry would be found.

We had, at best, an hour to get ourselves there, and into position. Trout fishing is an exacting pastime. Apart from precise detail being given to equipment preparation, there was as much attention given to every other aspect, and it did not surprise me at all that our target chose trout fishing as a diversion from his usual pursuits. One thing I knew about trout fishing was that early morning, just around dawn, was a preferred time for proponents of the sport; the period when the omnivorous hunting fish became active, searching for breakfast. We needed to get our skates on!

The streets were still steeped in darkness as we hurried from the guesthouse, and I remember thinking at the time how the landlady would be pleased no end to find us gone when she rose. We were into the countryside at the edge of town, crossing a stretch of open ground when a sound of a shotgun blast came to us, sounding more like a canon than a firearm for the way shattered the surrounding silence.

'Farmer Fishkin after a rabbit,' Took surmised, and I figured he was probably right. These folk lived of the land and a rabbit or two in the evening pot made a decent meal for farmer Fishkin and his kin.

We entered a thicket alongside the stream; the same stream as, further upstream our cottage was on, but not the one we wanted. The stream we were after was over the other side of a seriously steep hill, and with it being still very dark out here we needed to exercise caution in negotiating it, while making as good time as possible. There was already that predawn glow emanating low in the eastern sky.

'I'm glad we did that training back in Oz,' Took expressed, both of us breathing hard as we pushed forward, using arms and legs, like quadrupeds, to conquer the steep incline. 'You okay?' he enquired.

I scarce had breath enough in me to reply, 'Yeah,' considering quitting the cigarettes in that moment. 'No problem.'

We negotiated the peak as the horizon was becoming distinctly much paler, and I consulted the sketch map once more. 'Down that way,' I directed, and from where we stood it looked to me we were on the money. 'The footbridge we're looking for is a half mile from a road, down there—' and fortuitously, at that moment a pair of headlights were seen travelling along the road I mentioned.

With the position of our landmark established, I knew where the footbridge should be, and we continued on, down the slope at a pace I hoped would get us to our objective with plenty of time to spare. Distances out in the landscape can be deceiving if one is not used to it. A mile, for instance, viewed from the top of a lofty hill like this one, doesn't look like much. It's then you realize that distances on the ground are more formidable than they look. From our vantage to the footbridge, and on to our destination, true distance was deceiving.

'About three miles,' I told Took. 'We had better press on hard, buddy. If we get caught out in the open at sunrise. . . This guy won't be dangling a line by himself. You can bet on it. There'll be bodyguards and they'll be packing.'

The final distance was closer to four rather than three miles, but we were, in my defence, working from a sketched map. We discovered the footbridge where it was supposed to be, and the bend in the river we looked for, where three trees were described, was a further couple of miles from it.

The sun was about to breach the eastern quarter of the sky as we kept our cover, all the while pushing through the dense thicket growing along the hillside, descending at an angle making it difficult on the ankles, down to the valley floor and on to the bend in the stream which had been nominated.

Both of us breathing heavily, we dropped our bundles and near collapsed at a point near the bend where low bushes provided good cover.

'*Goddamnit,*' I gasped. 'My legs are like jelly.'

'Mine too,' said Took, laughing. 'And we have to climb back up that mother again, when we leave.'

'Just put a bullet in me and leave me here,' I answered, laughing as well. 'Maybe there's a boat around here, somewhere. A motorboat we can use?' I sat up to view the horizon in the distance, along the valley floor. The sun would light the valley in about an hour, I speculated. 'Let's get set up, quickly. If they're coming, they'll want to be here soon, when the fish are on the bite.'

It took us only a few minutes to assemble the M24 sniper rifle on its short tripod, load a clip full of 7.62mm, hollow-nose rounds and check that all ancillary equipment was functioning. Took loaded and primed the automatic he had brought along. A machine gun not dissimilar to the old World War II tommy gun, but shorter, like an Uzi, and capable of spraying lead at a phenomenal rate.

In the twilight I peered through the scope, made out only shadowy shapes. I would adjust the thing when daylight peeked through, but first things first, I pulled out the transceiver to make contact with our command post.

'Walrus to number one. Are you receiving, Number One?' I repeated and this time got a response.

'Number one to Walrus.'

'Walrus and Joker in position, over.'

'Glad to hear it. Sit tight. Call again upon arrival of target, to confirm identity.'

'How about a description, now?' I suggested. It seemed irregular not to have a photo, or at least verbal description to work from at this stage.

'Negative. Proceed as ordered. Have arranged aerial extraction for you guys upon completion. Out.'

'Aerial extraction,' Took repeated with immense relief. 'A chopper, do you suppose?'

'A balloon,' I told him, joking. I though we were going to have to traipse all the way back to the cottage on foot. I'm going to have a cigarette. Calm the nerves. My hands are shaking from the exertion.

Took nodded, understanding the necessity. What I did not need was to have shaky hands botch the job. That would put us in a real fix.

I rolled a cigarette and lit up, being careful to shield the lighter flame from sight of anyone who might be prowling around down there, perhaps reconnoitring in readiness for our target's fishing expedition. If they were coming, It wouldn't be long now.

We stretched out in the undergrowth, still bemused by how much the hike had highlighted our lack of physical fitness.

'This sort of thing is a younger man's job,' I mentioned, conversationally. 'Remind me to keep my nose out of other people's concerns in future, will you Took?

'So what? You done private detecting?'

'I think so. Maybe trout fishing is more my speed, these days. I might try it.'

'I can't see you sitting quietly by a stream, feeding the fish,' he observed. 'You could maybe help me restore motorcycles. There's good money in it. I could train you up, put you on apprentice wages.'

'And how much would that be?' I asked.

'Let me think. I once started a plumbing apprenticeship. I got fifteen dollars and fifty cents.'

'An hour? That's slave wages!'

'No, a week. I never dug so many goddamn trenches and ditches in all my life, and for fifteen fifty a week.'
'You finish the apprenticeship?'

'Fuck off. Not for fifteen fifty a week. In five years I would have been doing okay, charging the Earth for screwing in new taps or cleaning drains, but after six months of diggin' ditches. . . I was meant to sign indenture papers, committing to the five years training. Couldn't do it, man. I don't know what I was even thinking. I almost became one of them.'

'Them?'

'Normal, everyday people. I think that was the moment I realised I never would be one.'

From the distance came the sound of a motor, and we both sat up to peer along the valley, cast now in a kind of twilight as dawn continued to approach. A set of headlights emerged, and another, travelling cross-country, headed toward us from the west, on our side of the stream.

'This could be them,' Took said, and I lifted the rifle, began adjusting the scope in hope I might be able to see who it was approaching.

Illumination and therefore visibility was poor. I was able to make out a pair of Range Rovers, travelling single file over the terrain. In a few minutes they had arrived exactly where expected, on the bend of the water course, where a group of three trees, as described by the pencil drawn map, stood near the water's edge.

'This has been a long time coming,' Took expressed, pointedly, as we waited for the sun to emerge so that we might eyeball our target at long, long last.

'Yeah,' I agreed. 'Son-of-a-bitch has had this coming for awhile. I don't much come at this sniper thing, usually. Not exactly sporting, is it? But when I think of the lives this bastard fucked-up. . . The probable hundreds of thousands, or millions he intended on. . . Yeah, a long time coming.'

From where we crouched on the slope, behind cover, we watched people alight from the vehicles. Only shadows of people at the moment. They were preparing fishing poles and chairs and the like, but then I notice how some of the poles were not poles at all. Too short, and too substantial for skinny fishing poles. They were firearms; probably automatic weapons, judging by the way they were being handled, and of the four people there, three were armed and beginning to wander about, scanning the area.

'Wary bastard, ain't he?' I mumbled, employing the scope in hope of getting a better look. 'Come on daylight. Where are you? I checked my watch. A tad after five in the morning. 'The sun ought to bobbing up any moment now,' I uttered, becoming more tense and impatient with every passing minute.

There was not much difference in them, visually. They were still only dark shapes, although the telescopic sight brought them up close. The one I wanted was surely the one moving towards the water's edge, opening a steel framed stool, leaning his rod against the tree while he bent to select lures or live bait from his tackle-box.

'What's gong on down there?' Took wanted to know.

'The henchmen are wandering about, not doing a very good job of surveying the surroundings. Our man is baiting up, I think. About to cast his lure.'

'The hunter hunted,' Took quipped. '*Kinda* appropriate. Poetic, even. Bit of a pity, though, don't you think?'

'How do you mean?' I was already beginning the breathing technique taught to me decades ago, which would ensure a clear mind, reduce the need to breathe thereby unnecessarily causing unwanted movement as the trigger was squeezed.

'Well. . . Like you said, all the grief he caused, and he won't even know what it feels like to be fearful in the last moments. Not unless?'

'Forget it,' I responded, dismissing outright the suggestion. 'A clean kill and we're out of here.'

'What about the henchmen?'

'No witnesses. No survivors, Number One said. No point in having someone on our tail, radioing through to god knows how many hire d guns, and who would chase us down in no time.'

He apparently accepted my answer, having ceased the questioning. The light was ever so slowly increasing, but, any moment not the sun would be up and I could get this thing done, maybe start think about getting home to Janie. There was the extraction to get through first. Probably be flown back to the US airbase and leave the country from there. Then there was just the long flight home and. . .

What was I looking at here? The sun had emerged and was lighting the valley. The figure seen through the telescopic sight became quite well illuminated, dressed in dark waterproofs and peaked hat, but as I had been contemplating the trip home, the hat had been removed, fingers pulled through long, wavy locks of auburn hair. The face, pale, and through the lens I clearly could see red lipstick, mascara around the eyes, a silver necklace sparkling in the first rays of the day.

'*Fuck!*'

Took stared at me as I stared at him, gob-smacked and totally caught unawares.

'What?' he asked, concerned, sensing a major problem.

'Get Number One on the radio,' I ground out through clenched teeth, then remembered I had the thing clipped to my belt.

'Walrus to Number One. Walrus to Number One, over.' 'Number One here. Do you have the target in sight?' 'Describe target. Repeat, describe target, now.'

'Athletic build. Pale complexion. Five feet, nine inches. Hair, long, auburn. Blue eyes. Do you have the target?'

'You bastard,' I growled, and then depressed the trigger switch. 'What gender is our target? Repeat, what gender?'

There was a short wait, and then: 'Female. Target is female. Do you have the target in sight?'

'A woman?' Took mouthed, having overheard.

I paused, frozen by indecision, the transceiver still pressed against my ear. '*Muth-a-fuck-a,*' I growled into the mouthpiece, and dropped the instrument to the ground.

'Kinda shines a different light on things,' Took observed. Number One's voice continued to issue from the transceiver:

'Walrus. Confirm target acquisition.'

In all my years of service, I had not once, knowingly or intentionally killed a woman. The idea was anathema to me, and having to do so now violated whatever remained of a sense of control over my life.

'You are looking at Cassandra,' the voice continued, 'the vicious terrorist and cold blooded killer. It is within your grasp to stamp out an evil which will stop nothing to satisfy its lust for power, killing anyone in its way, bringing chaos, mayhem and misery to countless thousands. It's your objective, man. Get it done.'

So now a human being was being referred to as an *it*. Well, perhaps he had a point, in this case. As I thought on it the idea of a woman perpetrating the crimes I knew she was responsible for somehow made it worse. Women, to me, were mothers and nurturers, they stood for the best things in humanity. That this woman could be who she was, to my mind was a perversion of nature.

I bent and retrieved the transceiver. 'You should have told me, damn you. Wait for confirmation of completion, ' I said, and I passed the transceiver to Took.

'Let's do what we came here to do and get home,' I told him.

As I got onto my belly and positioned myself, reset the rifle, pressing the short tripod firmly into the ground, refocusing the scope and pumping a 7.62mm, hollo-nosed round into the chamber, Took checked the atmospheric conditions and distance, fed the information into the ballistics computer which he had become very proficient in using over the last few days.

Her minders seemed to have relaxed by this time, enjoying the outing now and forgetting their primary task. A couple of them had come together to light cigarettes, while the third, the only one left really doing his job, walked a wider perimeter, peering into the bushes along the escarpment, above which Took and I made our final preparations.

'One fifty seven metres,' he told me, in answer to my question of distance. 'Inclination at that distance, twenty percent humidity. . . ? It's barely five centimetres.'

I dialed it into the scope. There was no breeze, little humidity, the range was moderate. It didn't get any easier, and I wriggled into a comfortable position, the stock pushed firmly into my shoulder. As I began filling my lungs with air, I drew a bead on the woman who was manipulating the fishing rod, flicking with the wrist while feeding line out, trying to land the lure exactly where it was needed.

I brought her into sharp focus and adjusted the inclination angle, up a tiny bit. The safety released with a flick of the thumb. Her long, wavy hair shone in the morning light, and there was the hint of a smile on her face as the sun began to warm the day around us. She appeared effulgent, contented, relaxed in the moment and blissfully unaware as I inhaled a final time, began to breathe out, slowly, evenly, my finger poised, and then beginning to squeeze against the trigger. In my mind her face is captured forever in the moment, as the rifle kicked against my shoulder, the explosion shattering the tranquility of the idyllic scene, and the head erupted in a hideous display of exact ballistic physics, a brief moment after the projectile left the barrel.

Taking advantage of the lag time between registering an event and reacting, we continued the assault before the henchmen could respond. Took was on his feet and spraying lead, hitting the other two before I finished the tally with the third.

We speedily established confirmation of four kills before returning to where we had left the transceiver.

'Walrus to Number One. Come in Number One, over.' 'Number One, receiving.'

'*Target achieved*. Repeat, *target achieved*,' I reported, adopting *army-speak*; clinical terminology which somehow was meant to make killing a less atrocious act. 'Will await retrieval,' I added, needing to be sure we were all on the same page.

'Are you positive? Target achieved?' came the response.

'Target achieved,' I repeated yet again. 'Yes, *positive*, target achieved. *Dust-off*,' I hollered. 'How long for retrieval?'

We waited expectantly. A chopper coming to collect us was the requirement, but nothing came back over the radio.

'Walrus to Number One,' I tried, repeating several times, but to no avail. Dead air; they had cease transmission, leaving us out here surrounded by dead people and looking more than a little culpable.

We looked at one another, concernedly and with a terrible sinking feeling.

'What the fuck?' Took expressed entirely appropriately.

TWENTY FIVE

What followed were days of arduous, cross-country slogging over unfamiliar, muddy and very difficult territory we knew nothing about. We necessarily rid ourselves of all equipment tying us to the bloody event, and headed east, realising that the Polish border was our safest bet and probably within our physical ability to walk before exhaustion, or the authorities, claimed us both.

It was a grim affair of selecting a distant landmark dictated by its proximity to due east from our magnetic compass, and pushing toward it, grabbing what sleep could be had, occasionally lighting a fire at night to prevent our freezing to death, selecting the next landmark on the following day and repeating the procedure for as long as we were able to continue.

On the fourth day we trusted that we had crossed the boarder into Poland, and, on that assumption, we at last broke cover to emerge roadside, and within sight of a small rural town.

Took looked hard at the roadside signage as we entered the town, and on the basis of once having has a friend who was Polish, decided that the words *"looked Polish"* to him. Thank goodness he was right about that.

Neither of us had any local currency and we were starving hungry. We would have scrounged through bins, searching for anything looking even remotely edible had not a kindly old lady taken pity on us. We looked a sight, it must be said, after travelling far and sleeping rough for four days. My travelling companion had taken great sport in ribbing me about having been trained for survival in such circumstances. I didn't mind, his goading and making fun was a necessary distraction from circumstances, but he balked when I tore bark from a tree and gouged out a few grubs for his delectation.

The old lady bade us follow her home to her hovel, a mile outside of town, where she had on the ingle a pot of what was, I hope, mushroom and pork stew. Whatever it was, it was consumed with gusto and great appreciation, and while we rested a few hours, digesting the meal, she had disappeared.

She returned in the afternoon with a man driving a beaten up, blue truck; her son, as best I understood, who pointed to his truck, made gestures related to moving a steering wheel, and pointed eastward, saying "Warsaw, Warsaw, Warsaw." A measure of good fortune, *at last!*

Well, comparatively anyway. The son was travelling to a place somewhere near Warsaw, to a property owned by uncle Krzysztof. The fare price? That we catch and load eight free-range pigs into the back of the vehicle, a task much easier said than done. These pigs were big, uncooperative and tended more toward wild than free-range, I'm sure. Our benefactor, Gregor, laughed his damned arse off as he watched me and Took chase down, scrum-tackle and wrestle the cantankerous swine into the wooden pen arrangement on the back of his truck. When we looked about done, he pulled a sack of grain from the truck and began sprinkling it about. That done, he made with his pig call, a high pitched *wee-wee-wee* vocalization which drew the remaining animals in without any fuss, and after only a modicum of effort the pigs were loaded and ready for the drive. It would be an entertaining story he could tell his buddies at the pub, raise a few laughs and maybe solicit a free drink for the telling?

We drove through the night, with Gregor talking non stop and swigging from a half gallon flagon of Polish hillbilly moonshine. The more he drank, the more *entertaining* he became. The truck began to weave around a bit, but, for the most part, he did very well to keep that heap of rust, eight wild pigs and us on the road all the way to whatever one horse town we eventually arrived at.

We bailed out an hour after sunrise and started walking, waving our thumbs in the commonly understood international gesture every time a vehicle was heard to come from behind.

Our second ride took us into Warsaw. In the city we panhandled a few dollars, receiving some very strange looks from passers-by. Not speaking a word of the lingo, all we could do was stretch out one mit while, with the other, rub our stomachs and make noises suggesting hunger, but before too long we had enough in coins to make a phone call, and with even a few coins left over.

We called Janie, telling her of our plight. She promised to get immediately in touch with colonel Stanbridge. A retired colonel, he was a man I knew who was still able to make things happen, and I trusted him completely. From there, not wanting to waste daylight, we sought out the Australian Embassy, where we could speak to the consul, or ambassador or whatever the name was there in Warsaw. No easy task, it turned out, and we had to spin a major yarn even before managing to make an appointment to see the relevant person on the following day.

'Another night on the lamb,' I bemoaned. I was bone wearily, angry and becoming despondent.

Half a dozen bikers rolled by as I expressed this, catching Took's interest as they pulled up outside a club and backed their machines against the curb.

'Don't worry,' Took said, placing a hand on my shoulder. 'Twenty four hours and we'll be on our merry. What we need is a roof over our heads, a good meal and a nice, warm bed for the night. Take a break, buddy. Let me handle it, okay?'

'Handle it? How? We need cash.'

'We're on the streets, brother. I remember this shit. There are ways.'

He sounded confident. I had to give him that, and I was more than happy to let him take care of it. . . or not. I figured that whatever he had in mind would either succeed or fail mightily. It was his way, you might say. If he failed, at least I could count on an entertaining failure of sizeable proportion. It promised to be something unusual, and that was enough to raise my flagging spirits.

'Come on,' he said, tugging at my filthy coat. 'Opportunity knocks.'

I followed him along the sidewalk to where the bikers has assembled. A rowdy lot, they were engaging in horseplay, pushing and shoving one another, calling out in Polish, passing around a bottle of I don't know what and generally living up to public expectations of wild, anarchistic boys with no regard for convention. Your run of the mill, conventional biker boys, in other words.

As we approached the group of seven, another four bikes arrived, greeted with hooting and hollering. A couple who noticed our presence turned to us, saying, I guessed, 'What do you want?'

'Nice bikes,' Took started with, and was met with a moment's displeasure.

'*Brruumm, brruumm,*' he tried, miming riding a bike with ape-hanger handlebars, and nodding his head. 'Nice bikes, man'

The others began taking notice and converged. One imitated Took imitating riding a bike: 'Brruumm brruumm,' and began laughing.

'Norton eight-fifty Commando, Norton Atlas, seven-four-five,' Took named, pointing to each in turn. 'Ooh, man, and the old *Beeza!* BSA Gold Star. A classic. Whose machine is that?'

'My machine,' said a tall, wiry young man, in English, dressed in leather and grubby denim.

'These bikes are rare,' Took told him. 'Very nice, man.'

'BSA are making a new, updated version,' the guy said. 'You ride?' 'Some.'

'What you ride?'

'Black Shadow. Vincent. Fast and beautiful.'

Some of the throng had overheard and came over to listen in, with one of the members asking, 'How fast?'

'One hundred and fifty miles per hour, dude. The fastest motorcycle of its era, next to the Vincent Lightening, of course.'

'Look my bike,' said another, and stood aside to reveal his pride and joy. 'You know this one?'

The motorcycle located among the others, Took gasped. 'That's yours? Are you kidding me?'

He stepped off the curb to approach the motorcycle in question. 'I've never seen one up close before. It's beautiful.'

To me it was a just an old motorbike. Red/brown paint, chipped here an there, a low machine with wide bars and what looked to be a utilitarian, American style about it.

'You know it?' asked the tall, wiry, Warsaw native biker with long, black, greasy hair.

'Do you mind?' Took asked, demonstrating his need to touch it. The guy assented, and my bear sized friend stretched a leg over, and sat, a huge grin appearing. He leaned forward and wrapped his hands around the grips, bounced twice on the suspension, testing it.

'What's the deal with this one?' I asked him.

'Brother, this is a 1931 Indian 101 Scout. Around 370lbs. That's light, with low centre of gravity. I bet it handles,' he told the owner, who appeared to be enjoying Took's reaction.

'Is sweet,' the lad responded.

'Wow. You're a luck man,' Took told him, and turning to me, he said, 'The American army commissioned the manufacture of thousands of these during World War Two. Not many remain, making this an absolute gem.'

I nodded appreciatively, but wondering where all this was meant to lead, replied, 'Do these guys know where we can scrounge up some cash?'

'Thanks, man,' said Took, dismounting. 'You guys have got some really nice bikes. Me and my compadre are stranded here in the city without any money. I'm a mechanic. I could tune or do some repair work, if it's needed?'

Most of them didn't understand English and those who did had to translate to those with a puzzled look on their faces. They talked among themselves for a minute, before someone had an idea.

He regarded my companion, waving his hand over him, appearing to draw attention to his size. *'Walczacy. Das Walka! Tak?'*

There seemed to be consensus, and one who spoke English quite well, said to us, 'How much do you need money?

Was he asking how much money did we need, or how desperately did we need it? I wondered.

'A lot,' I replied, figuring it answered both, more or less adequately 'Do either of you fight?' He asked, now looking us over with a critical eye. 'You?' he asked me.

I shrugged. I was getting long in tooth, I knew, but what man is willing to admit it? Besides, I had a few tricks up my sleeve when it came to a scuffle.

'Sure,' I told him.

He then turned to my friend. 'You will fight?'

'What's it worth?' Took wanted to know, a question I should have asked, myself.

Our translator asked his comrades, answering the question with: 'Three thousand.'

'Three thousand what? *Drachmas?'* Drachmas were Greek currency, but it was all Greek to me at this point.

'Three thousand zloty,' he replied, not helping at all. 'Is that a lot?' It sounded like a lot, to me.

He scratched his head, consulted his brethren again before coming back with: 'One thousand US dollars . . . . *About,'* he added, not wanting to mislead anyone.

Somebody said something at the rear of the pack, gaining our friend's attention. *'Czy ty jasne*?' he responded.

'Tak,' the man replied, meaning *Yes,* I guessed.

He looked at his wristwatch. 'Want money? Must hurry. Must going. *The Nurkowac Klatka Szybowa* is across town. We will take you, but decide now.'

I looked to my companion for counsel:'Hey, we need money,' he correctly pointed out. 'Three thousand *zloty?* It's got to be a giggle. What else we going to do all day? Let's get it *on!'*

I agreed, wondering if this might be one of the less well thought out, dumb-bell decisions we had made recently.

Took and I climbed onto pillion seats behind our respective *"Wild Bunch"* Polish bikers. We were sped through the streets of Warsaw with an impressive roar accompanying our passage, in effort to arrive at *the Nurkowac Klatka Szybowa* before the contender registration deadline expired at 2pm.

He had said, "across town,"but we left town in our wake and were a couple of miles into the landscape before we turned onto a dirt track leading up to a farmhouse and a massive barn, in front of which were parked all manner of vehicles, including tractors, four wheel drives of every description, a dozen or more motorcycles and even a long, black limousine.

We entered the barn with time to spare. Inside the doorway a man dressed sharp, flanked by a couple of bruisers greeted us, asking: 'Co biznes?'

Our motorcycle friends explained why we were here, which appeared to greatly interest the man. 'So, you will fight?' he said, his English heavily cloaked in the local dialect. 'Very good. Write your name down here. You fight my man Otto and win the purse, perhaps?'

'What's that about?' I quizzed.

Our interpreter explained. 'He has his man, Otto. Anyone who can best Otto will take the purse.'

And the purse is how much?'

He asked the entrepreneur whose name, I later learned, was Horace Bernard, a well known chap who had his hand in about every moneymaking operation in the area, and doing quite well, I guessed. The brand new limousine out front was his, as were the goons and the whole fight club venture which had been running for years without intervention by the local constabulary.

'The purse is the purse,' Horace answered. 'Is depending on I am having good day. The more is the crowd loses, the more I like. The more I like, the more is the purse. Three thousand zloty is the minimum purse. Perhaps more, you understand?'

'Ivan,' he said to the big guy at his right shoulder. 'Take care of our new friends. Follow Ivan and he will give whatever you need,' he told us, and we followed Ivan to a changing room.

Beyond the entranceway, through a tattered red curtain, we entered the arena, otherwise known as the interior of the barn. A crowd of surprising size, around three hundred, I imagined, stood on the dirt floor surrounding a large metal cage at the centre. There was already a fight going on within the cage, but it was difficult to make out what was happening. We pushed through the throng with the assistance of big Ivan, and at the back of the barn were shown into a room partitioned by posts with timber boards nailed over them; another tattered red curtain draped over the doorway.

The space reeked of an unpleasant mixture of liniment, sweat and urine. There was a large wooden chest full of garments that we might choose to wear for the bout, but which we swiftly declined. We wanted to watch the action and get an idea of how we were going to survive this latest bout of foolishness.

'Would you find us something to hydrate with?' I asked Ivan, miming a man drinking, to make sure he understood. 'We will go out there to watch the fighting.'

'Ah, yes,' he replied, and left.

Took led the push towards the cage through the jubilant, rowdy spectators, some of whom were engaged in brawling of their own. After a struggle we emerged cage-side, in time to see some poor sod driven, headfirst into the cage of the ten metres square fight arena, constructed of two inch wide steel girding, spaced at around four inches, riveted together at the intersecting steel bands.

The combatants, both big chaps, wore tracksuit pants, one in a white singlet and the other wearing a Bon Jovi t-shirt. The man who had his head slammed into the cage climbed to his feet, looking groggy and disorientated, as the bigger man grabbed him by the head and began swinging him around; a version of the aeroplane manoeuvre I had seen performed by pro wrestlers on television, or by parents whose children enjoyed being spun around in this fashion. The guy being spun was in danger of having his feet come off the ground, leaving his neck to bear the full extent of the centrifugal force being applied.

'His head is about to pop off,' Took observed, but just as it was about to do just that, the guy doing the swinging released his grip, sending the poor bugga hurling once agin into the meshed steel bands.

There was a communal *'Woah,'* at the moment of release, and an 'Aaah,' when he slammed to a halt against the steel, and sunk to the dirt, defeated.

'I wonder what the rules are?' Took mused aloud, just as Ivan arrived with refreshments.

'No rules,' he said, and handed us a bottle of something. I had no idea what, but it wasn't water or an approved Olympic Games electrolyte replacement. It was, most likely, Ouzo, which would not be required until after the bout.

'Have we decided which of us is going in there?' asked Took, nodding toward the cage, where the last opponent was now being dragged out, feet first.

'Decide? It was your idea, pal. You're going,' I demanded, but he was already grinning ear to ear.

'Like I said, I'll take care of it. 'These guys are strong, but they ain't quick. Farm fed oaf aren't a major problem,' he said, confidently, but for whose benefit, I really wasn't sure.

We watched bout after bout for an hour, and eventually got a jug of water from Ivan, to hydrate my man with. The temperature was rising in here, becoming humid and kinda musky, with the noise, the rising dust and crazy action making the whole thing feel quite surreal.

Ivan had disappeared for a moment and came back over to us with a message. 'You will fight now.' He appeared to include the both of us in delivering the message, so I corrected him, to make sure there was no mistake.

'Just my friend,' I told him.

'Both,' he responded, and hooked a thumb over his shoulder. 'Mr Bernard say both of you.'

I looked over Ivan's shoulder to see Horace Bernard, nodding and smiling, holding up a drawstring purse as he raised two fingers on the other hand, suggesting twice the usual money.

'Both fight. Two times prize. Not one fight, two. Or go home,' he said, stubbornly, reminding me of those fake native American actors from dated television westerns.

'Fuck it,' said Took. 'We don't have to do this. It's only one more day on the street. No big deal.'

'Tell your boss, *No Problem*,' I told Ivan, feeling the effects of a rush of testosterone, emptying my head and puffing out my chest.

'No, man. It's cool,' Took advised, but I was not backing down. 'We're doing this thing,' I found my self saying, cementing the foolishness.

We were stripped down to the waist, wearing our canvas army footwear and cargos, standing at the centre of the fight cage, waiting to get a look at our opponents, and by this time the affect of the male hormone was beginning to fade. I figured a few stretching exercises were in order, and began limbering up to jeering and catcalling from the, by now, drunken, bloodthirsty crowd.

If you get tired,' said Took, coming up to talk tactics—'

'Just worry about yourself,' I cut him off, 'and think about that nice, warm bed tonight. Okay?'

He nodded and slapped me on the back, as the gate of our cage swung open, admitting our adversaries, one at a time.

'Twins,' I observed; over six feet in height and both a strange mixture of two hundred eighty pounds of muscle and lard combined. Thick, curly brown hair and thick beards, oddly calling to mind, Bluto, Popeye the sailor's constant nemesis.

'Got any spinach on you?' I asked, keeping a concerned eye on them, and the comment caused us both to burst out laughing.

The laughter immediately perplexed the *Blutos*, but served to dispel our uneasiness as they began circling us warily.

The circling continued until Took said, 'Fuck this. I'm not here to dance,' and advanced threateningly on the nearest.

I let him do his thing as I remained focussed on mine. We were close and I was watching for telltale signs of his first move. He made the mistake of transferring his weight to the back foot and raised his arms as if to say to the crowd, *Is this guy going to do something?*

I aimed my right hand high, meaning to bait him into a defensive move, raising his forearms to block. When he did, I ploughed into his belly with all I had, impacting him hard enough to force the air from his lungs as I tipped him onto his back. It was a great first move, and I was pleased with myself. I should have taken full advantage by stomping, hard, but I held back, seeing no reason to be so brutal, possibly crippling the poor bugga, but he quickly rolled himself like a beer barrel and was up on his feet again.

I had winded him pretty good, and while he tried to gather himself I chanced a look over to Took's situation. His opponent was holding his face, blood streaming down his chest while he held one arm outstretched, wanting to fend off anything else coming his way or asking Took to back off, but then he lunged forward, grabbing Took about the waist, lifting, squeezing, bending backward, trying hard to snap his spine.

I turned back in time to cop what felt like a hammer blow against the side of my head, spinning my entire world. Immediately afterwards I was ploughed into by two hundred and eighty pounds of muscle and lard. The guy had recovered faster than expected and retaliated with a similar move to my own, only he came down on top of me, pinning me under his weight.

I was able to pull my arms free from under him and twist his ears until they about came off. He cried out and roared but he would not desist, so I chopped him in the throat for good measure, which finally persuaded him to roll the fuck off of me.

I chanced another glance Took's way, to witness his man accepting a long lump of wood through the square gaps of the cage, clubbing Took with it. My man came at me again, and he, too, had a lump of wood in his had. It was an audience participation game, I realised. We should have gotten the rules straight from the get go. Both of us were fending off savage blows and avoiding, as much as possible, being brained or having our bones broken.

'Fuck these guys,' Took called out to me. 'Time to get serious.'

Serious? I thought I was being serious, but Took was right, I then realized. We thought we had been engaging in some kind of sport, or entertainment. Our mind set was all wrong. We were, in reality, very likely fighting for our lives. Whenever bloodletting is involved the mind becomes deadly focussed and serious, not only drawing on every bit of knowledge held in store, but improvised stuff, too, born out of animal survival, the organism adapting in the heat of the moment.

I saw Took lunge with a straight kick to his man's solar plexus, as, with an incoming fist the size of a ham-bone aimed at my face, I spun away, moving sideways and circling quickly, bringing my own left fist crashing behind my man's ear, where I knew it would cause temporary stupefaction.

I was behind him, my arm about his neck and squeezing, pilling him down to the ground. Took, I saw, was pummeling his guy with his fists and feet so that his adversary was on the verge of toppling, if I was any judge. My man was limp, at last, but I held him a moment longer before releasing the debilitating hold. Took gave his guy a final, haymaker with his full weight behind it. It connected the man's head, dead centre, and sent him sprawling to the ground, raising a cloud of dust and at last ending the contest.

The crowd seemed to have changed their mid about us and where much more enthusiastic, I was please to observe. Adding to the show, I grabbed my buddy's arm and we raised them in victory, even gave a couple of bows in appreciation of the applause, but I was all for getting out of there as soon as possible.

'Let's get our money and scoot,' I suggested, 'before friend Horace decides not to pay us.'

He did pay up. Our motorcycle enthusiast friends oversaw payment of our prize money: six thousand zloty, translating to forty two hundred Aussie dollars, we later calculated, a small portion of which we donated to the lads; transportation fees and services rendered.

'You come party now?' we were asked.

'No thank-you,' replied. I was already suffering the price of being clubbed repeatedly about the head and shoulders; my ribs, back and arms, too. 'A flop is what I'm in need of now.'

'Flop?' he repeated, puzzled by the word. 'Yeah. Somewhere to rest, you know? A room?'

'Aaah, *pokój!*' He appeared to have caught on. 'We take *flop.*'

TWENTY SIX

The lads dropped us off at the Sokoly, meaning *falcon*, a hotel owned by an acquaintance of theirs, and making sure he knew of our exploits before departing, asking him to take good care of us during our stay. Caleb Dabrowski, a be-suited small man of Jewish heritage, was only too pleased to oblige. We travelled together in the elevator, emerging on the top floor of the five story building, all the while with him extolling every facet of his hotel. We were not listening, only trying to decide which of our concerns in that moment was the most urgent. Sleep in a large, warm, comfortable bed, or eat in the fancy downstairs restaurant we had walked past while heading for the elevators?

He promised to provide us with suitable clothing as we closed the door on him and stood wearily, surveying the room we had purchased. It was five star, a plush and comfortable looking space, with two, snug king-sized beds beckoning to us. With dwindling energy reserves, we showered, and in my case, shaved, before climbing gingerly into our beds, both of us wincing and occasionally cursing the pain arising from the multiple impact sites and strained muscles, the cost of our earning money enough for this luxury.

In the morning we were to return to the Australian Embassy and try to convince them to find passage home for us. We had been dumped and left stranded by our team leader, opening us up to many perils, not the least of which was being discovered and charged with the assassination of a female national who was held in exceedingly high esteem by powerful entities, and not forgetting her hirelings. We had been lucky to get as far as we had to this point. We had to hope our luck would hold; we were only a step away from successfully escaping the scene, but dealing with the Embassy was still an unknown; a necessary evil, we both agreed, if ever we were going to get home.

Laying there, waiting for sleep to take us, I remembered my phone, from which I had removed the battery, days ago, at commencement of the operation. It would maybe need charging if I wanted to use it when I woke, so I dragged myself out of bed and dug it out from my kit, connected the charging cord and found an outlet near my bedside table before climbing back between the clean sheets.

From the bed alongside, Took asked, 'What do you suppose our chances are, tomorrow, at the Embassy? Is it even safe?'

'I was just wondering about that, myself.'

'You don't suppose we're walking into a trap, do you?'

'I was just wondering about that, myself,' I said again, becoming more concerned and annoyed that I had to be thinking about it right now. Sleep was all I wanted.

'There must be one hell of a manhunt going on,' he correctly mentioned. 'Can we trust the Embassy not to hand us over? Avoid a diplomatic situation or whatever it's called?'

'Do we have any options?' I returned, and lay thinking about it a while longer. 'It's a goddamn risk. We don't know if Number One was captured or what happened.'

'We know what didn't happen,' Took replied. 'No dust off. We were hung out to dry, well and truly.'

'We don't know that.' 'Don't we?'

Now my mind was beginning to pick up the threads again; doubts gnawing at me, possible scenarios as to why Number One had ceased communication with us being invented and discounted for lack of information. We were still in deep water, whichever way we cut it. As jaded and dull-witted as I felt, red flags were beginning to pop up all over the place. Had I accepted the consul's secretary's word in his offer of assistance purely out of a need to believe our problems were almost over? It was likely, because, right now the offer rung as hollow as an empty fifty gallon drum.

The phone on my bedside table *pinged*, meaning the battery was fully charged. I wondered if there was any useful information on it, rolled over and picked it up, checking for messages.

Janie had called twice and messaged once, so I went to messages and opened it, reading:

Hello darling. I hope you both are safe and well. A man named Willie Banks called. I wouldn't bother you with this, but it sounds important. He says Guido wants to talk to you, *urgently*. He said, he expects you have found yourself in hot water by now. He can get you out, he says, and there's a partial contact number. +61 08 203 He says you will know the remaining digits. They're scribbled on the back of the pad you took from Vincent. Don't trust anyone. He said Guido says that was important. That was the important thing. Good luck darling. All my love to you. And to Took.

I instantly remembered the old lag from Holdsworthy prison; the guy who said he could keep an eye out for us in there. Guido must have twigged he was working for me, but the message. . . ?

I needed the remainder of that number and immediately sent a return text to Janie, asking her to look for that number on the back of the pad Guido had mentioned. I had stuffed the pad into a drawer, at home, and she could text it to me when she received my reply. 'What you doin'?' Took wanted to know. 'It's hard enough to sleep as it is, without you fumbling around.'

'Guido sent us a message through Willy Banks. Remember him?' 'Of course. Willie *the peter thief* Banks. From Holdsworthy.'

'He delivered a message from Guido to Janie, intended for me. Saying as how we've probably found ourselves in trouble and not to trust anyone. Says he will help if we call him. I'm waiting for Janie to retrieve the number.'

'How would he know that?' Took asked, sitting up now, and looking troubled.

'Exactly. He knows too much to be guessing. What the hell is going on here?'

He laughed. 'I been asking myself that for a couple of weeks. And we're going to trust him?'

'As opposed to what? Walking into the embassy tomorrow, with our dicks in our hands and waiting for the hammer to drop?'

'Only asking, dude. No need to be testy. I gotta say I wasn't exactly convinced the Embassy was the best decision. I'm fine with hearing what the little man has to say. Are you?'

My phone *pinged* again, showing a new message from Janie. 'I am,' I told Took. I've got the number here. What time is it back in Oz? I'd like to think I'm disturbing his beauty sleep.'

I dialled the number and waited. 'This is you, Alex?' Guido asked. 'You will have recognized my caller ID. Of course it's me.'

'Things are not working out too well your you?'

The little sod was being cocky. 'I suspect you know the answer to that, Guido, and I would be interested to know how you know.'

'Aaah, I know much, my friend,' he continued, full of himself. 'Your military friends have deserted you by now, I suspect. Why else would you be calling me?'

'You mentioned something to Janie about getting us out,' I told him, wanting cut short his gloating and get to it. 'How the hell do you know what's going on over here?' I asked, unable to contain my incredulity a moment longer.

'We will talk about that another time, I think. Yes? Where are you at this moment, Alex? And your friend, mister Took. Is he with you?'

We're in Warsaw, considering going to the Embassy for assistance in the morning. That should tell you how jammed up we are, Guido. Our handler ditched us, left us in the lurch.'

'Oh dear. You are the *patsy*, is that the word? You did not do as they wished it and be caught. Good for you, Alex, but is political. You come home to what now?'

'I'll consider that on the way home. I know you're enjoying this, Guido, but we need a way out of here and you said something about helping. Remember?'

'Okay, you are as you say, jammed up. Yes, I help you and your friend, mister Took, to leave unobserved. Come see me when you return, won't you? I will explain things you want to know. And do bring Matilda with you again, and your wife. I would love again to see your wife, Janie. It will be a very nice visit. I think if you come to me before they know you have escaped capture, is much better.'

He was loving it. I could almost see him leaning back in his chair, feet up, puffing on an enormous cigar.

'Tell me, Alex. From the mouth of the horse, like they say. The person who is making all this trouble. *Is no more?*'

I had almost forgotten, Guido would be on tenterhooks regarding Cassandra's status. 'Why don't we discuss it when next we meet?' I suggested. 'Were *hot*, and time is wasting. I don't know that our door isn't about to be kicked down by the Polski police, the Belarusian Militia or some crazy eastern bloc mafia.'

I heard later that a squad of armed militiamen, dressed in black and wearing no identifying markings, had raided our hotel room barely ten minutes after we had left, early the following morning. Had I known of it much earlier, things would have played out very much differently. I would have suspected Guido of playing a hand and blown our departure plans all to hell.

At just after three in the morning, as Took and I still struggled for sleep, anguishing over the question of Guido's trustworthiness, the lock on our door was heard to release with a click, and in walked five scruffy individuals, looking as though they might have just finished work at the dockyard, and pulling trolleys on which two large trunks were mounted.

Tired and groggy, I was slow to react, fumbling to locate my needle gun from under my pillow, but the lead man had his hands half raised in an appeasing gesture, saying, 'Guido send, Guido send. Take you home, yes?'

They were in obvious haste and so we obliged, bundling our stuff together, as requested by our visitors, and climbing into the trunks into which airholes had thoughtfully been bored. We were rolled out of the room, taken down in an elevator, through the foyer and out through the main entrance of the building to be loaded into a waiting van.

Half an hour later, and still packed in our trunks, we arrived at a pier, loaded by way of cargo net and crane, down from the pier and into the hold of a massive steel barge, and finally released.

'Come, come,' invited a sailor, and he led us out of the hold via steps, gangways, watertight doors and narrow corridors to our cabin, a ten foot square, steel box containing a double bunk, washbasin, television set with a DVD player attached and a cupboard full of beta taped movies.

'Make comfort, here,' we were told. 'All okay.'

As he turned and departed, Took called after him. 'Hey, where are we going? You can't just dump us here without we know what's going on.'

The sailor was annoyed, but I guess he figured my friend was right. 'Okay, okay. Come, look,' he invited, making hand motions to follow him again.

A few paces away we came passed through a watertight door, out to a walkway at the side of the boat, into the fresh air. At the rail he pointed to the water, saying, 'Wisla.'

'Wisla,' I repeated, scratching my head, searching my memory for a connection.

'Rzeka, rzeka. Wisla rzeka,' and he pointed along the waterway.

Thank goodness the skipper appeared then, coming down from the wheelhouse onto the walkway. *'Dziekuje, Aleksander. Ty móc Isc wrócic do praca,'* and our frustrated guide went back to work.

'Hello,' greeted the captain. 'He was trying to tell you that you are on the Vistula river. We will take you out to the Black Sea, not far. Maybe five hours. Getting you out from the city is important. I hear there is a big search for you. Don't worry, all is arranged.'

And it was all arranged. Five hours later we switched boats, climbing into a speedboat; a machine that flew across the Black Sea waters at a phenomenal rate of knots, about crushing our spines and rattling internal organs inordinately for a full forty minutes until we landed sometime around midday at a small, fishing port town I have no idea the name of. Thankfully, things improved from there. We were taken by car to an airstrip where we boarded a light aircraft which took us to a major airport.

I had to hand it to Guido. He was no slouch when it came to paperwork and shady connections. After the light aircraft had landed we were asked to hand over our passports, which we did without argument. We had to trust those we met if we wanted out of here. We definitely want out, and inside ninety minutes our passports had been returned to us, after waiting at a little airfield cafeteria where we tried to relax with a sandwich and a milkshake.

The names on the passports had been changed. Anything more than that would have cost valuable time, and since any large scale manhunt which might have been mounted had only recently begun, it would take time for them to broadcast anything much beyond verbal descriptions and the fake names we provided at our last place of residence.

We were then transported to an international airport terminal some twenty miles away, given instructions and wished *bon voyage (in Polish)* before climbing aboard a flight to Morocco. From there we boarded a flight to Heathrow, London, and eighteen hours after that? A Qantas flight straight through to good old Adelaide, South Australia, taking another twenty four hours flying time.

By the time a taxi from the airport delivered us home, we were about dead on our feet. Took climbed out at his place, looking wobbly on his feet as he walked toward the front door, calling back to me, 'I'll see you at yours, when I've recovered.'

I walked through the front door at home to find Janie and Matilda in the kitchen, happily preparing a meal.

To their expressions of complete surprise, I replied, 'Hi girls. I'm home. Don't wake me for twelve hours,' and I didn't stop walking until I came up to the side of my bed and collapsed on top of it. The last thing I remembered before sleep took me was a vision of Bluto, the bully from Popeye cartoons, chasing after a caricature of myself. Bluto was angry. Smoke was coming from his ears and he was beating his chest, growling and yelling obscenities in Belarusian as he chased me. I could only hope he didn't catch up before unconsciousness did. . . and he didn't.'

TWENTY SEVEN

I awoke fourteen hours and twenty five minutes later, at seven fifteen in the morning. Janie knew to give me a wide berth at times like this. Sleep deprivation tends to bring out the worst in people, and I was appreciative of her not putting me in a position to make an arsehole of myself.

I lay on my back, staring at the ceiling for a long time, allowing bits and pieces of memory to fall into place of their own accord, until I judged everything was in place. The memory which stood out most of all, and way too clearly, was the one I wanted most to forget. The moment the round from the sniper rifle had impacted my target's head was freeze framed, perfectly captured in my mind's eye, and it unnerved me to think that it might haunt my dreams to the remainder of my life.

Cassandra had been a woman. The idea was shocking to me for many reasons, and that, too, was going to alter my world forevermore.

Even after fourteen hours of uninterrupted sleep I still wasn't feeling particularly refreshed; another one of those little indicators telling me that maybe it was time to pull my head in and settle into a less crazy way of living my life. Still, this damned thing wasn't yet over with. Loose ends to deal with, I reminded myself as I made the effort to rise, getting as far as sitting on the edge of the bed, looking out at the landscape beyond our bedroom window.

I was lucky to have come this far; to still be among the living, for one, to be married to a wonderful girl who didn't seem to mind me being who I was, for another, to be living in a beautiful location, surrounded by open countryside, fresh air, and I had to fuck it all up by allowing myself to be roped into this Cassandra thing once again. Well, the sooner I got these last items checked off of the agenda, the better it would be for all concerned.

I called Took, who did not answer, leaving a text message on his phone, telling him to drag his backside over here so we could keep things moving as fast as possible. That done, I showered, went through two disposable razor blades in removing the accumulated growth of beard from my face, and then accidentally doused myself with way too much cologne when the dispensing cap on the bottle came off as I tipped it towards myself. Jeans, t-shirt and jacket, wallet, pocketknife, tobacco and lighter in my pocket, and I was set.

I found Janie out in the back yard upon emerging into the day with a fresh brew of coffee in hand. She was planting bulbs into a freshly cultivated space in the garden, wearing a wide brimmed straw hat to keep the sun off her face.

'Morning dear,' she greeted, brightly. 'Did you sleep well?'

'Like the proverbial. It's nice out here,' I said, for lack of anything intelligent to say in the moment.

'It's a gorgeous day, isn't it?' she beamed, and there was something about her energy I couldn't put my finger on.

She backfilled the rich, dark soil around the final bulb, firmed the soil around it and watered it in. Rising then, she came over, pushed me back in my chair to sit on my lap and planted one on me. Not your average, everyday "morning hon" kiss, but the other kind, and any man reading this knows exactly the kind I mean.

'I've missed you,' she said. 'I've been worried and I'm glad to have you home again.'

'And with a greeting like that, I'm glad to be back,' I told her. 'The garden looks great.'

'Matty has been helping me out here. It's been fun, and it was nice having someone around to talk to while you two were away. Are you both okay? Did everything go well?'

'We made it back. That's the important thing.' I was going to leave it at that, but she needed more of a story and I figured I might as well elaborate.

'We got stranded and had to hotfoot it, cross-country over the border into Poland.'

'*Poland!* From where?'

'Belarus. . . but I shouldn't be telling you this, you know.' 'Stranded, how?'

'The support team disappeared and we couldn't raise them on the radio. Something fishy. It might have been bad but I guess we were lucky.'

She seemed satisfied for the moment, but she had to ask: 'And Cassandra?'

'Mission accomplished,' was all I said. Janie knew the meaning and she was wise enough to know not to ask for details.

'Dudes!' came Took's voice from the kitchen. He had, as usual, received no response at the front door and let himself in.

'Yeah, mate. Out here, the back verandah.'

'Can I make myself a coffee before I get there?' he asked. 'Go for it,' Janie called to him.

'Where's Matty?'

'I'm here,' she replied. 'I was just showering. 'I'd love a coffee, too.

Do you mind, Took?'

Matilda came out to the verandah to join us. 'Hello, Alex. Everything okay? You slept long enough. You looked worn out, in the brief moment we saw you.'

'I was, and it went well enough,' I answered.

'Did it, hell,' Took called out, which, for some reason evoked laughter from the girls.

'Well it didn't,' he said, emerging from the kitchen, handing Matilda her coffee and finding a chair for himself. 'How did you pull up?' he asked me.

'Don't ask.'

'Well I'm sore allover. What with the training program and having to walk halfway around the globe to get out, and not mentioning the terrible twins of Budapest or whatever.'

'Then spare a moment's thought for me,' I told him. I've got years on you, brother. How do you *think* I pulled up?'

'Just wanted to know,' he replied. 'You're getting grumpy in your old age, I aren't you?'

That didn't much amuse me, and I let it drop. 'Janie says you guys have been hard at it in the garden,' I said to Matilda. 'Looking good, too. Nice to know you're earning your keep,' I joked.

'I've really enjoy it,' she answered. 'But,' she gave a sideways glance to Janie before continuing with, 'we've both been worried since you text for uncle Guido's number. What was that about? Why was my uncle involved?'

I scoffed at that. 'Since when is uncle Guido ever *not* involved?' She replied sullenly, 'True enough. What did he do this time?'

'He saved our arses, is what!' Took answered. 'Yeah, I know. Guido saving our arses. Not a common occurrence, is it? But he did. We were in *diabolicals*, too. Abandoned in a strange land and the one option of going to the embassy was not so much an option as our desperate only choice, until Guido saved our bacon.'

'Wow,' she responded, delighting. 'Did he have a connection over there, maybe?'

'I'll say. He had us out of there lickety-split, and I'm still wondering how he knew so much of what was going on. The deal was, like, strictly hush-hush. It's got *me* stumped.'

'And me,' I enjoined. 'In a way, it began and ended with our little friend, Guido, and I doubt it's coincidence.'

Matilda was pensive, her eyes downcast, for the moment disconnected and wistful. Then, looking up, she said, 'I've not felt right about any of this since I first came to you, Alex. Your connection to my uncle, Guido's connection to Cassandra, and me to him and to you. And I've not yet asked you about. . . did you. . . you know. . . Is Cassandra. . . ?'

I nodded, and the answer cast a momentary dampener on our little gathering. 'Fuck it,' I said at last. She's responsible for so much death and misery in so many locations around the globe. She doesn't deserve a speck of sympathy.'

'*She?*' Janie and Matilda exclaimed in unison.

'Yeah,' Took confirmed. 'Who would have thought it?'

Again that image through the rifle scope came to mind. 'Dreadful,' I mumbled, without meaning to.

Janie reacted by placing a consoling hand on my knee. 'I know it was, dear, but you were just an instrument, nothing more,' she told me, soothingly, and it actually did help. 'Is that what caused you those awful nightmares last night?

'What nightmares?' I answered, unaware of anything of the sort. 'You were tossing and turning. You said something I didn't understand. Something about a neon dancer?'

'Nope,' I responded, but, in truth, yes. The neon dancer. I would never forget. Like a demon, I think. It was a nightmare I'd had many years ago. One which became repetitive and had well portrayed the abhorrence I felt back then, regarding the mass and so extraordinarily swift addiction to a substance known on the streets at the time as angel wings. The stuff had addicted many thousands, in Monarto alone, the apparent proving ground, we later discovered, in a plot which might have wreaked global havoc, killed millions had it not been detected early. It's evil nature lay in the fact that it had been produced in conjunction with another chemical compound, one that, when combining with the drug inside the human body, and surreptitiously delivered through the city's water supply, the result was instantaneous death. The whole scheme had been marketed as a means of population control, and aimed at countries where drug addiction and the resulting financial strain placed on society had become a major issue. In almost every country in the world, governments were squawking about the incurred cost of policing, the judicial system being cloyed and clogged, rising prison populations, erosion of the social fabric and added fiscal pressures regarding rising costs in wealthy countries providing national health care for its citizens. Cassandra's simple and inexpensive solution, while avoiding collateral damage to average citizens, had sparked much interest, especially in the poorer, more ruthlessly controlled countries. Took, Janie and I had stumbled over the insane plot in time to draw attention to it before millions were lost. The diabolical plan had greatly affected me, more than expected, at least. Recalling it all now, the guilt I had previously been feeling over my pulling the trigger diminished appreciably.

'She had it coming,' I muttered, emerging from my recollections. 'She did,' Janie assured me.

'Janie told me all about it,' said Matilda. 'It's almost impossible for me to comprehend people inventing so awful a thing, let alone setting the plan in motion. It was a terrible, terrible thing. I only hope nothing of the kind ever can happen again.'

'Let's hope so,' said Janie, as I held my tongue, thinking that as long as we continued ignoring rational methods of solving our problems and continued, instead, to choose the piecemeal, stopgap solutions, it was all but inevitable other crackpot fixes would be tried.

'So what now?' Took asked, attempting divert the conversation. 'I would like to close the books on this,' I replied in earnest.

'I want to know what happened, and why,' said Took. 'I've not once had a handle on this deal from the start. We might have taken out the root of the problem, and that's actually a good analogy. Like a rotten tooth, pulled, there's still the gunk and the sore gums. Although, now the rotten tooth has gone, it will heal, but you know what I mean, don't you? What caused the rotten tooth in the first place?' Took had puzzled himself and wasn't comfortable with how he had finished. 'There's a lot of unanswered questions,' he concluded.

'There are,' I agreed, 'and after our jaunt we don't know how much heat will be brought to bear against us. And the question remains, were we abandoned on purpose, or was our support team discovered and. . . *dealt with?*' I had almost used the word *executed*, but the girls were already apprehensive enough.

'Uncle Guido knows what's going on.' Matilda blurted out. 'I was telling Janie, earlier. I had the impression he was keeping something to himself. Something big, and I've known him long enough to know. He has always been secretive, and where I'm concerned, I know it's his way of being protective. This time though. No, he's being secretive, and there's a difference.'

'My thought's exactly,' I told her, 'and it just so happens we're invited back again, to Wordsworth, by he who knows way more about this game than any of us, and far more than he has been letting on.'

'Who we?' asked Janie.

'All of us *we*. The last time I spoke to him, he said to come see him as soon as we get back. He said, *all of us should drop by,* and that's exactly what we should do. You guys up for a plane ride tomorrow?'

TWENTY EIGHT

We booked the prison visit with Guido online, before leaving, and an early morning flight took us to Sydney. The next, to Ballina, and as we had done the first time around, we hired a car, this time something a bit more sedate, a late model Honda Accord, Euro, a comfortable cruiser with ample go in it. We even secured two rooms at the motel we had stayed in on the first trip, just a few mile short of Holdsworthy prison.

It was four in the afternoon by the time we arrived there, travel weary and much in need of a freshen up. Took and Matilda occupied the room beside Janie's and mine. After showering and throwing on a change of clothes, we gathered beside the pool at the rear of the motel to spend a couple of hours sunning ourselves, sipping cool drinks, chatting about mundane things—things not associated with the reason for our being there—and generally relaxing.

Around six o'clock or so, we drove down the road, looking for and finding a roadside restaurant where we enjoyed a halfway decent grilled steak, chips and salad before returning to our rooms where we hoped for a good night's sleep before the scheduled visit with Matilda's uncle Guido.

I say *'hoped for'* with good reason. At one in the morning I woke to the sound of . . . Well truth is, I don't know what woke me. Maybe it was a sound, but one of the six senses, I expect. The room *was* locked, I knew. I had secured the door, last thing, before Janie and I turned in. So why was there someone crossing the dark room, all stealthy like, in the wee hours; someone tall, silhouetted by the scarce illumination from outside, seeping through the pulled curtains?

My hand didn't need to move far in order to find the reassuring grip of *Lullaby*, my trusty needle gun, which I am in habit of slipping beneath my pillow, every night and wherever I might be. It might have been anyone, possibly Took, or Matilda. Janie was asleep beside me. That much I did know.

I was able to slide Lullaby out from under the pillow and line up on the target without giving myself away. I would give them one chance to identify themselves, I decided, but began with:

'Freeze*!'*

They disobeyed, and I saw an arm being raised, with something gripped by the hand.

Pft . . . The compressed-air-propelled needle found its target, and shortly after came the *thump,* as our night stalker hit the rug.

Janie had not stirred, meanwhile. I disliked having to wake her, but the light had to come on in order for me to discover what was going on. When it did, she complained without opening her eyes, and I whispered to her:

'Go back to sleep, hon. I'm getting a drink of water,' and, fortunately, it's what she did.

The person on the floor, dressed in black tracksuit, black sneakers and face-mask remained inert as I rifled his pockets, finding only a scrap of paper with the name of the motel written on it, in pencil. On the floor beside him lay the item he held before dozing off. A short nosed .38 revolver with silencer attached. On a whim I pulled off his left sneaker, finding a clue I had hoped for. The other was empty but the left one contained photo-id, and I had seen these before.

A small, printed card explained: ASIO. Australian Security Intelligence Organisation, it read, and with the kangaroo and emu insignia background, the name Alan Brubridge clearly printed.

'Okay, Alan my boy. *Upsidaisy*,' and heaving him onto my shoulder, I carried him next door. After tapping to gain entry, and the sound of rustling and sniggering coming from within, a dishevelled pair of fellow travellers stood, looking very much caught while at it, inside the opened doorway.

'Can I come in or do I have to stand here with this guy over my shoulder all night?'

They parted to make way as I dumped my catch on the small, uncomfortable, motel settee provided, telling them, 'Intruder.'

Matilda stood, wrapped under a blanket while Took, being Took, stood naked, with hands on hips. 'What are *we* supposed to do with him?'

'Too big to throw back,' I answered. 'He should be of some use, I expect.' I showed him the card I had found in the left sneaker.

'Yep, ASIO alright. How long will he be out?'

'Not much longer,' I replied, and slapped the visitor a couple of times in testing my estimate. A feeble hand half rose to fend off the blows. 'Couple more minutes.'

'Is Janie alright?' Matilda asked, concerned.

'She's still asleep,' I replied. 'She's a heavy sleeper,' but then came a soft tapping at the door.

Matilda let her in and we all stood around, waiting for CIA to wake up.

'When did all this happen?' Janie asked. 'Are you two alright?'

'It happened in your room,' they told her, and so she turned to me. 'In our room? And you didn't wake me?'

'Didn't see the point, really. He's coming around. Why don't you two go next door and have a cup of tea or whatever,' I suggested. 'Took and I can sort this out.'

They accepted the offer before our interloper became fully alert, leaving me with some hasty decisions to make. He woke to discover himself lying on the cheap and uncomfortable settee, Took and myself standing, looking down on him, no doubt scowling.

I pulled the ski mask from his head, discovering a short cropped military style crew. He was one of these square jawed, clean-cut types common to this kind of work. His brown eyes were beginning to focus.

'You're back with us?' I quizzed.

He gave groan before answering. 'I guess. What did you shoot me with, gin?'

'Sorry about that, but it'll pass soon enough,' I told him. 'It's a concoction I learned about in Central Africa. The Congo, actually. It stops gorillas, too, in slightly larger doses.'

'That's interesting, Jaeger,' he replied. 'You are Jaeger?'

'Last time I looked in a mirror. Who are you and who do you work for?'

He was hesitant, thinking things through, deciding to answer with, 'I'm the guy elected to stop you.'

Took said, 'I need a beer. Anyone want a beer?' and he went to the fridge to retrieve his cold one. 'Stop me doing what, exactly?'

The guy adopted a look suggesting disapproval, or something close to it. 'You going to tell me you don't know Captain Harris?'

'Never heard of a captain Harris,' Took replied for me, returning with his refreshment.

'The guy who trained you two, just a couple of weeks ago? Come off it, Jaeger.'

'Oh, you mean Number One. Tall guy, all starch and boot polish?' 'Whatever. They figured you'd be after his hide after he left you two to take the heat over there.'

'I knew he left us to die,' Took intervened. 'The bastard. I bet that was the plan all along. Do their dirty work for them and delete us, leaving no one alive to trace back to the source. Bloody typical.'

'It's not a trait of the military,' I defended. 'Those pricks we met. The panel or whatever. ASIO. It's exactly their style, which is to say, no fuckin' style at all.'

'They sent you? Trying to cover their tracks?' I asked.

He shrugged, unwilling to say more, meaning it was absolutely those mongrels.

'You got a name,' I asked.

'Jones.'

'Okay, Jones. Number One is Harris. Captain Harris. To tell you the truth, fellah, I hadn't considered Harris. I have enough on my plate right now, without adding the prick to the list of things to do. But you have solved the mystery. I was giving the bastard the benefit of the doubt, favouring the option he had been discovered and chased off the reservation. Come to think of it, he'll be catching hell for not making sure if we're still alive. Alive and dangerous, considering we link ASIO with Cassandra's demise. So screw Harris. There's undoubtedly a kick in the pants coming his way in any case. A demotion, I wouldn't wonder.'

Jones smiled at that, saying, 'He was put on a plane to Antarctica, the day after he returned. Guard duty at some shit-hole weather station down there.'

'Just deserts then,' I replied, 'but Jonesy, tell me, were you really going to shoot me in the head with that silenced thirty-eight?'

Again he shrugged. 'It's a job. Nothing personal, friend.'

Took tossed his empty stubby across the room, where it landed directly in the waste bin provided. 'Man, you gotta have eyes in your arse, these days. Every bastard out to kill you all the time. What is it with everyone?'

'It *is* getting to be a drag, ain't it,' I agreed. 'And always with the complications. What am I going to do with you, Jonesy?'

'Mind if I get my feet down onto the floor?' he asked. 'This thing is terribly uncomfortable.'

'Sure,' I said, and took a pace back, in case he had anything stupid in mind.

'So you guys were back-stabbed, left to die out there?' he asked, taking interest. Bloody ASIO,' he spat, when I nodded confirmation. 'They're always doing shit like that.'

'You're not ASIO?' Took asked.

'Hell no. I *was* special forces 'til I got too close to an exploding RPG.' He tapped his head. 'Unstable, they said, so now I, *er*. . . You know, freelance? Only a temp with ASIO.'

'Yeah,' I sympathised. 'Medical cover?'

He laughed. 'Being discharged as being unfit for duty made sure I have to go private, and paying top dollar.'

'That sucks,' again sympathising. 'You a single man?'

He raised his left hand, revealing a gold band. 'Six months, almost.' I looked to Took.

'He was going to blow your brains out, man.'

'Like the man said, and a man does what he has to do, right?'

'I suppose,' Took replied. 'You decide. It was your brains going to be splattered over the pillow.'

'Tell me, Jonesy, if I let you out of here. . . ?'

'They left you for dead, bloke. I don't much like working for these bastards anyway. The missus reckons I should go to art college. Graphic arts, you know? I'm handy with a pencil, and computer art, too. At least I wouldn't have to deal with arseholes like them anymore.'

'There's good money in that,' Took added. 'Graphic art? I have a friend does design bodywork on bikes and cars and he makes a packet. I could hook you up, if you like?'

'Really? I'd like that,' Jonesy, my would-be assassin responded. 'A regular job. I wouldn't have to be away from home all the time either.'

'I can't let you have your piece back,' I told him, 'but, Christ, do yourself a favour. Stop working with bastards like these. You can't trust them, as illustrated right now. The day will come you'll find you're the one hung out to dry, shadows creeping around *your* room in the middle of the night. I've spent years in the game, pal. It took me too long to wake up. Get a life you can say is your own.'

We all climbed back to bed at around three o'clock, after sending Jones on his way, complete with a contact number for Took's auto art and design buddy, who might help him get a start in the business. The girls were ruffled, but after explaining the situation they seemed okay with it. It had been an odd experience, but I felt good, imparting a grain of worthwhile advice to the young night stalker. Too bad no one had done as much for me when I was much younger. I probably wouldn't have listened though, being the smug son of a bitch I was back then. Still, it was better than putting the guy's mortal remains in a hole somewhere, in a field, maybe, in the middle of the night. And, hell, who wanted to dig a hole in the middle of the night? I was going to get little enough sleep as it was.

TWENTY NINE

Our interrupted sleep saw us arriving barely in time. Visitors were being allowed through as we parked, disembarked and walked up to the gate. Within the main gate a waiting officer greeted us, led us across the yard into A-Division, and once within the building, up to the barred barrier of Guido's wing. He unlocked the gate and we followed him along the corridor to his cell door. The guard thumped twice, called, 'Your visitors, Spinoza,' and left us to it.

Guido's bodyguard pushed open the heavy, girded door, gave us a visual once-over and allowed us entry, saying over his shoulder, 'Your niece and three others, boss.'

'Come, come, come,' Guido called excitedly as we entered.

'Find something to do for the next hour, Spike,' he told his minder.

Oh, did you fill the urns?

'Yes, boss,' he replied, and waited a second time to be dismissed. 'You go then,' and to us, 'Wonderful to see you all. Mattie, my favourite niece. How are you, dear? And Janie, wonderful to see you. Alex, mister Took, come in, find a seat. I've had extra seating brought in for the occasion.'

He had, too. There were two, large, comfortable couches, three armchairs and footstools as well. Where he had obtained the furniture from was anybody's guess. He came up to Matilda, and, as per the first time, she stooped to give her uncle a hug, while the rest of us maneuvered until everyone was seated: Janie and myself on a couch, Took found a large, mismatched armchair with extendable footrest, which he immediately employed in making himself comfortable. Matilda, as he insisted, seated herself near to him, on his left side, in a matching armchair to his own.

'Well, this is grand,' Guido proclaimed, weaving around between the furniture excitedly. 'Wonderful of you coming to visit me in this miserable place. You are all well?'

There were grunts and murmurings in response. 'I'm fine, uncle, Matilda told him.

'Not exactly hard time, is it?' Janie commented, looking over Guido's renovated, well equipped, comfortable environment.

'One does what one can,' he replied, either missing Janie's barb or dextrously parrying. 'I am so pleased,' he said, at last coming to rest in his own chair.

'I could not resist the invite,' I told him, wanting to get to it. I felt we were being used as props for his indefatigable ego, with us sitting in court, like vassals surrounding a bloated little runt of something akin to a feudal lord. I was sure this was what he had in mind, watching him sit there, smiling broadly, looking us over with that impossible to conceal superior attitude he carried everywhere, even in this place. Grudgingly, though, I had to hand it to him. He had done alright for himself. Most poor schmucks had to cut out their prison time the hard way. Not Guido. He was one of those rare birds who could fall into pig shit and come out smelling of lilac and jasmine.

'You could not resist, Alex. I know you could not.' He reached for a cigar from the humidifier on the table beside him, snipped off the end, making a big show of lighting the enormous thing with what I presumed was a Stirling silver, antique lighter.

'Where's Vinnie?' Took asked. Not joining us?'

'Yes,' Matilda enjoined. 'I must see dad. I cannot have come all this way—'

'Of course Vincent will be along, soon. We have been segregated. My nephew and I are not meant to spend time together, you see. The superintendent has his rules, but I have mine, and my methods. He did not approve at first, but this is special occasion, is it not? Vincent will be directly along. Is that right? Directly along?'

'Along, directly,' Matilda obliged. 'Good. I may not be able to visit again for some time.'

'Why is that?' he asked, pulling the fat cigar from between his lips. 'Are you going somewhere?'

'I've been thinking about it, uncle. I have not yet decided, for sure, but, with all that has been going on, I think I would like to go far away, think things over, maybe make a fresh start.'

'You are young. You have very much time to still choose. We should talk. Maybe I can help—'

'*No!*' It came out sharply, more sharply than she might have intended, but she continued. 'Not with your assistance, uncle. I have had enough of family interference.' She left it at that, leaving a telling vacuum which none of us felt in the least bit inclined to fill. I had hoped she might decide to cut loose of her manipulating family. Good for her, I remember thinking at the time.

'There are hot drinks and sandwiches, if anyone is hungry? He said, waving toward the cut sandwiches prepared on plates, and the steaming earns. Help yourselves, and Took immediately advanced on the sandwiches.

A knock was heard, coming from the cell doorway, and we all turned our head to see Vincent Zendell entering.'

'Ahh, Vincent. Glad to see you are joining us. We have been waiting for you. Find somewhere to sit, nephew.'

He barely acknowledged anyone's presence but for Guido and his daughter, to whom he instantly gravitated, embracing her warmly.

'Hello, Matty. It's good to see you again.'

'Hello, dad,' and she embraced him as warmly in return.

'Come, come, you two,' Guido expressed, impatiently. Sit over here, together.' He pointed to the unoccupied couch. 'We have much to talk about and not so much time. A pity, but the boss man. . . A little man, and no heart.'

When Matilda and her father had settled, I figured it was time to get proceeding under way.

'I want to start at the very beginning, Guido. Am I right in thinking you can provide the answers I want?'

'You are not wrong,' he answered, grinning around his cigar and looking particularly cunning. 'So, at the beginning, Alex. Where is it, the beginning?'

'For me, the beginning was the day Mattie walked into my office, wanting me to advise her on what to do about the threatening letter she received. A letter slid under her hotel suite door, in Melbourne, if I recall correctly.'

'That is *your* beginning, Alex. Okay. The letter. Why was letter put under door? I will tell you, this letter was a fake, Alex,' and he halted, looking for the my reaction.

It was Took who reacted first. 'A lure, right? A decoy? I knew it. ' 'What means, *alure?*'

'A ruse,' but when Guido continued to look uncertain, he tried again. 'A trap. You know what a trap is, don't you?

'A trap? You could say was a trap,' Guido answered. 'It is close, but think. Every trap has the thing to bring in the animal. The letter is the bait, mister Took. Bait.'

'No mister. Just Took, my friend clarified.'

'You cunning. . . How did I not see it?' I blurted out, dismayed at the depth of my own stupidity. It was the goddamn key to the whole thing, and I, numbskull that I was, had overlooked the possibility that the note to Matilda, threatening vengeance and quoting *'the sins of the father'*, had been bait, pure and simple. I sat there, piecing the whole thing together while Guido gloated his best gloat. Everything that had followed had been carefully thought through, playing on everyone's proclivities and proven traits. There was only one possible motive behind it, that I could fathom, but I had already proven my enormous fallibility and elected not to stick my oar in, preferring to hear it from the horse's mouth instead.

'Do you see now,' my boy? He aimed at me.

'I do, but I wouldn't want to deprive you of your moment, Guido. Go ahead,' I invited. 'The big reveal.'

A glance in Vinnie's direction told me he was as much in the dark as the others. Was it possible? I supposed it was. Guido had always treated his nephew, who was more talented in the areas of thuggery and coercion, as a dullard. Couldn't say I blamed him. Vinnie might have turned the delicate plan tits up, had he been in the know, and since Vinnie's daughter had been manipulated, to boot, he would have been tempted to reveal the truth to her, relieving her fear and anxiety which had set the whole thing in motion.

'The letter was a hoax,' I said, picking up the thread for Guido. '*The sins of the father are to be laid upon the children,*' I recited from memory. It frightened the wits out of your niece.'

'It was necessary.' He turned to Matilda. 'I'm sorry, my dear. It was necessary for you to believe in this danger, you see? Alex, he is a good man judging people. If you know, he will know. You went to him because, who else? You were to leave Melbourne and go to Monarto, save what you could after your mother, she die. God rest her soul. You knew the name Alex Jaeger. I know you remember the name from a little girl, yes?'

Matilda nodded, agreeing, but her eyes suggested mounting anger. 'Of course I searched out Alex. No one else would understand exactly what was behind that note.'

'Yes, and you convince Alex you are in danger and no one else can help me, you say to him. The most important, number one in this game.'

'You frightened the hell out of my daughter,' Vincent said, speaking at last, 'and me too, Guido. How could you?'

'Grow up, Vincent. Stop your whining. We are living in real world.'

Guido's reproach stung Vincent into temporary silence, leaving him sitting there, quietly simmering.

'And so, as you must, and as I know you will do, you come to me, Alex. You do not know if the letter it is real threat or if it has to do something with me. How could you decide? Come, talk to me, watch closely my behaviour? And Vincent, too, but he is knowing nothing and so cannot let loose the secret.'

'Clever,' Janie intoned, more in rebuke than felicitating. 'Using your own flesh and blood as a pawn. Frightening her that way.'

'Janie, you are woman. I understand. Me and Alex, we are in the real world. Real world it is dangerous, and need for doing this.'

'Cassandra,' she replied.

'Yes, Cassandra. Long ago we had agreement, but your husband and mister. . .' he checked himself, avoiding repeating his previous *faux pas*. . . 'Took. Alex,Took and yourself as well. You find out the big plan. I am left to look foolish, but this Cassandra? Not forgiving me, I know, and is now suddenly very dangerous time. This person has long memory, and, I know for sure, revenge is coming to me. I start to hear whispers and suddenly I must do something quickly. But what? I remember Alex. His weakness for rescuing, like you, the dames. . . Dames? Damsels, yes? In distressed? Matty will find Alex before too long, and Alex will find how to save her.

How? He must kill Cassandra. Who else but Alex Jaeger can do such a thing? But he must have clues.'

'I'm flattered that you hold me is so high regard, Guido'

'But you know already this. Haw many times I say? Come, work with Guido. Make much money. Live big life. Big, fat, good life,' he boasted, raising his arms as if to say, look at what I have made for myself, and apparently missing the irony.

'Anyone else want a coffee?' Took called out from the table, where he was spooning ingredients into a cup.

'I'll have one, thanks,' I replied.

Matilda raised a hand. 'I'd like a cup of tea, Took, if that's okay?' 'Don't let me interrupt your thing,' Took told Guido. 'Good story, man. So Alex came to the rescue. We come out here. . . No. I'm forgetting something. The small matter of the attempt on his life. Explain that to us, mother goose. The part where someone with a high powered rifle shoots my friend in the chest.'

A scowl crossed Guido's chubby little face. I wasn't sure if it was because of the mother goose crack or whether my being shot disturbed him.

'Unfortunate, Alex,' he said to me. 'I am sorry for this. An accident.' 'So I *was* the target?' I asked, needing this one point settled. 'No-no. Was to be like Matty the target. Idiot say he slipped and pulling the trigger, is accident. No one was meant to be shot, just look like. Convince you it was not hoax. Not just threat but real one. Then will you agree and take serious. Save Matty from *real* threat. I am sorry for it. You are okay though?'

I put my hand to my chest where the bruising had, only recently, faded away. 'You're sorry? I was damn near killed, you lunatic. It was nothing but a vague anxiety made me pull on my vest that morning.'

'Like a fox,' said Guido. 'Instinct.'

'Pure luck,' I grumbled, and winced as my fingers found the damaged nerve. 'And luck *does not* last forever, Guido. Remember that.'

'Aaah,' replied Guido, dismissing the idea. 'You are now doubting yourself?' He studied me. 'Too bad. You are older. All your life, out there, you are fighting all bad things in the world while the politicians, they talk and talk and they doing nothing? Now you are doubting yourself? Doubting yourself, what once you knew? Do you know what is said? Alex Jaeger, he is charming man. No,' he laughed at his error. 'Is charmed. Charmed life. Like the fox, and so lucky. But is not lucky. You are born with. It is something given by God. You hear? Like unicorn they are saying. When someone, a bad man, they hear that Jaeger is in town? *Ha!* Like the rabbit, running. Alex Jaeger the ghost. Cannot kill.' He turned to Janie. 'Do you know what is the meaning of Jaeger, miss Janie? *The hunter*. It is true.'

Sure, I had heard that stuff before, and there was a time I believed it, like an idiot, and that was the danger. Magical thinking, it's called. A great way to get yourself killed, but I was beginning to grow up and realise, at age forty-four, how self obsessed and deluded I have been all these years. How had I ever survived?

I could only shake my head. 'We both know it's nonsense, don't we,' I told him, giving him a look leaving no doubt in his mind.

'What happened next?' Janie asked, realising I had been keeping her in the dark over some of what had transpired.

'Is where Alex now go where I cannot,' said Guido, enjoying the telling. 'He has been shot and is now angry. He must do for Matty, and now also do for himself. He must be remembering how Cassandra he escape the first time, as I knew it would be. Where to go? Who to talk to that can give information you need.'

I interjected here. 'You're wrong about that,' I stated, happy to find fault. 'I was going to wash my hands of it. I could not get to Cassandra. I did not have the resources. Besides, I realised I was settled, a married man. I could go no further with it. Not, at any rate, without jeopardizing mine and Janie's marriage. I was happy to put all that behind me.'

The interjection put a crimp in Guido's story, and he paused, thoughtful for a while. 'But you still go?'

'I was going to dump it in the panel's lap and let them sort it out.'

Took chipped in: 'It turned out they had a problem with jurisdiction or whatever, and going through channels. Notifying others of a mission was a good way to compromise its success, and a sanctioned team through official channels was something they could not do. Obviously then, no paperwork no funding. But they could, if Alex and I agreed, send us in using undocumented funds to finance the thing; equipment, whatever outside connections and extra manpower became were needed. No paperwork necessary.'

'Nothing further would have happened, had we refused,' I underlined.

Guido laughed, saying, 'And of course you must go. You must finish what it was you begin long ago. It is just as I plan.'

He was beginning to get on my wick with his taking credit for everything. He had a point though. I don't recall having ever left a serious concern unreconciled in my life; a character trait Guido, no doubt, relied upon. If the panel had not offered support it would have eaten at me, endlessly, I most probably would have found *some* way of stopping the bastard; what I then perceived as a serious threat to Matilda's continued existence.

He was still smiling at me as I came to this conclusion, expecting me to concede the point, but then Janie posed a question.

'Who were these people?'

'The panel? I'm not entirely sure. Odd bods, maybe retired or still active brass from differing branches of national defence. ASIO was in the room, it turns out. Ample clout. Able to make arrangements off the record.'

'You got lucky,' I heard Vinnie say. Why he was here at all, escape d me, but for his daughter being here with us.

'You're right about that,' I responded, for some reason taking pity on the guy. Prison had really clipped his wings, and, as usual, he was still playing second fiddle to Guido. Perhaps third or fourth fiddle now, and being constantly reminded of his lowly position.

'Luck counts, Vincent,' Guido chided. 'A man makes his own luck.' 'I seem to remember *me* telling *you* that, long ago, Guido.'

He nodded. 'So now you go to, where is?' 'Belarus,' Took assisted.

'Yes, Belarus.'

'You know the rest,' I said, not keen on recounting our actions.

Guido was disappointed. 'I rescue you from across boarder, Alex.

Tell them how.'

'The how of it I'm not entirely privy to. You got us out, and we're grateful, I assure you. We might well be languishing in some damp dungeon of some long forgotten castle right now, if you hadn't gotten us out. It's not a thing either of us care to consider.'

'And now, Cassandra, she is no more problem. Thanks to you and your friend I must not more be afraid for her vengeance.'

'It's not why we did it, Guido,' I told him, bending the truth only a little. He was easy meat, in this place, and I guess I had taken his situation into consideration, among other things.

'I dislike loose ends,' I added. Anyway, Matty was my primary consideration. As my first client in my new job as a private detective, it would have been a piss poor start, had I failed. For you, though, it was about little more than you protecting yourself. Conniving and manipulative, as always.'

'You flatter me, as always,' he replied, grinning, enjoying the repartee. 'However way to look at it, Alex, you are saving my life. No one else could do this thing. I pay my debt.'

'Really? You realise that it cuts both ways. Cassandra was, for me, destined to be forever a bugbear. I think we did each other a favour.'

Just then a guard came to stand at the doorway, banging on the steel door with his baton and giving us a start. 'Alright people. Visiting time is over. Visitors are to be at the gate in five minutes, unless you want to stay?'

Ignoring the interruption, Guido leaned sideways to the table beside him, retrieved an envelope, stood and waddled over to me, handed me the envelope.

'Do not open the envelope until you are home,' he told me. 'You must promise.'

'Okay, but. ' I shrugged. 'I expect this is for services rendered?

Matilda's account?'

'Exactly,' he said. 'Is your fee.' He appeared happily surprised that I had accepted it.

'Thank-you,' I responded, as graciously as circumstances would permit. This I did not expect, but if he was going to reward our efforts, who was I to argue, regardless of how the money might have been obtained? Ill gotten gains, be damned. I have always maintained that a man should be paid for the work he does. I would, then, be splitting it with Took, I realised.

'There is a loose end, Guido.'

'There is?' He was thoughtful, trying to identify anything he might have overlooked. 'What?'

'Someone is sore about us slipping away and finding our way home. I had a chat with a guy about that very subject, early this morning. It seems Took and I are an embarrassment now. We obviously weren't meant to come home with what must be classified knowledge regarding an incident which never happened. We represent a serious danger to them. ASIO,' I clarified.

'I expected like this,' he said, having returned to his chair, sitting there like a mini version of king

Nebuchadnezzar. Would you like me to take care of this little thing for you, my boy?'

I would have told his to stop calling me, *my boy,* were he not about to offer ridding me of the last irritation stuck in my craw.

'You can do that?'

'Do you doubt?' he responded, deadpan.

'It would be helpful,' I conceded. 'Very,' I added, looking to Took.

'Then no worry more. Still I have friends, Alex. It could take one, two days. Be careful 'til then. I will have someone call you to say it is done.' He looked to Janie, imparted, *then,* what I interpreted as a sly and meaningful smile. 'What is it they say, miss Janie? Life it is having small surprises?'

What could I say then but, 'Thank-you,' adding, 'but we really don't need any more surprises at home, do we Janie?'

'We've had quite enough,' she agreed, seeming distracted.

'A shame to be out of time,' he expressed ingenuously, and oddly enough, I agreed. I likely wound not be seeing Guido again, with any kind of luck. Despite our differences, our opposite world views, differing opinions on just about anything one cared to mention, and despite what most others interpreted as a completely spurious relationship, we had actually formed an odd kind of friendship over the years. The little bugger had a way of growing on a person; but then, so too do melanomas, I reminded myself.

THIRTY

We arrived home around midnight, that same day. Took would normally have gone home to his cottage and sat by himself, eaten some kind of frozen, packaged meal, Janie imagined, watched television for a while before going to bed, but she had insisted he stay and have supper with us. He could either stay the night or slip off home after he had eaten and unwound a little.

He and Matilda had found a scrabble board and tiles pushed to the back of a shelf, and suggested we play. It seemed a good idea for lack of anything better. While we were momentarily alone in the kitchen, Janie whispered to me, 'I think they have *a thing* for one another. Have you noticed?'

I immediately cast my mind back to the previous night, when I had knocked on the door of their shared motel room with the intruder over my shoulder: the giggling and shuffling I had heard before the door had been opened, and him standing there in his birthday suit.

'Can't say I've noticed,' I lied.

'Then look,' she insisted, whispering hoarsely, grabbing my shirt to twist me about, pointing to the gap in the folding concertina panels on the breakfast bar. Through it I observed the pair in question, sitting close together at the table while waiting for the snack we two were preparing. Took's voice was low, as if not wanting especially to be overheard, with Matilda attentive, pouring over his every word.

'I don't believe it,' I whispered back, and I told her of the giggling and shuffling behind the door the previous night.

The night had become chilly, requiring that I light the kindling and firewood already prepared in the hearth, and we joined our guests, carrying trays with bowls of Chilli Con Carne on them, a pot of coffee and one containing tea which the girls had lately switched to.

A departure, by far, from what Took and I had recently been up to, the cozy atmosphere being generated saw me briefly disassociating myself from time to time, focusing on what there was, here, right in font of me. Friends, a simple, delicious meal and a board game, played while sitting among people I cared deeply about, and with the fire burning so cheerfully. I was as happy as I had ever been, and as Janie laughed that bright, full-of-happiness laugh of hers while contesting a triple word score, my heart near burst for the love I felt for her in the moment.

I was constantly being made aware of the growing attraction between Took and Matilda—made aware by Janie kicking me under the table every time they became extra attentive towards one another.

Hours passed without mention of turning in. The scrabble game had been played twice, won once by Matilda and by Janie the second time, while we laughed and talked about everything that had come to pass, and even of what we might all do in time to come.

'I really don't know,' Matilda had replied. 'My mother is dead and my father and uncle Guido are in prison.'

'I'm so sorry for you,' Janie had sympathized, and she was about to go on when Matilda explained:

'No, don't be sorry. It's not at all what I meant. I was about to say that with mum dead, dad in prison and my controlling uncle Guido too, for the first time in my life I realise I am totally free to do as I please. It's a liberating feeling. Really liberating. I have my whole life in front of me now, without anyone telling me what to do and how to do it.'

'What's happening about your father's properties and holdings?'

'We talked about that, yesterday, while you and uncle Guido were reminiscing,' she answered, wryly. 'He's having his lawyers sell off what remains after the courts took plenty in retribution. The money will be transferred to me. He told me he does not want my life to be hampered by financial concerns. He says I should find what I love best and to do it. To spread my wings and put the past behind me.' 'That's wonderful, dear,' Janie told her.

'Your father has changed,' I risked saying. 'It sounds as if he has been thinking for himself and discovering a few things.'

'It's true,' she replied, soberly. 'I'm surprised, too, but mostly relieved to see the changes in my father I had long hoped for but had never really thought would occur.

'So you have the whole world and the rest of your life in front of you.' I observed. 'Any ideas? Any long held dream you might now realise, perhaps?'

She became suddenly coy, and after looking to Took, responded, 'I've always just wanted to settle down somewhere. Somewhere nice, and have a *real* life, one without all the complications.'

'Well, you're almost there,' Took told her. 'We were talking,' he said, addressing Janie and I. 'Matty's got nowhere she has to be and nowhere special to go. She's going to come stay with me for a while, see how things go from there.'

'No kidding?' I said, making an effort not to say anything I might instantly regret. 'I hope you're handy with a spanner, Matty.'

She laughed. 'Yes, I know about his love of motorcycles.' 'And chainsaws?' said Janie.

'Yes, those too.'

'A quiet life in the country,' I sighed. 'Wouldn't that be something? It's what we set out to do, ourselves, but the world keeps on intruding as it does.'

She nodded, appearing to understand just what I meant. 'If I'm not overstepping the bounds of propriety, Alex, she began. I've been asking Adrien about how the two of you came together.' Her calling Took by his Christian name almost broke my concentration, but I managed to remain earnest and allowed her to continue. 'You two would seem a complete mismatch, ordinarily. Your backgrounds. I hope you don't mind me saying?'

Janie laughed, 'Go on, Matty, it's fine. You couldn't be more right about that, and, trust me, neither of us have thin skin. The truth is what we thrive on around here. We might have been offended if you *hadn't* described us that way.'

'But you're so wonderful together. Perfect,' she uttered, seeming to be confounded by the fact.

'Background has little to do with either of us,' I told her. 'Christ, were that the case, we wouldn't have stood a chance in hell. I don't know what to tell you, Matty. I'm no expert,' I confessed, laughing. 'There are no rules when it comes to matters of the heart.'

'Who *are* you?' Janie cracked wise. 'What have you done with my husband? Since when did you start talking like this?'

'The new, sensitive me,' I told her. You think I don't know about these things, woman? I ain't just handsome, virile and . . . handsome, you know?'

It made the girls laugh and I flexed my biceps for good measure. 'Prime male specimen, me. And this guy,' I added, including Took. 'Actually, did I hear someone call you near genius level, not so long ago,' I reminded him. Tidswell, was it? What happed to you?'

'Don't worry about it, man. It's still here,' he said, tapping the noggin. 'It's there when I deed it.

'And regarding these two?' he continued. 'Peas in a pod. Two halves of a single organism. I seen it right from the start, Matty. Mr death wish over there and miss down and out, almost for the count, but with a willpower I've never seen before. She's the only person I've ever heard of, let alone witnessed, who kicked a trilonite habit. People say it can't be done, but Janie? Living proof, right there. And now she's a qualified vet, would you believe?'

'Is that right?' Matilda gasped. 'That is impressive. How did you ever do it, Janie?

Janie smiled, telling her, 'I met *this* guy,' and she wrapped her arms around me, squeezing. 'The power of love, and it's no joke, Mattie. I fell for this lump of trouble the moment I met him. Okay, maybe the day after. Do you remember when you took me to the motel room to rest, after rescuing me at the Old Coach?' she asked me. 'You should have seen him, girl. Like an angel, he swooped in and changed my life forever. I beat the habit for him. For us both, and for the life we might have together.'

'Okay, guys. Break it up, will you?' I told them, which everyone found incredibly amusing.

'It's so romantic,' Matilda said, and turned then to Took. 'The two of you went beyond the call of duty for me. No one has ever done anything like it before. I'm so, so grateful.' She stroked Took's arm adoringly. 'I know there was no actual threat, but still, you didn't know that.'

Took looked only slightly uncomfortable, but he was lapping it up on the inside, I could tell. He wasn't a ladies man by a long stretch, but it occurred to me then that his tough upbringing had done him no favours in that department.

'So you two are going to make a go of it, eh? Good luck with it. It's about time someone tied down the big galoot.'

It wasn't long after that we all started displaying symptoms associated with a very long couple of days we had endured. The four of us chipped in together to clean up before turning in, so that we wouldn't have to wake up to the chore in the morning.

'You'll be staying over, won't you, Took?' Janie asked, to which he answered by giving Matilda a sideways glance, and scratching his head, answered, 'Yeah, if that's okay?'

Matilda grabbed his hand, saying, 'Good night everyone, and thanks for everything today. What a day it's been. I'm going to wake up tomorrow feeling very much different, I think.'

Matilda's room was equipped with a double bed, and Janie and I watched as the pair head for it. 'I wonder just how much sleep they'll get?' I commented quietly.

'More than you, mister,' was her reply, accompanied by a playful dig in the ribs.

The lights were switched off, the open fire checked to make sure no logs could roll out during the night as we rested. I switched off my phone, too. No one was going to disturb me tonight. There was nothing scheduled; no matters to attend to, and Janie even sent a text to her staff, telling them not to expect her in at the clinic for a while, meaning days on end, together, enjoying all the relaxing downtime I for one had been looking forward to for a very long time.

The evening for me had been something special, I realised. For so long I had lived always looking forward, attempting to predict the problems which would greet me the following day and making plans to defeat them. There was something about these past several weeks; not just the challenges, the obstacles and adrenalin fuelled moments we had been through. That for me was nothing new and had for most of my life been just the way it was. I had done quite a bit of soul-searching in recent times, having realised I had overlooked many things in life which were at last coming into focus for me. I guess I had gotten so used to living life on the edge and at speed, I simply never noticed what I had been overlooking. When Janie had gotten her veterinary qualifications and opened the her own clinic, I had become lost, with far too much time on my hands. My wild, lawless days had been taken from me by the restrictions placed on me by the law courts and the watchful arms of the Government whose job it was to deprive a man of continuing doing the things he felt he was born to do. Still, the time had to come, I suppose, and if it had not, I might never have been forced into taking a long, hard look at myself, and discovering, at last, how blind I had been, and for so long.

Age, too, had caught up with me, and I fought it as long as I could. There was an impending feeling of great loss as I began noticing the changes. I had intended on living forever. A foolish notion, but life was just too much fun ever to consider I might grow older, to the point of having to slow down, anyway. I had tried to fool myself that I was different to everyone else and that time would never catch up. A damn fool, I saw I had been. Of course it catches up and of course I am no different to others in that regard. I had learned a lot about myself during these past weeks. Learned too that while some things are lost in the aging process, much is also gained. Only now was I really seeing it. What is gained in the process is well worth the trade, I only had to look at the things recently come into my life to know that was true.

I had considered that what I felt for Janie was love, up until recently. Suddenly I realised that, although I did love the girl—and there was no doubt of it—my capacity to love and to cherish that love had grown almost exponentially. There was no real loss in the aging process, only new and better things. If that was the sort of thing I had to look forward to as time progressed, bring it on, I told myself.

We climbed in between the sheets and moved up close together, with her resting her head on my chest as we luxuriated in the comfort of our expensive, superduper, spine supporting mattress which Janie had bought, after seeing a television advertisement declaring, *'The best night's sleep you will ever have,'* and right then I didn't doubt it. I was tired enough and satisfied enough that I could have slept standing on my head.

I was about to drift off when Janie sat bolt upright.

'The envelope,' she said. 'The envelope Guido gave you. We didn't see what's inside. Where is it?'

Luckily it was in my jacket pocket, the jacket lying folded over the back of a chair within arm's reach. Anywhere else and it would certainly have waited until morning.

I switched on my bedside lamp, rolled toward it, reaching to discover the envelope still tucked away in the pocket. 'I bet it's a lottery ticket,' I bemoaned, withdrawing my hand and clenching the envelope. 'Exactly Guido's idea of a joke.'

I tore open the flap, slid out a card contained within. In the low light of my bedside lamp I made out the word, *Congratulations*, followed by the words, *It's a baby!* There was a cartoon drawing of a baby in a basket, or something like it, flanked by caricatures of two very surprised looking parents, their hands stuck to their faces and with mouths agape in shock and surprise.

I read it out loud and handed it over to Janie, telling her, 'I told you so.'

'There's a cheque inside the card,' she said, switching on her own lamp and touching it again until it was much brighter. I was expecting her to read out the amount but there was only silence, so I sat up to join her.

'Well, how much is it?'

She handed it back to me to read for myself. 'Goddamn—' I could not believe my eyes. 'Five hundred thousand dollars?' but Janie didn't appear to be so taken by it, inspecting the card instead.

'Joke card. Typical,' I said, chuckling, but still, she remained silent, until at last saying, ' How could he. . . ?'

'How could he what?' I asked, with sudden difficulty, on account of my mouth becoming incredibly dry.

I looked from the card to her, took possession of it, opening it up to read, *"Janie, Alex and family to be. You have been blessed with a baby.* Congratulations, uncle Guido." 'A joke, right?' I stated.

Janie smiled, kissed me on the lips. 'I have something to tell you, Alex. How he found out, I don't know, but it's true, dear. You're going to be a father, and a wonderful father you'll be.'

I was stunned. What man is not, when receiving the news? Stunned and overjoyed. It was the best news the universe could have given me, and I was so ready for this.

She kissed me again, softly, the biggest fool on God's green Earth that I was, and I kissed her right back. Alex Jaeger, father. It was wonderful news and life had just become so much grander.

end